Dedalus European Classics
General Editor: Mike Mitchell

The Mystery of the
Yellow Room

Gaston Leroux

The Mystery of the Yellow Room

with an Afterword by Terry Hale

Dedalus

Published in the UK by Dedalus Limited,
24–26, St Judith's Lane, Sawtry, Cambs, PE28 5XE
Email: info@ dedalusbooks.com
www.dedalusbooks.com

ISBN printed book   978 1 873982 38 9
ISBN e-book   978 1 907650 24 6

Dedalus is distributed in the USA and Canada by SCB Distributors,
15608 South New Century Drive, Gardena, CA 90248
email: info@scbdistributors.com   web: www.scbdistributors.com

Dedalus is distributed in Australia by Peribo Pty Ltd.
58, Beaumont Road, Mount Kuring-gai, N.S.W. 2080
email: info@peribo.com.au

Publishing History
First published in France in 1908
First Dedalus edition in 1997
Second Dedalus edition in 2003, reprinted in 2008 and 2012
First e-book edition 2012

Translation copyright © Dedalus 1997
Afterword copyright © Terry Hale 1997

Printed in Finland by WS Bookwell
Typeset by RefineCatch Ltd

A C.I.P. listing for this book is available on request.

CHAPTER I

In which we begin not to understand

It is not without emotion that I here begin to relate the extraordinary adventures of Joseph Rouletabille. Up until now he had so firmly opposed my doing so that I had given up hope of ever being able to publish the most extraordinary detective story of the past fifteen years. The public might never have known the whole truth about the mystery of the Yellow Room with which my friend was so closely involved, if, apropos of the recent nomination to the rank of Grand Cross of the Legion of Honour of the illustrious M. Stangerson, an evening paper had not revived a terrible drama which Joseph Rouletabille had told me he wished for ever forgotten.

The Yellow Room! Who now remembers an affair that, fifteen years ago, caused so much ink to flow? Things are so very quickly forgotten in Paris. Have not the very name of the Nayves trial and the tragic story of young Ménaldo's death completely passed out of mind? Yet then, the public were so deeply interested in the details of the trial that a ministerial crisis that happened at the same time went totally unnoticed. The Yellow Room trial, which preceded the Nayves case by a few years, caused an even greater sensation. For months, the whole world pondered this obscure problem, the most obscure, to my knowledge, that has ever challenged the perspicacity of our police or taxed the consciences of our judges. Everyone was bent on finding a solution to this puzzle. It was a drama which fascinated both Europe and America. In truth – and I may say this, since there can be no question of personal pride in the matter, for I do nothing more than transcribe certain facts on which some exceptional documents in my possession enable me to throw a new light – in truth, I do not think that you could find anything to compare with the mystery of the Yellow Room in the domain of fact or fantasy, not even amongst the inventions of Edgar Allen Poe and his imitators.

Young Rouletabille, aged eighteen, then a junior reporter on a leading newspaper, succeeded in discovering what no one else could. But when, at the trial, he gave the key to the whole case, he did not tell the whole truth. He told only what was necessary to explain the inexplicable and to ensure the acquittal of an innocent man. The reasons for his reticence no longer exist. Moreover, my friend ought now to speak out fully. You are about to learn the whole truth and, without further preamble, I shall now place before you the problem of the Yellow Room exactly as it was placed before the eyes of the entire world on the day after the tragedy at the Chateau du Glandier.

On 25th October, **1892** the following note appeared in *Le Temps:*

'A fearful crime has been committed at Professor Stangerson's house in Glandier, on the edge of the forest of Ste-Geneviève, near Epinay-sur-Orge. Last night, whilst the Professor was in his laboratory, an attempt was made on the life of Mademoiselle Stangerson, who was sleeping in an adjoining room. The doctors fear for Mlle Stangerson's life.'

One can easily imagine the sensation that this news caused throughout Paris. The world was already fascinated by the work of Professor Stangerson and his daughter. They were the first to perform experiments in radiography and, later on, the results of their studies were to lead the Curies to the discovery of radium. Moreover, the Professor was shortly to read before the Academy of Sciences a sensational paper on his new theory: the Dissociation of Matter, a theory destined to shake the foundations of all official science, which has so long been based on the famous principle that nothing is lost and nothing is created; this reading was eagerly anticipated.

The next morning, the newspapers were full of the tragedy.

Le Matin, amongst others, published the following article, entitled:

A SUPERNATURAL CRIME

'Here are the only details' – explained the anonymous writer – 'that we have been able to obtain concerning the crime at the Chateau du Glandier. Professor Stangerson's despair and the impossibility of garnering any information from the lips of the victim, have made our investigations and those of the police so difficult that, for the present, we cannot form any clear idea of what took place in the Yellow Room in which Mlle Stangerson, in her nightdress, was found lying on the floor, on the point of death. We have, however, been able to interview Old Jacques – as he is called in the neighbourhood – an old servant in the employ of the Stangerson family. Old Jacques entered the Yellow Room at the same time as the professor. This room adjoins the laboratory. The laboratory and the Yellow Room are in a pavilion at the far end of the park, about four hundred yards from the chateau.

"It was half-past twelve at night," the good old man told us, "and when the tragedy happened, I was in the laboratory, where Monsieur Stangerson was still at work. I had spent the evening cleaning and putting away various scientific instruments and was waiting for Monsieur Stangerson to finish work before going to bed. Mademoiselle Mathilde had worked with her father up until midnight. Just as the clock struck midnight in the laboratory, she had risen, kissed M. Stangerson and bade him goodnight. She bade me goodnight too as she pushed open the door of the Yellow Room. We heard her lock the door and shoot the bolt. I could not help laughing, and I said to Monsieur: 'There's Mademoiselle double-locking the door. She must be afraid of the Good Lord's beast!' Monsieur did not even hear me, for he was deep in thought. Just then I heard a fearful miauling and I immediately recognised the cry of the Good Lord's Beast. It made me shiver. 'Is that cat going to keep us awake again all night?' I said to myself; for I must tell you, sir, that until late October, I live in the attic, right over the Yellow Room, so that

Mademoiselle is not left alone through the night in the park. It is Mademoiselle's fancy to spend the spring, summer and part of the autumn in the pavilion; she obviously finds it more pleasant than the chateau, and for the last four years – that is, ever since the place was built – she has always taken up her lodging there in the early spring. When winter comes, Mademoiselle returns to the chateau, for there is no fireplace in the Yellow Room.

We remained in the pavilion, then, M. Stangerson and I. We made no noise. He was seated at his desk. As for me, I was sitting on a chair, for I had finished my work, and I was watching him and thinking: 'What a man! What brains! What knowledge!' I attach considerable importance to the fact that we made no noise since, given the silence, the murderer must have thought that we had left the place. Then, suddenly, while the clock was striking half-past midnight, a desperate scream came from the Yellow Room. It was the voice of Mademoiselle, crying 'Murder! Murder! Help!' Immediately afterwards, shots rang out, and there was a great noise of tables and furniture being overturned, as if in the course of a struggle, and again we heard the voice of Mademoiselle screaming 'Murder! Help! Father! Father!'

As you may imagine, we sprang up, and M. Stangerson and I threw ourselves upon the door. But, alas, as I told you, it had been firmly locked on the inside by Mademoiselle herself with key and bolt. We tried to force it open, but it would not budge. M. Stangerson was like a madman, and, truly, it was enough to make anyone mad, for he could hear Mademoiselle still hoarsely calling out, her voice ever fainter now, 'Help! Help!' M. Stangerson rained terrible blows on the door; he wept with rage and sobbed with despair and helplessness.

It was then that I had an inspiration. 'The murderer must have got in through the window!' I cried, and I rushed out of the pavilion and ran like a madman.

Unfortunately, the window of the Yellow Room looks out on to the park, so that the park wall, right next to the pavilion, blocked my path to the window. To reach it, it was first of all necessary to go out of the park. I ran towards the gate and, on my way, met Bernier and his wife, the caretakers, who were hastening to the pavilion, obviously drawn there by the sound of gunshots and by our cries. In a few words I told them what had happened. I instructed the concierge to join M. Stangerson at once, and told his wife to come with me and open the park gates. Five minutes later, she and I were standing before the window of the Yellow Room.

The moon was shining brightly, and I saw quite clearly that the window had not been touched. Not only were the iron bars that protect it intact, but the shutters behind were closed exactly as I had closed them myself on the previous evening, as I did every day, although Mademoiselle, knowing that I was tired and had much to do, had told me not to trouble myself, saying that she would close them herself. They were just as I had left them, fastened with an iron catch on the inside. The murderer, therefore, could not have entered that way and could not possibly escape that way. But I could not get in either.

That was terrible – enough to turn one's brain! The door was locked on the inside and the shutters of the only window were also fastened on the inside, and, as well as those shutters, there were iron bars so close together that you could not even have got your arm through them. And there was Mademoiselle still calling for help or, rather, no, she had ceased to call. She was dead, perhaps. But I could still hear her father in the pavilion trying to break down the door. The concierge and I then ran back to the pavilion. In spite of the furious attempts of M. Stangerson and Bernier to break it down, the door was still holding firm. At length, it gave way before our united and frenzied efforts, and then what did we see?

I ought to tell you, by the way, that the concierge's wife was standing behind us holding the laboratory lamp – a powerful lamp that lit the whole room.

I must also tell you, sir, that the Yellow Room is quite small. Mademoiselle had furnished it with a fairly large iron bedstead, a small table, a night-commode, a washing-stand and two chairs. We took all that in at a glance by the light of the big lamp. Mademoiselle, in her nightdress, was lying on the floor in the midst of the most incredible disorder. The table and chairs had been overturned, showing that there had been a violent struggle. Mademoiselle had clearly been dragged from her bed. She was covered with blood and had terrible marks on her throat – scratches made by someone's finger-nails – and from a wound on her right temple, a thread of blood trickled forth, making a little pool on the floor. When M. Stangerson saw his daughter in that terrible state, he threw himself on his knees beside her, uttering a cry of despair. It was really pitiful to hear him. He checked that she was still breathing and devoted all his attention to her. As for us, we searched for the wretch who had tried to kill our mistress, and I swear to you, sir, had we found him, it would have gone hard with him!

But how could he not be there, how could he have escaped? It beggars the imagination. There was no one under the bed, no one behind the furniture. All we found were traces of his presence there; the bloodstained marks of a man's large hand on the walls and on the door; a large handkerchief red with blood, but with no initials; an old cap and many fresh footprints on the floor – the prints of a man with large feet, whose boots had left a sort of sooty impression. How had this man got in? How had he vanished? Don't forget, sir, that there is no fireplace in the Yellow Room. He could not have escaped by the door, for it is narrow, and besides, the concierge was standing on the threshold with the lamp in her hand while her husband and I were searching for the murderer in this small square room, where no one could possibly hide. As we discovered at once, there was no one behind the door, which we had forced open. No escape would have been pos-sible through the window, still firmly secured, the shutters closed and the iron bars untampered with. What then? Well, to be honest, I began to suspect the Devil's work.

Then, on the floor, we found my revolver – yes, my own revolver! That brought me back to reality with a jolt. The Devil would not have needed to steal my revolver to kill Mademoiselle. The man who had been there had first gone up to my attic and taken my revolver from the drawer where I keep it, and had used it afterwards against Mlle Mathilde. We then ascertained, by counting the cartridges, that the murderer had fired two shots. When you come to think of it, sir, it was very fortunate for me in those awful circumstances that M. Stangerson was in the laboratory when the crime occurred, and that he saw with his own eyes that I was there with him, for otherwise, with this business of the revolver, there is no telling what would have happened.

Very likely I would already be under lock and key. After all, what the law most wants is to be able to send a man to the scaffold!"

The editor of *Le Matin* added the following lines to this interview:

'We have allowed Old Jacques to tell us all that he knows about the crime committed in the Yellow Room. We have reproduced it in his own words, only sparing the reader the endless lamentations with which he adorned his narrative. We should have liked to put some questions to Old Jacques, but just as we were about to ask those questions, he was sent for by the judge, who was carrying out his enquiries in the hall of the chateau. We found it impossible to gain admission to Glandier and, as for the oak grove, it is encircled by detectives and gendarmes, eagerly searching out any footprints leading to the pavilion, and which may, eventually, lead to the discovery of the murderer.

We would also have liked to question the caretakers, man and wife, but they are nowhere to be found. Finally, we waited in a roadside inn, not far from the chateau gates, for the departure of Monsieur de Marquet, the judge of Corbeil. At half-past five, we saw him and his clerk, and, before he entered his carriage, we were able to ask him the following questions:

"Can you, Monsieur de Marquet, give us any information about this affair without prejudicing the course of your inquiry?"

"Impossible!" was the reply. "All I can say is that this is by far the strangest affair I have ever known. The more we think we know something, the further we are from knowing anything at all!"

We asked Monsieur de Marquet to be good enough to explain his meaning, and this is what he said – the importance of which will be evident to all:

"If nothing is added to the material facts so far established, I really fear that the mystery which surrounds the abominable crime of which Mlle Stangerson has been the victim will never be brought to light, but it is to be hoped that the examination of the walls, ceiling and floor of the Yellow Room – an examination, which I shall undertake tomorrow, together with the builder who built the pavilion four years ago – will afford us the proof we need. For the problem is this: We have to find out how the murderer gained entry. He entered by the door and hid himself under the bed, awaiting Mlle Stangerson. But how did he leave? There lies the problem. If no trap, no secret door, no recess or hiding-place, no opening of any sort is found, if the sounding of the walls – even if that involves the demolition of the pavilion – does not reveal any passageway through which a human being or any other being could pass; if the ceiling shows no crack, if the floor conceals no tunnel, we will really have to start believing, as Old Jacques says, that this is the Devil's work." '

And the anonymous writer in *Le Matin* mentions in this article – which I selected as the most interesting of all those published about the mysterious affair that day – the fact that the judge laid stress on those words.

The article concluded with these lines:

'We wanted to know what Old Jacques meant by the cry of the Good Lord's Beast. The landlord of the Tower Inn explained to us that it is the particularly sinister cry that is occasionally heard at night and which is the cry of a cat belonging to an aged woman, known locally as Old Mother Agenoux. Mother Agenoux is a sort of saint, who lives in a hut in the heart of the forest, not far from the grotto of Ste-Geneviève.

The Yellow Room, the Good Lord's Beast, Mother Agenoux, the Devil, Ste-Geneviève, Old Jacques – here is an amazingly complex crime which the stroke of a pickaxe in the wall of the pavilion may unravel for us tomorrow. Let us at least hope so. Meanwhile, it is feared that Mlle Stangerson – who has not yet emerged from her delirium and can say only one word distinctly, 'Murderer! Murderer!' – will not live through the night.'

In conclusion, in its late edition, the same newspaper announced that the head of the Secret Police had sent a telegram to the famous detective, Frédéric Larsan, who was in London investigating the theft of some securities, ordering him to return to Paris at once.

CHAPTER II

In which Joseph Rouletabille appears for the first time

I remember young Rouletabille's arrival in my room that morning as clearly as if it had happened yesterday. It was about eight o'clock and I was still in bed, reading the article in *Le Matin* about the Glandier crime.

But before going any further, I must introduce my friend to the reader.

I first met Joseph Rouletabille when he was a junior reporter. At that time, I myself was a very young lawyer, and often met him in the anterooms of the judges at the Law Courts. He was, as they say in France, 'une bonne bille' – a good sort, but, literally, 'a good ball'. Indeed, he seemed to have taken his head, round as a bullet, out of a box of billiard balls, and I presume that is why his fellow journalists – all keen billiard players – had given him that nickname, which he was to retain and eventually make famous. He was always red as a tomato, one moment happy as a lark, the next grave as a judge. How was it that this boy – he was only sixteen and a half when I saw him for the first time – already managed to earn his living as a journalist? That was what everyone who came in contact with him might have asked, had his beginnings not been quite so well known. At the time of the Rue Oberkampf affair in which the body of a woman was found cut into pieces, he had brought to the editor of *L'Epoque* – a paper then rivalling *Le Matin* in its swift and comprehensive news coverage – the woman's left foot, which was the only part missing from the basket in which the gory remains had been discovered. The police had spent the whole week searching for that left foot, and Rouletabille had found it down a drain, where no one else had thought to look. To do this he had used the equipment of a sewer-man, a member of one of the emergency teams engaged by the City of Paris administration after serious damage caused by the flooding of the Seine.

When the editor found himself in possession of the precious foot and heard the string of intelligent deductions that had led the lad to it, he was filled with admiration for such detective cunning in the brain of a sixteen-year-old, and delighted at being able to exhibit in the 'morgue-window' of his paper the left foot of the victim of the Rue Oberkampf murder.

'With this foot,' he cried jocularly, 'I'll make the headlines.'

Then, having handed the ghastly parcel to the forensic expert attached to the journal, he asked the youth, who was soon to become Rouletabille, what he would expect to earn as a junior reporter on *L'Epoque*.

'Two hundred francs a month,' the youngster replied modestly, dumbfounded by the unexpected proposal.

'You shall have two hundred and fifty,' said the editor. 'only I want you to tell everybody that you have been on my paper for a month. Let it also be made quite clear that it was not you, but *L'Epoque* that discovered the woman's foot. Here, my young friend, the individual is nothing and the newspaper everything.'

He then asked the new reporter to withdraw, but before the youth reached the door, he called him back and asked him his name. The young man replied:

'Joseph Joséphin.'

'That's not a name,' said the editor. 'But since you won't be signing anything you write, it's of no matter.'

The beardless junior soon made many friends, for he was hardworking and gifted with a good humour that delighted the most surly and disarmed the most envious of his colleagues. At the café where the reporters assembled before going to the Courts or to the Prefecture in search of that day's crime, he began to gain a reputation as an unraveller of intricate cases, which even reached the ears of the head of the Criminal Investigation Department. When a case was worth the trouble, and Rouletabille – for that was how he was known by then – had been set on the trail by the editor, he often got the better of even the most renowned detectives.

It was in that café that I became more fully acquainted with him. We chatted and I soon felt a great liking for the young fellow. His intelligence was so wonderfully keen and original; he was the most methodical and able person I have ever met.

Some time after this I was put in charge of the legal news on *Le Cri du Boulevard*. My entry into journalism could not but strengthen my ties with Rouletabille. After a time, my new friend having meanwhile undertaken a little court reporting for *L'Epoque*, I was able occasionally to furnish him with the legal terminology he needed.

Nearly two years passed in this way, and the more I got to know Rouletabille, the more I loved him, for beneath his mask of joyous extravagance, I found him to be unusually serious and thoughtful. On several occasions, I, who was used to seeing him happy – often perhaps too happy – found him plunged in deep melancholy.

When I tried to question him as to this change of mood, he merely laughed, but made no reply. One day, after I had questioned him about his parents, of whom he never spoke, he turned away, pretending not to have heard what I had said.

It was at that stage of our friendship that the famous case of the Yellow Room occurred – a case which was not only to place him in the first rank of newspaper reporters, but also to prove him to be the greatest detective in the world – a double rôle which it was not that surprising to find played by the same person, considering that the daily press was already fast becoming what it is today – the gazette of crime.

Some people may complain of this; for myself, I regard it as an excellent thing. We can never have too many weapons, public or private, against criminals. Some people, however, contend that by devoting so many column inches to crime, the newspapers actually encourage it, but then some people are never satisfied.

Rouletabille, as I have said, came into my room that morning, 20th October **1892**. His face was redder than usual, his eyes were staring, he was short of breath, and he appeared to be in a state of extreme excitement. Brandishing *Le Matin* in one trembling hand, he said:

'Well, my dear Sainclair, you've read about . . .'

'The Glandier crime?'

'Yes, the Yellow Room! What do you think of it?'

'I think it was the work of either the Devil or the Good Lord's Beast.'

'Be serious.'

'Well, I must confess that I can't really believe in murderers who make their escape through solid brick walls. I think Old Jacques did wrong to leave behind him the weapon with which the crime was committed and, since he occupies the attic immediately above Mlle Stangerson's room, the search of the building ordered for Friday by the judge will give us the key to the enigma, and we shall soon know by what secret door the old fellow was able to slip in and out, and immediately return to the laboratory to M. Stangerson without his absence being noticed. What else can I say? Of course, I'm only surmising.'

Rouletabille seated himself in an armchair, lit his pipe, and then replied in a tone of great irony:

'Young man, you are a barrister, and I have no doubt of your ability to save the guilty from conviction; but if you ever become a judge on the bench, you will have no problem at all in condemning innocent people! You really are a most gifted young man!'

For a while, he puffed energetically on his pipe, then he went on:

'No hiding-place will be found, and the mystery of the Yellow Room will become more and more mysterious. That's why it interests me. The judge is right: there has never been a stranger crime than this.'

'Have you any idea how the murderer escaped?' I asked.

'None,' replied Rouletabille, 'none as yet. But I already have some ideas about the revolver. For example, the revolver was not used by the murderer.'

'Good heavens! By whom then?'

'Why – by Mlle Stangerson.'

'I don't understand,' I said.

Rouletabille shrugged his shoulders.

'Has nothing in the article in *Le Matin* particularly struck you?'

'Nothing. I found the whole story utterly bizarre.'

'What about the door being locked on the inside?'

'That's the only perfectly natural thing in the article.'

'Really! And the bolt?'

'The bolt?'

'The bolt – again inside the room – further securing the door? Mlle Stangerson took a lot of precautions. To me it seems obvious that she was afraid of someone. That was why she took those precautions. She had even taken Old Jacques' revolver without telling him. No doubt she did not wish to alarm anyone, least of all her father. The thing she dreaded happened, and she defended herself. There was a struggle and she used the revolver skilfully enough to wound the assassin in the hand – which explains the large, bloody handprint on the wall and on the door, left by the man groping for a way out; but she did not fire soon enough to avoid the terrible blow she received on the right temple.'

'It was not with the revolver, then, that she was wounded on the right temple.'

'The newspaper does not say so, and, personally, I don't think it was – because it seems logical to me that the revolver was used by Mlle Stangerson against the murderer. Now, what weapon did the murderer use? The blow on the temple seems to show that the murderer wished to stun Mlle Stangerson – after he had unsuccessfully tried to strangle her. He must have known that Old Jacques lived in the attic, and that was one of the reasons, I believe, why he used a silent weapon – a club, maybe, or a hammer.'

'None of this explains how the murderer got out of the Yellow Room,' I observed.

'Evidently,' replied Rouletabille, rising. 'And as that is the very thing that requires explanation, I am off to the Chateau du Glandier and I came here to fetch you and take you there with me.'

'Me?'

'Yes, dear friend, I want you. *L'Epoque* has entrusted this case to me, and it is up to me to solve it as quickly as possible.'

'But how can I be of use to you?'

'M. Robert Darzac is at the Chateau du Glandier.'

'That's true. He must be in a state of utter despair.'

'I must talk to him.'

Rouletabille said that in a tone that surprised me.

'Do you think he may have something of interest to tell you?' I asked.

'Yes.'

That was all he would say. He withdrew to my sitting-room, urging me to dress quickly.

I knew M. Robert Darzac, having been of great service to him in a civil action, while I was secretary to Maître Barbet Delatour. Robert Darzac, who was, at the time, about forty years of age, was a professor of physics at the Sorbonne. He was intimately connected with the Stangersons, since, after courting Mlle Strangerson assiduously for seven years, he was now about to marry her. She must have been about thirty-five then, but was still remarkably good-looking.

While I was dressing, I called out to Rouletabille, who was impatiently pacing up and down in my sitting-room:

'Have you any idea as to the social class of the murderer?'

'Yes,' he replied, 'I believe him to be an extremely well-connected person, a man belonging, at the least, to the upper middle classes. That, again, is only an impression.'

'What makes you think that?'

'Well,' my friend replied, 'the greasy cap, the common handkerchief and the bootprints on the floor.'

'I see,' I said. 'One does not leave so many clues behind one when they tell the truth.'

'We shall make something of you yet, my dear Sainclair,' concluded Rouletabille.

CHAPTER III

A man passed through the shutters like a shadow

Half an hour later, Rouletabille and I were on the platform of
Orléans station, awaiting the departure of the train which was
to take us to Epinay-sur-Orge.

We witnessed the arrival of the Corbeil court, represented
by M. de Marquet and his clerk. M. de Marquet had spent the
night in Paris in order to watch the final rehearsal of a little
revue, of which he was the author, though he signed himself
simply 'Castigat Ridendo'.

M. de Marquet was getting on a bit. Generally, he was
extremely polite and good-tempered. He had had but one
passion all his life: the theatre. Throughout his career on the
bench, he was interested solely in cases that might furnish him
with material for plays.

So it was that, when I met him, I heard M. de Marquet say
to his clerk, with a sigh:

'Let us hope, my dear Monsieur Maleine, that this
builder with his pick-axe does not destroy such a wonderful
mystery.'

'Have no fear,' M. Maleine replied, 'his pick-axe may well
demolish the pavilion, but it will leave our case intact. I have
sounded the walls and studied the ceiling and floor, and I
know all about these things. I am not to be deceived. We need
fear nothing, for we shall discover nothing.'

Having thus reassured his chief, M. Maleine then drew
M. de Marquet's attention to us with a discreet movement
of his head. The judge frowned, and, as he saw Rouletabille
approaching him, hat in hand, he sprang into one of the
empty carriages, saying loudly to his clerk: 'No journalists!'

M. Maleine replied: 'I understand,' and endeavoured to
prevent Rouletabille from stepping into the judge's

compartment: 'Excuse me, gentlemen, this compartment is reserved.'

'I work for *L'Epoque*,' said my young friend with the utmost politeness and a number of salutations, 'and I have a word or two to say to M. de Marquet.'

'M. de Marquet is busy. His inquiry . . .'

'Ah, his inquiry, believe me, is a matter of absolute indifference to me! I am no mere reporter of petty events,' said Rouletabille, with a look of utter contempt for the literature of the news columns, 'I am the dramatic critic of *L'Epoque* and, since I shall have to give a little account of the revue at La Scala this evening . . .'

'Step in, please, Monsieur,' said the clerk courteously.

Rouletabille was already inside the compartment. I followed him and seated myself next to him. The clerk stepped in as well and closed the carriage door.

M. de Marquet looked severely at his clerk.

'Oh, Monsieur,' Rouletabille began, 'do not be angry with the young man. I know I joined you in spite of your instructions to him, but let me tell you that it is not with M. de Marquet that I wish to have the honour of speaking, but with M. Castigat Ridendo. Allow me, as the dramatic critic of *L'Epoque*, to congratulate you.'

M. de Marquet was nervously stroking his pointed beard. He explained to Rouletabille that he was too modest an author to desire the veil of his pseudonym to be publicly raised, and that he sincerely hoped his enthusiasm for his work as a playwright would not lead him to inform the world that Castigat Ridendo was none other than the judge of Corbeil.

Then he added, after a slight hesitation: 'The work of the author might be injurious to that of the judge. Especially in the provinces, far from Paris; people are rather narrow-minded and conventional . . .'

'You may rely on my discretion,' Rouletabille exclaimed.

The train was now in motion.

'We're off!' said the judge, surprised that we should be making the journey with him.

'Yes, Monsieur,' said Rouletabille, with a happy smile, 'the

Truth is on its way to the Chateau du Glandier. A remarkable case, M. de Marquet, a most remarkable case!'

'Indeed! In fact, an incredible, unfathomable, inexplicable affair. And my only fear, M. Rouletabille, is that you journalists will interfere and try to explain it all away.'

This thrust went home.

'Yes,' he quietly replied, 'you are right to be afraid. These journalists get everywhere. As for myself, Monsieur, mere chance has placed me in your path and had me travel in your carriage.'

'Where are you going, then?' asked M. de Marquet.

'To the Chateau du Glandier,' replied Rouletabille, without a flicker.

M. de Marquet was taken aback.

'You will not be allowed in, Monsieur Rouletabille.'

'Will you stop me?' said my friend, already prepared for the fray.

'Certainly not. I am too fond of the press to be in any way disagreeable to them, but M. Stangerson has given orders for his door to be kept closed to everyone, and it is well guarded. Not a single journalist was able to get as far as the gates of Glandier yesterday.'

'So much the better!' Rouletabille retorted. 'I have come in time.'

M. de Marquet bit his lip and seemed determined to remain obstinately silent. He only relaxed a little when Rouletabille told him that we were going to Glandier in order to visit an old and intimate friend, M. Robert Darzac, whom Rouletabille had perhaps met once in his life.

'Poor Robert!' he said. 'This dreadful affair could be the death of him – he is so deeply in love with Mlle Stangerson.'

'M. Darzac's grief is indeed painful to see,' M. de Marquet muttered, as if sorry to speak at all.

'But it is to be hoped that Mlle Stangerson will be saved.'

'Let us hope so. Her father was telling me yesterday that, were she to die, he would not be long in following her. What an incalculable loss that would mean to science!'

'The wound on her temple is serious, is it not?'

'Indeed, and it is a miracle that it has not proved fatal. The blow was given with such tremendous force.'

'So she was not wounded with the revolver,' said Rouletabille, giving me a triumphant look.

Monsieur de Marquet appeared greatly embarrassed.

'I have said nothing, I do not wish to say anything, and I shall say nothing.'

He then turned towards his clerk, as if he no longer knew us.

But Rouletabille was not to be so easily shaken off. He moved closer to the judge, and, showing him a copy of *Le Matin*, which he drew from his pocket, said:

'There is one thing, Monsieur, which I may inquire of you without being indiscreet. Did you read the account given in *Le Matin*? It is absurd, is it not?'

'Not in the least, Monsieur.'

'What! The Yellow Room has but one barred window, the bars of which have not been moved, and only one door, which had to be broken down – and the murderer was not found?'

'That is so, Monsieur, that is so. That is how the problem stands.'

Rouletabille said no more, but immersed himself in thoughts known only to himself and remained thus for a quarter of an hour.

When he returned to us, he said, again addressing the judge:

'How was Mlle Stangerson wearing her hair that evening?'

'I don't see what that has to do with anything,' replied M. de Marquet.

'It is an extremely important point,' said Rouletabille. 'Her hair was parted in the middle, wasn't it? I am convinced that on that evening, the evening of the tragedy, she had her hair parted in the middle and looped back over her forehead on either side.'

'Then, Monsieur Rouletabille, you are quite mistaken,' replied the judge. 'That evening Mlle Stangerson had her hair drawn up in a knot on the top of her head. It must be her usual way of dressing it. Her forehead was completely uncovered, I can assure you, for we have carefully examined the wound. There was no blood on her hair, and Mlle Stangerson's coiffure has not been touched since the crime was committed.'

'You are sure? You are quite sure that, on the night of the crime, she did not have her hair looped over her forehead?'

'Perfectly sure,' the judge continued, smiling, 'for I remember the doctor saying to me, while he was examining the wound, 'It is a great pity that Mlle Stangerson was in the habit of wearing her hair off her forehead. If she had worn it differently, the blow she received on the temple would have been softened.' It seems rather odd that you should attach so much importance to this point.'

'Ah, if only she had worn her hair over her forehead!' said Rouletabille, looking discouraged. 'What a mystery! And I must solve it.' And he really did look desperate.

'And is the wound to her temple very serious?' he asked presently.

'Very.'

'What weapon did the attacker use?'

'That, my dear sir, is a secret of the investigation.'

'Have you found the weapon?'

The judge did not answer.

'And what about the injuries to her throat?'

M. de Marquet informed us that the injuries were such that, according to the doctors, had the murderer kept the pressure up for a few seconds longer, Mlle Stangerson would have died of strangulation.

'The case, as reported in *Le Matin*,' said Rouletabille, as keen as ever, 'seems to be more and more inexplicable. Can you tell me, Monsieur, what doors and windows there are in the pavilion?'

'There are five,' replied M. de Marquet, having coughed once or twice, giving way at last to the desire he felt to recount the whole fantastic mystery of the case he was investigating. 'There are five: the door to the hall, which is the only entrance to the pavilion; this door is always closed and cannot be opened, either from outside or in, except by two special keys that Old Jacques or M. Stangerson always keep with them. Mlle Stangerson has no need of a key, since Old Jacques lives in the pavilion, and since, during the daytime, she never leaves her father's side. When all four of them rushed into the Yellow Room, after breaking down the bedroom door, the door in the hall was closed as usual. Old Jacques had one of the keys in his pocket and M. Stangerson the other.

As for the windows in the pavilion, there are four – one in the Yellow Room, two in the laboratory and one in the hall. The window in the Yellow Room and those in the laboratory look out over open countryside. The only window looking out over the park is the one in the hall.'

'That was the window he must have escaped through!' exclaimed Rouletabille.

'How do you know that?' asked M. de Marquet, fixing my young friend with a strange look.

'We'll see later on how the murderer escaped from the Yellow Room,' replied Rouletabille 'but he must have left the pavilion by the hall window.'

'Once more, how do you know that?'

'How? Why the thing is simple! Since it is quite obvious that he could not escape through the door to the pavilion, it is clear that he must have climbed through a window, and for him to do that, there must be at least one window with no iron bars. The window in the Yellow Room is secured by iron bars, because it looks out over the countryside; the two laboratory windows are evidently protected in a like manner for the same reason. Since the murderer got away, I imagine that he found a window that was not barred, and that must be the hall window, which opens on to the park, that is, on to the property itself. One doesn't need witchcraft to find that out.'

'Yes,' said M. de Marquet, 'but as you might have guessed, that window, the only one which is not barred, has solid iron shutters. Now those iron shutters remained fastened with an iron latch, and yet we have proof that the murderer made his escape from the pavilion through that very window. Traces of blood on the inside wall and on the shutters, and footprints on the ground – footprints which are identical to those I found and measured in the Yellow Room – establish the fact that the murderer made his escape through that window. But, then, how did he do it, seeing that the shutters remained fastened on the inside? He passed through the shutters like a shadow. And, finally, the most bewildering part of it all is that it is impossible to form any idea as to how the criminal got out of the Yellow Room, or how he passed through the laboratory to reach the hall, for he had to go that way. Ah, yes, M. Rouletabille, it is altogether a fine case, a bewildering and fascinating case. And the key to it will not be found for a long time, I hope.'

'You hope, Monsieur?'

M. de Marquet corrected himself.

'I do not hope, I think. That is what I meant.'

'Could that window have been closed and refastened after the flight of the murderer?' asked Rouletabille.

'Of course, that seems the most natural explanation to me at present, though that in itself remains inexplicable, for it would imply an accomplice – or even accomplices – and I don't see . . .'

After a short silence, he added:

'Ah, if only Mlle Stangerson were well enough today to allow us to question her!'

Following up his thought, Rouletabille asked:

'And what about the attic? There must be some opening in that attic!'

'Yes, I forgot all about the attic. There is, in fact, a window – or, rather, a skylight – which, since it looks out over the countryside, M. Stangerson has had barred, like the other windows. Those bars, like all the windows on the ground floor, remained intact, and the shutters, which naturally open inwards, remained closed. Besides, we have not found anything that could lead us to suspect that the murderer passed through the attic.'

'It seems clear to you then, Monsieur, that the murderer escaped – though how no one knows – through the hall window?'

'Everything seems to indicate that.'

'I think so myself,' declared Rouletabille gravely. After a brief silence, he continued:

'If you found no trace of the murderer in the attic – for example, footprints similar to those found on the floor of the Yellow Room – you must conclude that it was not he who stole Old Jacques' revolver.'

'There are no traces in the attic other than those left by Old Jacques himself,' said the judge, with a significant turn of the head. And he completed his thoughts by saying: 'Luckily for Old Jacques, he was with M. Stangerson in the laboratory. So what part did his revolver play in the attack? It seems very clear that the weapon did less injury to Mlle Stangerson than to the murderer.'

Without replying to this question, which doubtless embarrassed him, M. de Marquet told us that two bullets had been found in the Yellow Room – one in the wall stained with the print of a man's large hand – and the other in the ceiling.

'Ah-ha, in the ceiling!' muttered Rouletabille. 'In the ceiling! That is most interesting! In the ceiling!'

He puffed away on his pipe for a while in silence, shrouding himself in clouds of smoke. When we reached Epinay-sur-Orge, I had to give him a tap on the shoulder to rouse him from his reverie and remind him to step out on to the station platform.

There the judge and his clerk bowed politely, and gave us to understand that they had seen quite enough of us; then they quickly got into a trap that was awaiting them.

'How long does it take to walk to the Chateau du Glandier?' Rouletabille asked one of the porters.

'About an hour and a half to an hour and three-quarters easy walking,' the man replied.

Having looked up at the sky and found its appearance satisfactory, Rouletabille took my arm and said:

'Come on, I need a walk.'

'Well,' I asked, 'are things becoming less confusing?'

'Not a bit of it,' he said, 'the whole affair seems more confusing than ever! I have an idea though.'

'What idea?'

'I can't say anything just now. My idea is one that involves the life or death of at least two people.'

'Do you think there are accomplices?'

'I don't.'

We fell silent. Presently, he went on:

'It was a bit of luck our falling in with the judge and his clerk. By the way, was I not right about the revolver?'

His head was bent, he had his hands in his pockets, and he was whistling. After a while, I heard him murmur:

'Poor woman!'

'Is it Mlle Stangerson you pity?'

'Yes, she's a fine woman and worthy of being pitied! She is a woman of great strength of character, and I fancy – I fancy . . .'

'You know her, then?'

'Not at all. I have seen her but once.'

'Why, then, do you say that she is a woman of great strength of character?'

'Because she bravely faced the murderer; because she courageously defended herself; and, above all – oh, above all – because of that bullet in the ceiling!'

I looked at Rouletabille and wondered to myself whether he was not mocking me, or whether he had not suddenly taken leave of his senses. But I soon saw that he had never seemed less inclined to joke, and the brightness of his keen, clever eyes assured me that he still had all his wits. Then, too, I was getting used to his broken way of talking, which, most of the time, left me puzzled as to his meaning, till suddenly, with a few rapidly spoken sentences, he made his idea quite plain to me. Then everything became quite clear. The words he had spoken, apparently devoid of sense, became so thoroughly logical, their meaning so transparent, that I could not understand how I had not seen it sooner.

CHAPTER IV

Amidst wild nature

The Chateau du Glandier is one of the oldest chateaux in the Ile-de-France. It stands a few hundred yards from the road which leads from the village of Ste-Geneviève to Monthéry. A collection of somewhat incongruous structures, it is dominated by a tower, which is supposed to contain the remains of Ste-Geneviève, the patron saint of Paris.

When M. Stangerson bought the estate, about fifteen years before the drama with which we are concerned took place, the Chateau du Glandier had been unoccupied for a long time.

Another old chateau in the neighbourhood was also empty, so that the region was practically deserted. There were a few small houses on the road leading to Corbeil and an inn, called the Tower Inn, which offered hospitality to passing waggoners; these were the only remnant of civilisation in that out-of-the-way place.

M. Stangerson was already famous. He had just returned from America, where his work had made a tremendous impact. The book which he had published in Philadelphia on the dissociation of matter through the use of electricity had aroused controversy throughout the whole of the scientific world. M. Stangerson was a Frenchman, but of American origin. Some complicated legal affairs to do with an inheritance had kept him in the United States for several years, and there he had continued the work that he had begun in France, whither he had finally returned in possession of a large fortune. This fortune was most welcome to him for, although he might have made millions of dollars merely from exploiting two or three of the chemical discoveries he had made regarding new dyeing processes, it was always repellent to him to use

29

for personal gain the wonderful gift of invention which he had received from Nature. He did not regard this gift as his. He owed it to mankind and this philanthropic view meant that everything that his genius brought into the world belonged in the public domain.

He did not try to conceal his satisfaction at coming into possession of this large fortune, which would enable him to devote himself to his passion: pure science, and it seemed that he had further reasons for rejoicing. At the time that her father returned from America and bought the Glandier estate, Mlle Stangerson was twenty years of age. She was exceedingly pretty, having both the Parisian grace of her mother – who had died in childbirth – and all the vigour of her American grandfather. William Stangerson, a citizen of Philadelphia, had been obliged to become a naturalised Frenchman for family reasons at the time of his marriage to a French lady – the future mother of the illustrious Professor Stangerson. This explains the professor's French nationality.

At twenty, Mathilde Stangerson was one of the most beautiful girls of marriageable age in either the old or the new world – a charming blonde, with blue eyes and a milk-white complexion. It was her father's duty – in spite of the sorrow which any separation from her would cause him – to think of her marriage and to give her a dowry. Instead he buried himself and his child at Glandier at the very moment when his friends were expecting him to introduce her into society. Some of them expressed their astonishment. To their questions, the professor answered:

'It is my daughter's wish. I can refuse her nothing. She chose Glandier herself.'

When questioned, the young girl calmly replied:

'What better place for our work than here amidst this solitude?'

For Mlle Stangerson already helped her father in his work, though it could not then be supposed that her passion for science would lead her so far as to discourage all the suitors who presented themselves to her over a period of more than fifteen years. However secluded the life led by both father and daughter, they still had to appear at a few official receptions and, at certain times of the year, in the drawing rooms of two or three friends, where the professor's reputation as a scientist and Mathilde's beauty caused a sensation. The young woman's attitude did not at first discourage suitors, but after a few years, they tired of the quest.

Only one persisted, with tender tenacity, and earned the name of 'the perpetual fiancé', which he accepted with melancholy resignation; he was M. Robert Darzac. Mlle Stangerson was no longer young and, having found no reason to marry in all her five-and-thirty years, it seemed that she never would. But such arguments evidently meant nothing to M. Robert Darzac, who continued to pay court – if the delicate and tender affection with which he ceaselessly surrounded this woman can be called courtship – in the face of her declared intention never to marry.

Suddenly, some weeks before the events with which we are concerned here, a rumour spread around Paris. No one attached much importance to it, since it seemed too incredible to be true. It was said that Mlle Stangerson had, at last, consented to marry M. Robert Darzac! It was only when M. Robert Darzac himself made no denial of this rumour of impending matrimony that people slowly began to see that this unlikely report might be true. Finally, as he was leaving the Academy of Science one day, M. Stangerson declared that the marriage of his daughter to M. Robert Darzac would be celebrated in the privacy of the Chateau du Glandier, as soon as he and his daughter had put the finishing touches to the paper which would be the summation of all their work on the dissociation of matter, that is to say, on the return of matter to ether. The new couple would settle down at Glandier, and the son-in-law would help in the work to which father and daughter had devoted their lives.

The world of science had not yet had time to recover from this news, when it learned of the attempted murder of Mlle Stangerson in the fantastic circumstances which we have already related, and which our visit to the chateau will now enable us to ascertain with yet greater precision.

CHAPTER V

In which Joseph Rouletabille addresses a few words to M. Robert Darzac and gets a strange reaction

We had been walking for several minutes, Rouletabille and I, along a wall enclosing M. Stangerson's estate, when our attention was drawn to a man half-bent over the ground, so absorbed in what he was doing that he did not see us coming towards him. One moment he stooped so low that he almost touched the ground, the next he drew himself up and peered at the wall; then he stood studying the palm of his right hand, then walked away with long strides, broke into a run, and again looked into the palm of his own hand. Rouletabille brought me to a halt with a gesture.

'Hush! It is Frédéric Larsan at work! We mustn't disturb him.'

Joseph Rouletabille had a great admiration for the celebrated detective. I had never seen Frédéric Larsan before, but I knew him well by reputation.

He had become a well-known figure after he solved the mysterious case of the theft of the gold ingots from the Paris Mint and after his capture of the gang who had cracked the safe in the vaults of the Banque de Crédit Universelle. He was considered at the time to be the most skilful unraveller of the most mysterious and complicated crimes. His reputation had spread throughout the world. It will thus surprise no one that, at the very outset of the mystery of the Yellow Room, the head of Sûreté should have wired to him to return immediately. Frédéric, who was known at the Sûreté as 'the Great Fred', had made all speed, doubtless knowing by experience that the Sûreté would only interrupt his work if he were urgently needed in another quarter. As Rouletabille said, Larsan was already at work. We soon discovered what that work involved.

It was his watch that he kept looking at in the palm of his right hand and he seemed to be timing something. Then he turned back, again breaking into a run and stopping only when he reached the park gate, where he again consulted his watch. He put it away in his pocket, gave a discouraged shrug of his shoulders, pushed open the gate, entered the park, closed the gate, and locked it. When he looked up, he saw us through the bars. Joseph Rouletabille rushed forward, and I followed. Frédéric Larsan was waiting for us.

'Monsieur Fred,' said Rouletabille, raising his hat, 'can you tell me whether M. Robert Darzac is at the chateau at the moment? This is a lawyer friend of his from Paris who would like to speak to him.'

'I really don't know, M. Rouletabille,' replied Larsan, shaking hands with my friend, whom he had met several times in the course of some of his more difficult inquiries. 'I have not seen him.'

'The caretakers will doubtless be able to tell us,' said Rouletabille, pointing to the lodge.

'The caretakers will not be able to tell you anything, M. Rouletabille.'

'Why not?'

'Because they were arrested half an hour ago.'

'Arrested!' cried Rouletabille. 'Are they the murderers then?'

Frédéric Larsan shrugged his shoulders.

'When one cannot arrest the murderer,' he said, with an ironic air, 'one can always indulge in the luxury of discovering accomplices.'

'Is it you who had them arrested, Monsieur Fred?'

'No, no, not I. I didn't have them arrested. In the first place, because I am pretty sure that they have nothing to do with the case, and also because . . .'

'Because of what?' asked Rouletabille eagerly.

'Oh, nothing,' said Larsan, shaking his head.

'Because there are no accomplices,' whispered Rouletabille.

Frédéric Larsan started and looked at him intently.

'Aha! You have an idea, then, about this matter? Yet you

33

have seen nothing, young man. You have not yet gained admission here.'

'I will though.'

'I doubt it. There are strict orders to allow no one in.'

'I shall gain admission if you let me see M. Robert Darzac. Do that for me! We are old friends, Monsieur Fred. Please! Remember the fine story I wrote about you and the case of the gold ingots!'

Rouletabille's face was truly comic to observe. It expressed such an irresistible desire to cross the threshold beyond which the prodigious mystery had occurred. There was such eloquence not only in his lips and eyes but in every feature, that I could not help but burst out laughing. Frédéric Larsan could not keep a straight face any more than I could.

Meanwhile, behind the gate, he calmly put the key in his pocket. I studied him.

He was a man of about fifty. He had a fine head of greying hair, a pale complexion and a strong profile. His forehead was high and bulging; his chin and cheeks were clean-shaven; his upper lip – without a moustache – was finely delineated. His eyes were rather small and round, and he looked at people in a way that was at once searching and disquieting. He was well-built and of medium height, and had a pleasant, elegant air about him. There was nothing of the vulgar detective in his appearance. He was a great artist in his way; he knew it, and one felt that he had a high opinion of himself.

Larsan turned his head at the sound of a vehicle which had come from the chateau and had just reached the gate behind him. We recognised the trap that had conveyed the judge and his clerk from the station at Epinay.

'Well,' said Frédéric Larsan, 'you wanted to speak to Robert Darzac. There he is.'

The trap was at the gate and Robert Darzac was asking Frédéric Larsan to open it for him, since he was pressed for time if he was to catch the next train to Paris, when he recognised me. While Larsan was unlocking the gate, Darzac asked what had brought me to Glandier at such a tragic time. I then noticed his deathly pallor, the deep sorrow etched on his face.

'Is Mlle Stangerson better?' I asked.

'Yes,' he said 'they may be able to save her. She must be saved.'

He did not add, 'or it will be the death of me,' but the words trembled on his pale lips.

Rouletabille then intervened.

'You are in a hurry, Monsieur. Yet I must speak to you. I have something of the greatest importance to tell you.'

Frédéric Larsan interrupted them.

'May I leave you?' he asked of Robert Darzac. 'Have you a key, or do you want me to leave you this one?'

'Thank you, no. I have a key myself and will lock the gate behind me.'

Larsan hurried off in the direction of the chateau whose imposing mass was visible a few hundred yards away.

Robert Darzac was frowning, and already showing signs of impatience. I introduced Rouletabille as a friend of mine, but as soon as he learnt that the young man was a journalist, M. Darzac looked at me reproachfully and, explaining that he had to be at Epinay in twenty minutes, he bowed and whipped on his horse. To my amazement, though, Rouletabille seized the bridle and stopped the horse, meanwhile pronouncing these, to me, utterly meaningless words:

'The vicarage has lost none of its charm nor the garden its brightness.'

These words had no sooner left Rouletabille's lips than I saw Robert Darzac falter. Pale as he was, he grew paler still. His eyes were fixed in terror on the young man, and he immediately stepped from the trap in an inexpressible state of agitation.

'Let us go!' he stammered. 'Let us go!'

Then, all of a sudden, with a sort of fury, he repeated:

'Let us go, Monsieur! Let us go!'

And he turned back down the road leading to the chateau, while Rouletabille followed him, still holding the horse's bridle. I said a few words to M. Darzac, but he did not answer me. I looked at Rouletabille questioningly, but he did not see me.

CHAPTER VI

In the depths of the oak grove

We reached the chateau, and, as we approached it, saw four gendarmes pacing up and down in front of a small door on the ground floor of the tower. We soon learned that this was where Bernier and his wife, the caretakers, were confined.

M. Robert Darzac led us into the modern part of the chateau by a large door. Rouletabille, who had left the horse and trap in the care of a servant, never took his eyes off Darzac. I followed the direction of his gaze and found that it was fixed on the Sorbonne professor's gloved hands. When we found ourselves in a small sitting-room, M. Darzac turned to Rouletabille and said rather sharply:

'Speak! What do you want?'

The reporter answered in an equally sharp tone:

'I want to shake hands with you.'

Darzac shrank back.

'What does that mean?'

He evidently understood what I then understood myself – that my friend suspected him of being responsible for the abominable attempt on Mlle Stangerson's life. He suddenly remembered the bloody handprint on the walls of the Yellow Room. I took a close look at this man, with his noble features and usually frank gaze, who, at this moment, was so strangely troubled. He held out his right hand and, pointing to me, said:

'You are a friend of M. Sainclair who once rendered me a great service in a lawsuit, Monsieur, and I see no reason to refuse you my hand.'

Rouletabille did not take the extended hand. He said, lying with the utmost audacity:

'Monsieur, I have lived for several years in Russia, where I have learned never to shake any but an ungloved hand.'

I thought then that the Sorbonne professor was going to give vent to his rage, but, instead, he managed to calm himself, remove his glove and present his hand to Rouletabille. There was not a mark on it.

'Are you satisfied?'

'No,' replied Rouletabille. 'My dear friend,' he said, turning to me, 'I must ask you to leave us alone for a moment.'

I bowed and withdrew, amazed at what I had just seen and heard. I was at a loss to know why M. Robert Darzac had not already shown my impertinent and stupid friend the door. I was, at the time, angry with Rouletabille on account of his insulting suspicions, which had led to the extraordinary incident with the glove.

For some twenty minutes, I strolled up and down in front of the chateau, trying to connect the different events of the day, and failing to do so. What was going on in Rouletabille's mind? Did he really think that M. Robert Darzac was the attacker? How could anyone think that this man, who was shortly to have married Mlle Stangerson, could have gained entry into the Yellow Room in order to murder his own fiancée? Besides, no one had as yet managed to explain how the criminal managed to escape from the Yellow Room; and so long as that mystery, which appeared to me so inexplicable, remained unsolved, I thought it the duty of all to refrain from suspecting anybody. And then, what was the meaning of that seemingly senseless phrase: 'The vicarage has lost none of its charm nor the garden its brightness,' which still rang in my ears? I was anxious to rejoin Rouletabille and question him about that mysterious sentence.

At that moment, the young reporter emerged from the chateau, together with M. Robert Darzac, and, extraordinary though it may seem, I saw at a glance that they were the best of friends.

'We're going to the Yellow Room. Come with us,' Rouletabille said to me. 'By the way, old fellow, I'm keeping you with me all day. We'll lunch together locally.'

'You'll lunch with me here, gentlemen . . .'

'No,' replied the young man, 'thank you kindly, but we'll lunch at the Tower Inn.'

'You'll fare very badly there.'

'Do you think so? Well, I hope to learn something there,' Rouletabille replied. 'After luncheon, we'll set to work again. I'll write my article, and you'll be so good as to take it to the office for me.'

'Will you not return to Paris with me?'

'No, I shall remain here overnight.'

I turned to Rouletabille. He spoke quite seriously, and M. Robert Darzac did not appear to be in the least surprised. We were passing the tower and heard wailing voices. Rouletabille asked:

'Why have these people been arrested?'

'It's partly my fault,' said M. Darzac. 'I remarked yesterday to the judge that it was impossible to account for the fact that the caretakers had had time to hear the revolver-shots, get dressed and run from their lodge to the pavilion in the space of two minutes; for that is all the time that elapsed between the firing of the shots and the arrival on the scene of Old Jacques.'

'That is indeed suspicious,' said Rouletabille.

'And they were dressed?'

'That's just it. It seems so incredible. They were fully dressed. The woman wore clogs, but the man had boots on — laced up. Now, they declare that they went to bed at their usual time of half-past nine. When he arrived this morning, the judge brought with him from Paris a revolver of the same calibre as that used in the case. He made the clerk fire two shots in the Yellow Room with the doors and windows closed. We were with him in the caretakers' lodge; we heard nothing; nothing *could* be heard from there. The caretakers lied. There can be no doubt about that. They were already near the pavilion, waiting for something. Of course, we do not accuse them of being the authors of the crime, but it seems likely that they were accomplices. M. de Marquet had them arrested at once.'

'If they had been accomplices,' said Rouletabille, 'they would have arrived in a dishevelled state or, rather, they would not have arrived at all. When people throw themselves into the arms of the law with so many proofs of their complicity about them, it is because they are *not* accomplices. I don't believe there are any accomplices in this affair.'

'Then, why were they abroad at midnight? Let them explain themselves.'

'There is obviously some reason why they will not speak. What that reason is remains to be seen. But, even if they are not accomplices, it may be important to know that reason. Everything that takes place on such a night is important.'

We had just crossed an old bridge over the Douve, and were entering the part of the park known as the oak grove. This place, where Mlle Stangerson lived for part of the year because she found it cheerful, appeared to us sad and dreary. The soil was black and muddy from the recent rain and the decaying leaves around the trunks of the trees were black; the dull, dark sky was thick with heavy clouds as if in mourning.

It was in this desolate retreat that we found the white walls of the pavilion. A strange building indeed, without a window to be seen from where we stood. Only a small door marked the entrance. As we came nearer, we were able to make out its plan. The building took all the light it needed from the south – that is to say, from the open country. When the small door that gave on to the park was closed, M. and Mlle Stangerson must have found there an ideal prison in which to live with their work and their dreams.

I will now give the plan of the pavilion. It had but one floor – the ground floor – which was reached by a few steps and, above it, an attic with which we need not concern ourselves. It is, then, the plan of the ground floor in all its simplicity which I here submit to the reader.

This plan was drawn by Rouletabille himself and I have ascertained that it was complete, and that there was not a line missing in it that might have led to the solution of the problem then set before us.

Before mounting the three steps leading up to the door of the pavilion, Rouletabille stopped, and said point-blank to M. Darzac:

'So what was the motive for the crime?'

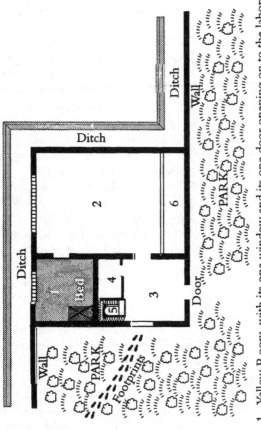

1. Yellow Room, with its one window and its one door opening on to the laboratory.
2. Laboratory, with its two large barred windows and its two doors, one opening on to the hall, the other on to the Yellow Room.
3. Hall with its unbarred window and door opening on to the park.
4. Washroom.
5. Stairs to the attic.
6. The pavilion's large and only fireplace, used for experiments in the laboratory.

40

'Speaking for myself, Monsieur, there can be no doubts on the subject,' said Mlle Stangerson's fiancé, greatly distressed. 'The fingermarks and the deep scratches on Mlle Stangerson's chest and throat show that the wretch who attacked her tried to commit a dastardly crime. The medical experts who examined those marks yesterday declare that the hand that made them was the same as the hand that left the print on the wall – an enormous hand and much too large to fit my glove, Monsieur,' he added with a bitter smile.

'Could not that red mark,' I broke in, 'have been left by Mlle Stangerson, who, as she fell, leant against the wall and left on it, as she slid to the ground, an enlarged impression of her blood-stained hand?'

'There was not a drop of blood on either of Mlle Stangerson's hands when she was found lying on the floor,' replied M. Darzac.

'It is clear, then,' I said, 'that it was Mlle Stangerson who was armed with Old Jacques' revolver, since she wounded the murderer in the hand. Was she in fear of somebody or something?'

'Probably.'

'There is no one you suspect?'

'No,' replied M. Darzac, looking at Rouletabille.

Rouletabille then said to me:

'I must tell you, my friend, that the inquiry is a little more advanced than M. de Marquet chose to tell us. It is not only known that the revolver was the weapon with which Mlle Stangerson defended herself, but the other weapon used to attack and strike Mlle Stangerson has been known from the first. It was, so M. Darzac tells me, a cudgel made from a sheep's bone. Why is M. de Marquet being so mysterious about this bone? Is it with the object of helping the investigation? Probably. He imagines perhaps that its owner will be found amongst those who are known in the criminal haunts of Paris to use this instrument of crime, the most terrible that nature has invented. But who knows what goes on in the mind of an judge,' Rouletabille added, with contemptuous irony.

'A cudgel was found in the Yellow Room, then?' I asked.

'Yes, Monsieur,' said Robert Darzac, 'at the foot of the bed. But, I beg you, don't say anything about that, for we have promised M. de Marquet not to mention it.'

I nodded.

'It is an enormous bone, the top of which – or, rather, the joint – was still red with blood from the wound inflicted on Mlle Stangerson. It is an old bone, which, according to appearances, must have been used for other crimes. So thinks M. de. Marquet, who has had it taken to the Municipal Laboratory in Paris to be analysed. In fact, he thinks he has detected on this bone, not only the blood of the last victim, but the dried bloodstains from previous crimes.'

'A cudgel like that in the hands of a skilled murderer is a terrible weapon,' said Rouletabille, 'more efficient than a heavy hammer.'

'The scoundrel has made that clear enough,' said M. Robert Darzac painfully. 'The joint of the bone fits the wound perfectly. My belief is that the wound would have been fatal had Mlle Stangerson not fired the revolver. Wounded in the hand, her attacker dropped the bone and fled. Unfortunately, the blow had already been struck, and Mlle Stangerson was stunned, after having first been nearly strangled. If she had succeeded in wounding the man with the first shot, she would doubtless have escaped the blow. She obviously picked up the revolver too late, and, in the struggle, the first shot she fired became lodged in the ceiling. It was only the second that hit home.'

M. Darzac then knocked at the door of the pavilion. My impatience to enter the place where the crime had been committed may easily be imagined. I was trembling with excitement and, in spite of the great interest I took in the account of the attack, it irritated me to find that our conversation was becoming protracted, and that the door of the pavilion remained firmly closed.

At last it was opened.

A man, whom I recognised at once as Old Jacques, stood on the threshold.

He appeared to be well over sixty years of age. He had a long, white beard and silvery hair; he wore a Basque beret. He looked rather surly and cross, but his expression lightened as soon as he saw M. Darzac.

'Friends of mine,' our guide said simply. 'Is anyone in the pavilion, Jacques?'

'I am not supposed to allow anybody to enter, Monsieur Robert, but, of course, the order does not apply to you. Besides, what do they mean by their secrecy? Those officials have seen everything there was to be seen, and taken enough sketches and drawn up enough reports . . .'

'Excuse me, Monsieur Jacques. One question before anything else,' said Rouletabille.

'What is it, young man? If I can answer it, I will.'

'Did your mistress that night wear her hair parted in the middle and looped back?'

'No, young man. My mistress has never worn her hair in that fashion, neither on that day nor on any other. She had her hair combed back, as usual, so that you could see her beautiful forehead.'

Rouletabille grunted, and at once set about examining the door. He inspected the catch. He satisfied himself that it could not possibly remain open, and that a key was required to open it.

Then we entered the hall, a small, well-lit room, paved with square red tiles.

'This is the window by which the murderer escaped!'

'So they say, Monsieur, so they keep on saying! But if he had gone off that way we would have seen him. We are not blind, neither M. Stangerson nor I, nor the caretakers whom they've put in prison. Why don't they put me in prison, too, on account of my revolver?'

Rouletabille had already opened the window, and was examining the shutters.

'Were these closed at the time of the crime?'

'Yes. They were fastened with the iron bar inside,' said Old Jacques, 'and I am pretty well certain that the murderer did not get out that way!'

43

'Are there any bloodstains?'

'Yes there are, on the stones outside. But what kind of blood?'

'Ah,' said Rouletabille, 'I can see the footprints on the path there; the ground must have been very damp. I'll examine them presently.'

'Nonsense!' said Old Jacques. 'The murderer did not go that way!'

'Indeed? Well, which way, did he go then?'

'How should I know?'

Rouletabille was looking at everything, sniffing everything. He went down on his knees and rapidly examined the tiled floor. Old Jacques went on:

'Ah, you won't find anything there, young man! Nothing has been found. Besides, it's all dirty now; too many people have been in here. They won't let me wash the floor. But on the day of the crime I had washed it thoroughly – I, Old Jacques; and if the murderer had walked through here with his dirty boots, I would have seen it. He left enough footprints in Mademoiselle's room.'

Rouletabille rose, and asked:

'When did you last wash the floor?'

And he fixed his searching eyes on Old Jacques.

'Why, as I told you, on the day of the crime, at about half-past five. The next day the judge came and saw all the marks there were on the floor, as plainly as if they had been made with ink on white paper. Well, there were no footprints to be found either in the hall or in the laboratory, which were both as clean as a whistle! Since they were found outside this window, he must have got into the attic above the Yellow Room then cut a hole through the roof and dropped to the ground right outside the hall window. But there's no hole either in the ceiling of the Yellow Room or in the roof of my attic. So you see, no one knows anything, nothing. And nothing will ever be known. It is a mystery of the Devil's own making.'

Rouletabille knelt down again, almost in front of a small washroom at the back of the hall. He remained in that position for almost a minute.

'Well?' I asked him when he got up.

'Oh, nothing very important, just a drop of blood.'

He then turned to Old Jacques.

'When you began cleaning the laboratory and the hall, was the hall window open?'

'No, Monsieur, it was closed, but after I had finished washing the floor, I lit some charcoal for Monsieur in the laboratory furnace. I used some old newspapers to light it, so there was a bit of smoke and I opened the two windows in the laboratory and this one, to create a through draught, then I shut the windows in the laboratory, left the hall window open, and went out. When I returned to the pavilion this window had been closed, and Monsieur and Mademoiselle were already at work in the laboratory.'

'M. or Mlle Stangerson had, no doubt, shut it?'

'No doubt.'

'You did not ask them?'

'No.'

After a close inspection of the little washroom and of the staircase leading up to the attic, Rouletabille went into the laboratory. It was, I confess, in a state of great excitement that I followed him. Robert Darzac kept his eyes fixed on my friend, but my eyes went straight to the door of the Yellow Room. It was closed and, as I immediately saw, badly battered.

My young friend, who went about his work methodically, was silently studying the room in which we were standing. It was large and well-lit. Two large windows – almost bay windows – fitted with strong iron bars, looked out upon a large sweep of open country.

The whole of one side of the laboratory was taken up by a vast fireplace, with crucibles, furnaces, retorts and other instruments used for chemical experiments. There were tables laden with phials, documents, and a small electrical machine, an apparatus, as M. Darzac informed me, which was used by Professor Stangerson to demonstrate the dissociation of matter under the action of sunlight, etc.

Along the walls there were cabinets, with or without glass

fronts, full of microscopes, special cameras, and an amazing quantity of chemical crystals.

Rouletabille was ferreting around in the fireplace. He investigated the contents of crucibles with the tip of his finger. Then he suddenly drew himself up, holding a piece of half-consumed paper in his hand. He came over to where we were standing talking by one of the windows, and said:

'Keep that for us, Monsieur Darzac.'

I bent over the piece of scorched paper which M. Darzac had just taken from the hand of Rouletabille, and read the following words – the only ones still legible:

'. . .The vicarage has lost none of its charm nor the garden its brightness.'

Underneath was a date: 23rd October.

That was the second time that those same meaningless words had struck me, and for the second time I saw the effect they had on M. Darzac. M. Darzac immediately glanced across at Old Jacques, but the latter had not seen us, being busy over at the other window. Then, trembling, Mlle Stangerson's fiancé opened his pocket-book, placed the piece of paper in it and said with a deep sigh:

'My God!'

Meanwhile, Rouletabille had clambered into the fireplace – that is to say, he had got onto the bricks at the back. He was intently examining the chimney, which grew narrower as it went up, and which, about three feet above him, was closed with sheets of iron fastened into the brickwork, through which passed three small pipes, each six inches in diameter.

'Impossible to get in or out that way,' he said, jumping back into the laboratory. 'Besides, even if 'he' had attempted it, he would have brought all that iron-work down with him. No, that is not where we should look.'

Rouletabille next examined the furniture, and opened the doors of the cabinets. Then it was the turn of the windows, through which he declared no one could possibly have passed, and through which no one had passed or attempted to pass. At the second window he found Old Jacques still in contemplation.

46

'Well, Old Jacques,' he said, 'what are you staring at?'

'I'm watching the detective there. He keeps going round and round the lake. That's another fellow who'll find out nothing!'

'You don't know Frédéric Larsan, Old Jacques, or you wouldn't speak of him in that way,' said Rouletabille, in sombre tones. 'If there is one person here who will find the murderer, it is he.'

And Rouletabille heaved a deep sigh.

'Before they can catch the criminal, they'll first have to find out how they lost him,' said Old Jacques stolidly.

At last we came to the door of the Yellow Room.

CHAPTER VII

In which Rouletabille makes investigations under the bed

Having pushed open the door of the Yellow Room, Rouletabille paused on the threshold and said in an emotional voice I was only to understand much later:

'Ah, the perfume of the lady in black!'

The room was dark. Old Jacques wanted to open the shutters, but Rouletabille stopped him.

'Did the drama take place in total darkness?' he asked.

'No, young man, I don't think so. Mlle Stangerson always insisted on having a nightlight on her table, and it was I who lit it every evening before she went to bed. I was a sort of chambermaid, you understand, when the evening came. The real chambermaid only came here in the morning. Mademoiselle works late into the night.'

'Where did the table with the nightlight stand? Far from the bed?'

'Some way from the bed.'

'Can you put a match to the nightlight?'

'It's broken and the oil in it was spilled when the table was upset. Besides, all the things in the room have been left just as they were. I have only to open the shutters and you shall see for yourself.'

'Stop!'

Rouletabille went back into the laboratory, closed the shutters of the two windows there, and the door of the hall as well. When we were in complete darkness, he lit a taper, gave it to Old Jacques, and told him to move to the middle of the room with it, to the place where the nightlight was burning that day.

Old Jacques, who was in his stocking feet – he generally left his clogs in the hall – went into the Yellow Room holding the taper, and we had a vague impression of a floor strewn with various objects, of a bed in one corner, and, in front of us to the left, the gleam of a looking-glass hanging on the wall near to the bed.

Rouletabille said:

'That'll do. You may now open the shutters'

'Don't come any further,' Old Jacques said. 'You might make marks with your boots, and nothing must be disturbed or altered. That at least is what the judge said, though he will not need to come into this room again now.'

He opened the shutters. Pale daylight filtered in, casting a ghostly gleam on the saffron-coloured walls. The floor – for, although the laboratory and the hall were tiled, the Yellow Room had wooden flooring – was covered with a yellow carpet which covered nearly the whole surface, even under the bed and the washstand, the only pieces of furniture still standing. The round table, the bedside table and the two chairs had been overturned. There was also a large bloodstain on the carpet, made, as Old Jacques informed us, by blood from the wound on Mlle Stangerson's forehead. Indeed there were drops of blood everywhere, following as it were the would-be murderer's large, black footsteps. Everything led one to believe that these drops of blood came from the wound of the man who had, for a moment, pressed his red hand against the wall. There were other traces of the same hand on the wall, but much less distinct. They were quite obviously the marks of a man's large hand.

I could not help crying out:

'Look at this blood on the wall! The man who pressed his hand so heavily upon it in the darkness must have believed that he was pushing at a door! That's why he pressed so hard, leaving his handprint on the yellow wallpaper like a terrible accusation; for there cannot be many hands of that sort in the world. It is big and strong, and the fingers are nearly all of the same length, apart from the thumb, which is missing; we have only the palm print. And if we follow the track of this hand,' I continued, 'we can see how it groped its way along that side, felt for the door, found it and then felt for the lock.'

'No doubt,' said Rouletabille, chuckling. 'Except there is no blood on the lock or on the bolt.'

'What does that prove?' I retorted, with a degree of logic of which I was quite proud. 'He probably drew the bolt and opened the lock with his left hand, which would have been quite natural, since it was his right hand that was wounded.'

'He didn't open it at all!' said Old Jacques. 'We are not fools, you know! And there were four of us here when we broke down the door!'

I went on:

'What a strange hand though!'

'It's a normal hand,' said Rouletabille, 'it's just that the imprint of it was distorted as it slipped on the wall. The criminal must be a man of about five-foot-eight.'

'How do you know?'

'By the position of the handprint on the wall.'

My friend was concerned next with the round bullet hole in the wall.

'This bullet,' said Rouletabille, 'was fired straight – I mean, neither from above nor from below.' And he further remarked that it was a few inches lower on the wall than the red handprint.

Rouletabille went back to the door and carefully examined the lock and the bolt, and satisfied himself that the door had certainly been broken down from the outside, for the lock and bolt were still on the door – one locked, and the other pulled in from the wall – the two sockets were nearly torn off, and only held in place by a screw or two.

The young reporter examined them, looked at both sides of the door, ascertained that the bolt could not be reached from the outside, that the key had been found in the inner side of the lock, and, finally, that, with the key in the lock and on the inside, it was impossible to open that door from without with any other kind of key. Having made sure of all these details, and also that the door did not close automatically – that it was, in fact, the most ordinary of doors, fitted with a solid lock and bolt, which had remained closed – he said at last: 'That's better!' Then, sitting down on the floor, he rapidly took off his boots.

The next thing he did was to rise and examine the overturned furniture. We watched in silence. Old Jacques kept on saying, ever more ironically:

'Young fellow, you're putting yourself to a great deal of needless trouble.'

Rouletabille raised his head,

'You're quite right, Old Jacques,' he said, 'your mistress did not have her hair parted in the middle that evening. I was a fool to have believed that she did.'

And, supple as a serpent, he slipped under the bed.

Old Jacques then remarked:

'Is it not amazing to think that the murderer was hidden under there? He must have been under that bed at ten o'clock when I came in here to close the shutters and light the nightlight, since neither M. Stangerson, Mlle Mathilde nor I moved from the laboratory afterwards until the moment of the tragedy.'

Presently, we heard Rouletabille shout from under the bed.

'Someone has moved the carpet. Who did it?'

'We did, Monsieur!' Old Jacques exclaimed. 'When we couldn't find the attacker, we wondered whether there was a hole in the floor.'

'There isn't,' replied Rouletabille. 'Is there a cellar?'

'No, there is no cellar. But that didn't stop us and it didn't stop the judge and his clerk from studying the floor, board by board, as if there was a cellar.'

The reporter then reappeared. His eyes were sparkling, his nostrils quivered. He remained on his hands and knees. In fact, I could find no better comparison in my mind than that of an admirable pointer on the scent of some wonderful piece of game. Indeed, he did scent the footsteps of a man, the man whom he had sworn to hand over to his chief, the editor of *L'Epoque*, for it must not be forgotten that Rouletabille was a journalist.

Still on hands and knees, he made his way to each of the four corners of the room, sniffing, so to speak, and studying every object in the place, everything that we could see – which was not much – and everything we could not see – which, it seemed, was considerable.

The washstand was a simple table standing on four legs. Nothing could possibly transform it into a hiding place. There was no wardrobe, for Mlle Stangerson kept her clothes at the chateau.

Rouletabille's hands and even his nose progressed along the walls, which were made of solid brick. When he had done with the walls and passed his nimble fingers over every portion of the yellow paper covering them, he reached the ceiling, which he was able to touch by mounting a chair he had placed on the washstand, moving this ingeniously-constructed ladder from place to place. After he had finished his scrutiny of the ceiling, where he examined the mark left by the other bullet, he went over to the window and examined the iron bars and shutters, all of which were solid and intact. At last, he uttered a sigh of relief and satisfaction and declared that, now, he was quite at ease.

'Do you realise now how securely the unfortunate young lady was locked in when they tried to murder her, when she was calling out for help?' Old Jacques asked mournfully.

'She was indeed!' said the young reporter, wiping the perspiration from his brow. 'The Yellow Room was as securely locked as an iron safe!'

'Exactly,' I said. 'And that is just what makes this mystery the most puzzling I've ever known, even in the realms of the imagination. Even Edgar Allan Poe invented nothing to compare with this in *The Murders in the Rue Morgue*. There the scene of the crime was secure enough to prevent the escape of a man, but there was a window through which a monkey – the perpetrator of the murders – could slip away; but here there can be no question of an opening of any sort. With the door and the shutters fastened and the windows closed, as they were, not even a fly could either enter or escape.'

'In truth,' Rouletabille said, as he mopped his brow, 'in truth, it is a very great, very fascinating and very beautiful mystery.'

'The Good Lord's Beast,' Old Jacques muttered, 'the Good

Lord's Beast itself, had it committed the crime, could not have escaped. Listen! Do you hear? Hush!'

Old Jacques was making a sign for us to keep silent, and with his arm outstretched towards the forest, he was listening to something we could not hear.

'It's gone!' he said at length. 'I shall have to kill that beast. Its cry is too awful – but it is the Good Lord's Beast, and every night, they say, it goes to pray on the tomb of Ste Geneviève, and no one dares touch it lest Mother Agenoux should cast an evil spell on them!'

'How big is this Good Lord's Beast?'

'About the size of a small retriever; it's a monster, I can tell you. Ah, I've more than once wondered whether it was not the beast that took our poor Mademoiselle by the throat with its claws! But the Good Lord's Beast does not wear boots or fire revolvers, nor does it have a hand like that!' exclaimed Old Jacques, again pointing to the red hand on the wall. 'Besides, it would have been shut up in the room and we would have seen it, just as we would have seen a man!'

'Obviously,' I said. 'At first, before we had seen the Yellow Room, I also wondered whether Mother Agenoux's cat . . .'

'What, you too!' cried Rouletabille.

'And you?' I asked.

'Not for a moment! Ever since I read the article in the *Le Matin*, I knew that there was no animal involved. No, a fearful tragedy has been enacted here . . . But you say nothing about the beret or the handkerchief found here, Old Jacques.'

'The judge took them, of course,' the old man answered, hesitantly.

The reporter said to him, very gravely:

'I have seen neither the handkerchief nor the beret, yet I can tell you what they are like.'

'You are very clever!' said Old Jacques, coughing and embarrassed.

'The handkerchief is a large one, blue with red stripes, and the cap is an old Basque beret, like the one you are wearing now!'

'It is true; you must be a sorcerer,' said the old servant,

trying to laugh, but failing. 'But how do you know that the handkerchief is blue with red stripes?'

'Because, if it had not been blue with red stripes, it would not have been found at all.'

Paying no further attention to Old Jacques, my friend took from his pocket a piece of paper and a pair of scissors; he bent over the footprints, placed the paper over one of them, and began to cut. In a short time he had a perfect pattern of it, which he handed to me, begging me not to lose it.

He then returned to the window, and pointing to Frédéric Larsan, who had still not left the shore of the lake, asked Old Jacques whether the detective had, like himself, been working in the Yellow Room.

'No,' replied Robert Darzac, who, since Rouletabille had handed him the piece of scorched paper found in one of the crucibles, had not uttered a single word. 'He says that he does not need to examine the Yellow Room, that the murderer made his escape from it in a perfectly natural way, and that he will explain how he did it this evening.'

Hearing M. Darzac's words, Rouletabille turned pale – a most unusual thing.

'Has Frédéric Larsan actually discovered the truth which I am only just beginning to guess at?' he murmured. 'Frédéric Larsan is a great man, a very great man, and I admire him. But what has to be done today is something more than mere detective work, it requires more than what mere experience can teach us. The man who is to unravel this mystery will have to be logical, as logical as two plus two equals four. He must use his powers of reasoning.'

And the reporter rushed out, frantic at the thought that the great and celebrated Fred might discover, before him, the solution to the mystery of the Yellow Room.

I caught up with him at the door of the pavilion.

'Calm yourself, old chap,' I said. 'Are you not satisfied with your progress?'

'I am,' he said to me, with a deep sigh of satisfaction. 'I am extremely pleased to have learned so many things.'

'Moral or material?'

'Some moral and one material. Take this for example.'

And rapidly he drew from his waistcoat pocket a folded piece of paper, which he must have put there while he was under the bed. In that fold of paper was a blonde hair from a woman's head.

CHAPTER VIII

The judge takes Mlle Stangerson's evidence

Five minutes later, Joseph Rouletabille was bending over the footprints discovered in the park, under the hall window, when a man, who must have been a servant at the chateau, came striding towards us, calling out to M. Darzac, who was coming out of the pavilion:

'Monsieur Robert, the judge is interrogating Mlle Stangerson.'

M. Darzac muttered a vague excuse, and set off at a run towards the chateau, the servant following him.

'If the lady talks,' I said, 'matters will become interesting.'

'We must know,' said my friend. 'Let us go to the chateau.'

He drew me with him, but, at the chateau, a gendarme stationed in the entrance hall denied us access to the stairs leading up to the first floor. We had to wait.

Meanwhile, this is what happened in the victim's room.

The family doctor, finding that Mlle Stangerson was much better, but fearing a fatal relapse which would no longer permit of her being interrogated, had thought it his duty to inform the judge, who decided to proceed immediately with a brief interrogation. M. de Marquet, the clerk, M. Stangerson and the doctor were present. Later, I procured the text of the interrogation. Here it is in all its judicial dryness:

Question: Are you able, Mademoiselle, without too much fatigue, to give us a few necessary details of the frightful attack of which you have been the victim?

Answer: I feel much better, Monsieur, and I will tell you all I know. When I entered my room I did not notice anything unusual there.

Q. If you will allow me, Mademoiselle, I will ask the

questions and you will answer them. That will tire you less than making a long report.

A. As you please, Monsieur.

Q. How did you spend the day of the attack? I want you to be as minutely precise as possible. I would like to know everything you did that day, if that is not asking too much of you.

A. I rose at ten o'clock, for my father and I had returned home late the previous night, having been to the dinner and reception given by the President of the Republic in honour of the Philadelphia Academy of Science. When I left my room, at half-past ten, my father was already busy in the laboratory. We worked together until midday. We then walked for half an hour in the park, as we always do before lunch at the chateau. After luncheon, we went for another half-hour stroll before returning to the laboratory. There we found my chambermaid, who had just cleaned out my room. I went into the Yellow Room to give her some important instructions and, directly afterwards, she left the pavilion, and I resumed my work with my father. At five o'clock we again went for a walk in the park, and had tea.

Q. Before leaving the pavilion at five o'clock, did you go into your room?

A. No, Monsieur, but my father did; he went, at my request, to fetch me my hat.

Q. And he found nothing suspicious in the Yellow Room?

M. Stangerson. Absolutely not, Monsieur.

Q. Besides, it is almost certain that the attacker was not yet concealed under the bed at that time. When you went out, the door of the room had not been locked?

A. No, we had no reason to do so.

Q. How long had you been absent from the pavilion, M. Stangerson and yourself?

A. About an hour.

Q. It was during that hour, no doubt, that your attacker got into the pavilion. But how? No one knows. True, footprints have been found in the park – footprints which lead away from the hall window, but none have been found going towards it. Did you notice whether the hall window was open when you went out?

A. I don't remember.

M. Stangerson. It was closed.

Q. And when you returned?

Mlle Stangerson. I didn't notice.

M. Stangerson. It was still closed. I remember it quite well, for I remarked out loud: 'Old Jacques might have opened that window while we were out!'

Q. How very strange! Remember, M. Stangerson, that Old Jacques, during your absence, and before going out, *had* opened it! Anyway, you returned to the laboratory at six o'clock. Did you resume work?

Mlle Stangerson. Yes, Monsieur.

Q. And you did not leave the laboratory from that hour until the moment when you entered your room?

M. Stangerson. Neither my daughter nor I did, Monsieur, The work we were engaged on was so pressing, we lost not a moment, neglecting everything else on that account.

Q. You dined in the laboratory?

A. Yes, for the same reason.

Q. Do you usually dine in the laboratory?

A. We rarely do.

Q. Could the attacker have known that you would dine in the laboratory that evening?

M. Stangerson. I doubt it. It was only when we returned to the pavilion, at about six o'clock, that I decided to dine in the laboratory with my daughter. At that moment, my game-keeper arrived and detained me a moment to ask me to accompany him on an urgent tour of inspection of a part of the woods which I have decided to thin. I had no time then, and put the thing off until the next day, and begged the game-keeper, as he was going to the chateau, to tell the butler that we would dine in the laboratory. He left me to carry out my orders and I joined my daughter, who was already at work.

Q. At what time, Mademoiselle, did you go to your room, while your father continued to work?

A. At midnight.

Q. Did Old Jacques enter the Yellow Room in the course of the evening?

A. Yes, to close the shutters and to light the nightlight.

Q. Did he notice anything suspicious?

A. He would have told us. Old Jacques is a good man, who is very fond of me.

Q. You affirm, Monsieur Stangerson, that Old Jacques afterwards remained with you all the time you were in the laboratory?

M. Stangerson. I am sure of it. I have no suspicions on that side.

Q. When you entered your room, Mademoiselle, did you immediately shut the door and lock and bolt it? Why so many precautions when you knew that your father and your servant were there. Were you afraid of something?

A. My father would be returning to the chateau very soon, and Old Jacques would be going to bed. Besides, I *did* fear something.

Q. So much so that you borrowed Old Jacques' revolver without informing him?

A. That is true. I did not want to alarm anybody, the less so since my fears might have been childish.

Q. What was it you feared?

A. I can hardly say now. For several nights recently, I thought I heard, both in the park and outside the park, near the pavilion, unusual sounds, sometimes footsteps, at other times the cracking of branches. The night before the attack, when I did not go to bed before three o'clock in the morning, on our return from the Elysée Palace, I stood for a moment before my window, and I felt sure I saw shadows.

Q. How many?

A. Two, moving round near the lake, then the moon went behind the clouds and I lost sight of them. By this time of the year, I have generally returned for the winter to my apartment in the chateau, but this year I decided not to leave the pavilion until my father had completed the summary of his work on the dissociation of matter for the Academy of Science. I did not want this important work, which was to have been finished in a matter of a few days, to be impeded by a change in our daily habits. You can see why I did not wish to mention my childish fears to my father, nor even to Old Jacques, who, I knew, would have been unable to keep it to himself. Knowing that he had a revolver in his room, I took advantage of his absence and borrowed it, placing it in the drawer of my bedside table.

Q. Have you, to your knowledge, any enemies?

A. None.

Q. You understand, Mademoiselle, that we find the elaborate precautions you took somewhat surprising?

M. Stangerson. Such precautions were very strange, my child.

A. As I said, I had been feeling uneasy, very uneasy, for two nights.

M. Stangerson. You should have told me about it, then this terrible misfortune could have been avoided.

Q. When the door of the Yellow Room was locked, Mademoiselle, did you go to bed?

A. Yes, and since I was very tired, I fell asleep at once.

Q. Was the nightlight still burning?

A. Yes, but only feebly.

Q. Tell us, Mademoiselle, what happened afterwards.

A. I don't know how long I had been asleep, but I suddenly woke up and uttered a loud cry.

M. Stangerson. Yes, a terrible cry – 'Murder!' It still rings in my ears.

Q. You uttered a loud cry . . .

A. A man was in my room. He sprang at me, seized me by the throat and tried to strangle me. He might well have succeeded had I not been able to reach into the drawer of my bedside table and grab the loaded revolver I had placed there. By then, the man had forced me to the foot of the bed and was brandishing a sort of club above my head. I fired and felt a terrible blow strike me on the head. All that, Monsieur, happened more quickly than I can tell – and after that I knew nothing more.

Q. Nothing? You have no idea as to how the murderer managed to escape from your room?

A. None whatsoever. I know nothing more. One does not know what is happening around one when one is unconscious.

Q. Was the man you saw tall or short?

A. I only saw a shadow, which seemed to me to be huge.

Q. You cannot give us any description?

A. I know nothing more, Monsieur. A man threw himself upon me and I fired at him. I know nothing more.

Here ended Mlle Stangerson's evidence. Joseph Rouletabille waited patiently for M. Robert Darzac, who soon appeared.

He had heard the interrogation from a room near Mlle Stangerson's and came to report it to my friend with great accuracy, revealing a retentive memory and a degree of tact which really surprised me. Thanks to the notes he had scribbled down, he was able to reproduce almost word for word the questions asked and the answers given.

Indeed, M. Darzac might have been taken for my young friend's secretary. He behaved as if he would refuse him nothing, or, rather, as if he were his employee.

The fact of the closed window struck the reporter as it had struck the judge. Rouletabille asked Darzac to repeat once more the father's and the daughter's accounts of the way they had spent their time on the day of the tragedy. The dinner in the laboratory seemed to interest him deeply, and he had it repeated to him three times, to make absolutely sure that the gamekeeper was the only person who knew that the professor and his daughter were going to dine in the laboratory, and how he had come to know of it.

When M. Darzac stopped speaking, I said:

'Her evidence does not get us very far.'

'It sets us back,' said M. Darzac.

'It throws new light upon it,' said Rouletabille thoughtfully.

CHAPTER IX

Reporter and detective

All three of us turned back towards the pavilion. At some distance from the building, the reporter made us stop, and, pointing to a clump of bushes to the right, said:

'That's where the attacker came from when he entered the pavilion.'

As there were other similar clumps of bushes between the great oaks, I asked why he should have chosen that one rather than any of the others. Rouletabille answered me by pointing to the path, which ran quite close by the thicket and led to the door of the pavilion.

'That path,' he said, 'is gravelled, as you see. Since no footprints have been found on the soft ground, on his way to the pavilion, the man must have passed along it to go there. That man did not have wings. He walked, but he walked on the gravel in which his boots left no impression. The gravel has, in fact, been trodden.'

'I would like to kill him with my own hands!' cried Mlle Stangerson's fiancé, with a vehemence that amazed me.

'I believe you,' said Rouletabille gravely, 'but you have not answered my question.'

We were walking past the thicket of which the young reporter had spoken to us a minute before. I went into the thicket and pointed out to him evidence of a man having been hidden there. Once more Rouletabille was right.

'Yes, yes,' he said. 'We are dealing with a human being, who does not use any other means than those we would use ourselves, and everything will be revealed in the end.'

He then asked me for the paper cut-out of the other footprint which he had previously handed to me, and applied it to a clear print behind the shrubs. Then he stood up and said: 'Of course!'

I assumed that he would now follow the footprints left by the attacker in his flight from the hall window, but he led us far to the left, saying that it was pointless splashing around in the mud and that he was sure now of the route taken by the criminal.

'I know he went along the wall, fifty yards away from the pavilion. Then he jumped over the hedge and across the ditch there, just opposite the little path leading to the lake. It is the easiest way of getting out of the estate and reaching the lake.'

'How do you know that he went to the lake?'

'Because Frédéric Larsan has not left its shores since this morning. There must be some unusual tracks there.'

A few minutes later we reached the lake.

The great Fred must have seen us coming, but we were doubtless of very little interest to him, for he took scarcely any notice of us, merely continuing to stir with his stick in something we could not see.

'Look!' said Rouletabille. 'Here are more of the fugitive's footprints. They skirt the lake at this place, return, and finally disappear just before this path, which leads to the main road to Epinay. The man continued his flight towards Paris.'

'What makes you think that,' I asked, 'since there are no footprints on the path?'

'What makes me think that? Why, these footprints here, which I expected to find!' said Rouletabille, pointing to the sharply-defined imprint of an elegant boot. 'Look!' And he called out to Frédéric Larsan.

'Monsieur Fred, these footprints have been here ever since the discovery of the crime.'

'Yes, young man, and a careful note has been made of them,' replied Fred, without looking up. 'You see, there are steps leading in both directions, coming and going.'

'And the man had a bicycle!' the reporter exclaimed.

Then, after having looked at the tracks left by the bicycle, which accompanied the comings and goings of the elegant footprints, I thought I might intervene.

'The bicycle explains the disappearance of the larger footprints, the attacker's prints,' I said. 'The murderer, with his huge hob-nailed boots, got on a bicycle. His accomplice, the man with the elegant boots, had been acting on his account.'

'No, no!' replied Rouletabille, with a strange smile. 'I have been expecting to find these elegant footprints from the start, I am pleased I've found them. They are the footprints of the attacker.'

'So there were two of them?'

'No, there was but one, and he had no accomplice.'

'Very good! Very clever!' said Frédéric Larsan.

'Look!' the young reporter went on, showing us where the ground had been disturbed by someone's large, heavy feet. 'Here is where the man sat down and took off his hob-nailed boots, which he had worn only for the purpose of misleading the police and then, probably taking them with him, he got up, with his own boots on, and quickly headed for the main road, pushing his bicycle. He couldn't risk riding it on the rough path. Besides, the lightness of the impression made by the wheels on the path, in spite of the softness of the ground, proves what I say to be right. If the man had been riding the bicycle, the wheels would have sunk deep into the earth. No, no, there was but one man here, the attacker, on foot.'

'Bravo! Bravo!' Fred cried again, and coming suddenly over to us, he planted himself in front of M. Robert Darzac and said to him:

'If we had a bicycle here, we could demonstrate the correctness of the young man's reasoning. Is there one at the chateau, do you happen to know?'

'No,' replied Darzac, 'there isn't. I took mine to Paris four days ago, the last time I came to the chateau, before the crime took place.'

'A pity,' replied Fred, in an extremely cold tone of voice. Then, turning to Rouletabille, he said:

'If you go on like this, we shall both come to the same conclusion. Have you any idea as to how the attacker escaped from the Yellow Room?'

'Yes,' my friend replied, 'I do.'

'So have I,' said Fred, 'and it is probably the same as yours. There are no two ways of reasoning in this affair. I will await the arrival of my chief, before offering my explanation to the judge.'

'Ah, the Chief of the Sûreté is coming?'

'Yes, this afternoon, to be present at the judge's interrogation of all those who may have played a part in the tragedy. It should be very interesting. It's a pity you won't be there.'

Oh, but I shall,' said Rouletabille confidently.

'Really! You're a very remarkable young man,' replied the detective, in a tone not wholly free from irony. 'You would make a wonderful detective if you had a little more method; if you were less guided by your instincts and the bumps on your forehead. I have had occasion to observe already, Monsieur Rouletabille, that you reason far too much. You do not allow yourself to be guided enough by observation. What do you say to the blood-stained handkerchief and the red handprint on the wall? I have only seen the handkerchief. Speak!'

'Bah!' said Rouletabille, slightly taken aback. 'The murderer was wounded in the hand by Mlle Stangerson's revolver.'

'Ah, you see, a purely instinctive observation. Take care! You rely too much on logic, Monsieur Rouletabille; logic will do you a bad turn if you use it indiscriminately. You are right when you speak of Mlle Stangerson's revolver. There is no doubt that the victim fired a shot, but you are wrong when you say that she wounded the murderer in the hand.'

'I'm sure of it!' cried Rouletabille.

Fred, imperturbable, interrupted him.

'Lack of observation, Monsieur, lack of observation again. My examination of the handkerchief, the numerous little round stains – left by drops of blood – which I found on the footprints, at the moment when the foot touches the ground, prove to me that the murderer was not wounded at all. The murderer, Monsieur Rouletabille, had a nosebleed!'

The great Fred spoke most seriously. However, I could not refrain from uttering an exclamation.

The reporter looked gravely at Fred, who looked gravely back at him. And Fred immediately gave his conclusion:

'The man, who was bleeding into his hand and handkerchief, wiped his hand on the wall. The fact is highly important, because there is no need for him to have been wounded in the hand for him to be the murderer.'

Rouletabille seemed to be thinking deeply, then he said:

'There is something much more dangerous, Monsieur Frédéric Larsan, than the misuse of logic, and that is the disposition of mind in certain detectives which makes them, in perfectly good faith, bend that logic to the needs of their preconceived ideas. You already have your idea about the murderer, Monsieur Fred. Don't deny it. And your theory requires the murderer not to have been wounded in the hand, otherwise your idea would come to nothing. And so, you have searched and found nothing else. It is a dangerous system, a dangerous system, Monsieur Fred, to start from the idea you have formed of the murderer and thus arrive at the proofs that you need. That may well lead you astray. Beware, Monsieur Fred, a miscarriage of justice awaits you.'

And, laughing a little, his hands in his pockets. Rouletabille fixed his bright eyes on the great Fred.

Frédéric Larsan silently considered the youth who presumed to be a better detective than he, then he shrugged his shoulders, bowed and walked quickly away.

Rouletabille watched him depart and then turned to us, with a joyous and triumphant look on his face.

'I shall beat him!' he exclaimed. 'I shall beat the great Fred, clever as he is! Rouletabille is smarter at this game than all the rest of them! The great Fred reasons like a child!'

He performed a little dance, then stopped abruptly. My eyes followed his eyes. They were fixed on M. Robert Darzac, who had turned deathly pale and was staring at the impression left by his feet alongside those elegant footprints. They were identical!

We thought he was going to faint. His eyes, dilated with terror, avoided ours, while his right hand nervously stroked the beard on his honest, gentle and despairing face. At length, he regained his composure, bade us farewell and left us, saying in a strained voice that he was obliged to return to the chateau.

'What the devil . . .' said Rouletabille.

He too appeared to be deeply concerned. He took from his pocket-book a piece of white paper, as I had seen him do before, and, with his scissors, cut out the shape of the elegant bootmarks left on the ground. Then, he applied this new paper pattern to M. Darzac's footprints. It fitted perfectly. Presently, he said: 'Yet I believe M. Darzac to be an honest man.'

And he led me to the Tower Inn, less than a mile away down the road.

CHAPTER X

'From now on we shall have to eat red meat!'

I saw at once that the Tower Inn was at least two centuries old, perhaps older. Under its ancient, rustic signboard, a man with a crabbed-looking face was standing on the threshold, apparently lost in gloomy thoughts.

He only deigned to look at us when we were standing quite close to him, and he asked, in a rather disagreeable manner, what we wanted. He was obviously the landlord of this pretty place. As we expressed the hope that he would be good enough to let us have some luncheon, he declared he had no provisions whatsoever, and that it would be impossible for him to satisfy our wish. As he spoke, he looked at us with open suspicion.

'You have nothing to fear from us,' Rouletabille said to the fellow. 'We are not the police.'

'I'm not afraid of the police, I'm not afraid of anybody,' the man replied.

I was already making signs to my friend, giving him to understand that we would do better not to insist, but Rouletabille, who was clearly very keen to enter the inn, slipped under the man's arm and stepped in.

'Come on,' he said, 'it's quite cosy in here!'

A great fire was blazing in the hearth, and we held out our hands to warm them, for the weather was rather chilly that morning. The room was fairly large and was furnished with two heavy tables, a few stools, and a counter filled with bottles of cordials and liqueurs standing in rows.'

'Here's a fine fire for roasting a chicken,' said Rouletabille.

'We have no chicken here,' the landlord replied, 'not even a miserable rabbit!'

'I know that,' said my friend, with an ironic smile. 'I know that from now on we shall have to eat red meat.'

I confess I did not in the least understand what Rouletabille meant. Why had he said to the landlord: 'From now on
we shall have to eat red meat'? Why did the innkeeper, as soon
as he heard the words, utter a terrible curse, then control
himself and place himself at our disposal as obediently as
Robert Darzac had done when he heard those other magic
words: 'The vicarage has lost none of its charm nor the garden
its brightness'? My friend certainly had a gift for getting
through to people by using utterly incomprehensible phrases!
I told him as much and he smiled. I should have preferred
some explanation, but he placed a finger on his lips, which
evidently meant that he did not wish to speak, and enjoined
me to remain silent too.

The landlord had pushed open a little side door and called
to somebody to bring out half a dozen eggs and a piece of
beefsteak. The order was quickly executed, and there
appeared at the top of the staircase a very pretty woman, with
beautiful blonde hair and large, gentle eyes.

The innkeeper said to her roughly:

'Get out! And if the Green Man comes, don't let me see
you about!'

She disappeared. Rouletabille took the eggs, which had
been brought to him in a bowl, and the meat which was on a
dish, and put them down carefully beside him in the fireplace.
He took down a frying-pan and a gridiron, and began to beat
up our omelette before proceeding to grill our beefsteak. He
further ordered two bottles of the man's best cider, and
seemed to take as little notice of the landlord as the landlord
did of him. The man, however, kept looking sideways, first at
Rouletabille, then at me, with obvious nervousness. He let us
do our own cooking, and laid out the table near one of the
windows.

Suddenly, I heard him mutter:

'Here he comes!'

His face changed and his expression became one of fierce
hatred. He went and stood with his nose pressed to one of
the windows, watching the road. There was no need for me
to draw Rouletabille's attention to the fact; he had already

abandoned our omelette and joined the landlord at the window. I followed him.

A man dressed entirely in green velveteen, wearing a huntsman's cap of the same colour, was walking towards us at a leisurely pace, smoking a pipe. He carried a gun slung over his shoulder, and there was an almost aristocratic ease about his gait. He must have been about forty-five. He wore a pince-nez and his hair, as well as his moustache, was turning grey. He was remarkably handsome. As he passed by the inn, he seemed to hesitate, as if wondering whether or not he should come in. He glanced at us, took a few puffs on his pipe, and then resumed his walk at the same nonchalant pace.

Rouletabille and I looked at our host. His flashing eyes, clenched fists and trembling lips told us of his tumultuous feelings.

'He has done well not to come in here today!' he hissed.

'Who is that man?' asked Rouletabille, returning to his omelette.

'The Green Man,' growled the innkeeper. 'You don't know him? So much the better for you. You are better off not making his acquaintance. He is M. Stangerson's game-keeper.'

'You don't seem to like him very much?' said the reporter, pouring his omelette into the frying-pan.

'Like him! No one here likes him, Monsieur. He's one of those conceited fellows who has known better days, who had money – once. He hates everybody because he has been forced to become a servant to earn his living – for, after all, a gamekeeper is only a servant, don't you think? Upon my word, you would think he was the master of Glandier, and that all the land and woods belonged to him. He won't even allow a poor devil to sit down on the grass – his grass – and eat a morsel of bread!'

'Does he often come here?'

'Too often. But I'll make it quite clear that I don't like the look of him. Up until about a month ago he didn't bother us – the Tower Inn didn't even exist for him. He didn't have time, he was far too busy then, courting the landlady of the

Three Lilies at St-Michel. Now that he's finished with her, he wants to spend his time here. He's a real bad'un, always after the girls. There's not an honest man can bear him. Why the caretakers of the chateau themselves can't stand him – the Green Man!'

'Are the caretakers at the chateau honest people then, landlord?' asked Rouletabille.

'Call me Mathieu, that's my name. Well, as sure as my name is Mathieu, yes, I believe them to be honest!'

'Yet they've been arrested?'

'What does that prove? But I don't want to get involved in other people's business!'

'And what do you think of the crime?'

'What? Of the attempt on the life of poor Mlle Stangerson? A good girl, I tell you, and dearly loved all around here! What can I think of it?'

'Tell us your opinion.'

'Well, I think nothing at all and a lot of things. But that's no one else's business.'

'Not even mine?' insisted Rouletabille.

The innkeeper looked at him sideways, and said gruffly: 'No, not even yours!'

The omelette was ready. We sat down at table and were silently eating, when the door was pushed open, and there appeared on the threshold an old woman dressed in rags, a staff in her hand, her head doddering, her white hair hanging limply over her wrinkled brow.

'Ah, there you are, Mother Agenoux! We haven't seen you in ages!' said our host.

'I've been very ill, near to death,' said the old woman. 'Have you, by chance, anything for the Good Lord's Beast?'

She entered the inn, followed by a cat larger than any I had ever imagined to exist. The beast looked at us and mewed in such a melancholy way that I could not help but shudder. I had never before heard such a lugubrious sound.

As if drawn by that cry, a man came in after the old woman. It was the Green Man. He greeted us with a wave of his hand and seated himself at a table next to ours.

'Give me a glass of cider, Mathieu!' he said.

When the Green Man came in, the innkeeper started violently, but now he visibly checked his anger.

'I have no cider; I gave the last bottles to these two gentlemen,' he replied.

'Then give me a glass of white wine,' said the Green Man, without showing the least surprise.

'There's no white wine left, there's nothing left!' said Mathieu in a hollow voice.

'How is Madame Mathieu?'

The innkeeper clenched his fists, and I thought he was about to strike the Green Man. Then he said:

'She's fine, thank you!'

So the young woman with the large, gentle eyes, whom we had just seen, was the wife of this brutal rustic, who, to his physical shortcomings added that moral defect: jealousy.

Slamming the door behind him, the landlord left the room. Mother Agenoux was still there, leaning on her staff, her huge cat by her feet.

The Green Man asked her:

'Have you been ill, Mother Agenoux? We haven't seen you for the last week?'

'Yes, Monsieur. I've only been out of my bed three times, and that was to go and pray to Ste Geneviève, our good patroness. The rest of the time, I've been in bed. There was no one to nurse me but the Good Lord's Beast.'

'It never left your side?'

'Leave me? No, neither by day nor night!'

'You are sure of that?'

'As sure as I am of Paradise.'

'Then how was it, Mother Agenonx, that during the night on which the crime was committed, the cry of the Good Lord's Beast was heard again and again?'

Mother Agenoux went and planted herself in front of the gamekeeper, and struck the floor with her staff.

'I know nothing about it!' she declared. 'But I'll tell you one thing. There is no other cat in the world with a cry like this one. On the night of the crime, I, too, heard the cry of the

Good Lord's Beast outside and yet she was sitting on my lap and didn't mew once! I swear it! I crossed myself when I heard it, as if I had heard the Devil!'

I looked at the gamekeeper while he was asking the last question, and I am much mistaken if I did not detect a mocking smile on his lips.

At that moment, the noise of a sharp quarrel reached us. We even thought that we heard the dull sound of blows, as if somebody was being felled. The Green Man rose resolutely to his feet and hurried to the door alongside the fireplace. But the door was suddenly wrenched open, and the landlord appeared, and said laughingly to the gamekeeper:

'Don't alarm yourself! It's only my wife. She has bad toothache! Here is some meat for your cat, Mother Agenoux.'

He handed a small parcel to the old woman, who took it eagerly and went out by the door, closely followed by the Good Lord's Beast.

The Green Man asked:

'You'll not serve me then?'

Mathieu could no longer suppress his anger.

'There's nothing for you here, nothing at all! Clear out!'

The Green Man bowed to us and went out. He had no sooner crossed the threshold than Mathieu banged the door after him, and, turning towards us – foaming at the mouth, his eyes bloodshot – he said hoarsely to us, shaking his clenched fist at the door he had just slammed on the man he hated:

'I don't know who you are, but if you want to know, *that is the attacker!*'

As soon as he had said that, Mathieu left us. Rouletabille returned to the fireplace, and said:

'Now, let's grill our steak.'

We saw no more of Mathieu that day, and deep silence reigned in the inn as we left, having placed five francs on the table in payment for our meal.

Rouletabille at once took me on a three-mile walk around M. Stangerson's estate. He stopped for ten minutes at the corner of a narrow road, in that part of the forest bordered by the road from Epinay to Corbeil. He told me that the murderer had certainly passed that way – thus accounting for the state of his rough boots – before entering the park and concealing himself in the little clump of trees near the pavilion.

'You don't believe, then, that the gamekeeper had anything to do with the crime?' I asked.

'We shall see that later on,' he replied. 'For the present, I won't bother about the innkeeper's words. He spoke out of hatred. It was not on account of the Green Man that I took you to the Tower Inn.'

Having said that, Rouletabille, stole – and I behind him – towards the little building, which, being near the park gate, was used as a lodge by the caretakers who had been arrested that morning. With the skill of an acrobat, he climbed in by a sort of garret window, which had been left open, and returned ten minutes later, exclaiming 'Of course!', words which, in his mouth, were always highly significant.

Just as we were about to take the road leading to the chateau, there was a commotion at the park gate. A carriage had arrived and several people were hurrying from the chateau to meet it. Rouletabille indicated to me the gentleman getting out.

'That is the head of the Criminal Investigation Department – the Chief of the Sûreté!' he said. 'Now we shall see what Frédéric Larsan has up his sleeve, and whether he really is cleverer than all the rest of us!'

The Chief of the Sûreté's carriage was followed by three other vehicles filled with reporters, who also tried to gain entry to the park, but there were two gendarmes stationed at the gate with directions to admit no one. The Chief of the Sûreté calmed their impatience by promising that, later that evening, he would let the Press have all the information he could, without prejudicing the judge's inquiry.

CHAPTER XI

In which Frédéric Larsan explains how the murderer was able to get out of the Yellow Room

Amongst a mass of papers – legal documents, notes and newspaper-cuttings which I possess – relative to the Mystery of the Yellow Room, there is one extremely interesting piece – an account of the famous interrogation that took place that afternoon in Professor Stangerson's laboratory in the presence of the Chief of the Sûreté. This account is from the pen of M. Maliene, the clerk, who, like the judge, devoted his spare time to literary work. This document was to have been part of a book – never published – entitled: *My Interrogations*. It was given to me by the clerk himself, some time after the case's astonishing denouement, unique in legal history.

Here it is. It is not a mere transcription of questions and answers. The clerk often sets down in it his personal impressions.

The Clerk's account

We, the judge and I, had spent a whole hour in the Yellow Room, together with the builder who built the pavilion according to plans drawn up by Professor Stangerson himself. The builder had a workman with him. M. de Marquet had had the walls laid entirely bare, that is to say, he had had them stripped of the yellow paper which covered them. Soundings with the pick-axe in different places had satisfied us that there was no opening of any kind. The floor and the ceiling had been minutely examined. We had discovered nothing – there was nothing to be discovered. M. de Marquet looked delighted and kept repeating over and over:

'What a case, gentlemen, what a case! You'll see, we shall never know how the murderer was able to get out of this room!'

Suddenly, M. de Marquet, who was beaming with joy because he was unable to solve the mystery, remembered that it was, in fact, his duty to try and solve it. He called to the officer in charge of the gendarmes:

'Go to the chateau,' he said, 'and ask M. Stangerson and M. Robert Darzac to join me in the laboratory, and Old Jacques too. And have your men bring the two caretakers here.'

Five minutes later, these people were all assembled in the laboratory. The Chief of the Sûreté, who had just arrived at Glandier, joined us at that moment. I was seated at Professor Stangerson's desk ready for work, when M. de Marquet made the following little speech – as original as it was unexpected:

'With your permission, gentlemen,' he said, 'since interrogations tend to give such poor results, we will, for once, abandon the old system. I will not have you brought before me in turn, individually. No, we shall all remain here, as we are – M. Stangerson, M. Robert Darzac, Old Jacques, the two caretakers, M. the Chief of the Sûreté, M. the Clerk, and myself. And we shall all be on the same footing. The caretakers may for a while forget that they are prisoners. We are going to hold a conversation. I have called you together to confer. We are on the very spot where the crime was committed; well, what should we talk about if not about the crime? Let us talk about it then quite freely, intelligently, or even foolishly. Let us say anything that occurs to us. Let us speak without method – for method, so far, has not helped us much. So I put my trust in Chance. And now, let us begin!'

Then, as he passed near me, he said in a low voice:

'What did you think of that, eh? What a scene! Could you have imagined that? I'll make a little play out of it for the Vaudeville Theatre!'

And he rubbed his hands in glee.

I looked at M. Stangerson. The hope he had been given by the doctors' latest reports declaring that Mlle Stangerson might survive her wounds, had done little to erase from his noble features the great grief weighing on him.

'Now, M. Stangerson,' said M. de Marquet, rather pompously, 'kindly place yourself exactly where you were when Mlle Stangerson left you to enter her room.'

The professor rose and, standing about two feet from the door of the Yellow Room, he said, in a voice that was without accent or emphasis, a voice which I can only describe as 'dead':

'I was here. At about eleven o'clock I moved my desk to this place, for Old Jacques, who spent all evening cleaning the apparatus, needed all the space behind me. My daughter worked at the same desk with me. When she got up, after kissing me and bidding Old Jacques goodnight, she had, in order to enter her room, to pass between my desk and the door, which was not easy. You may gather from this that I was very near the place where the crime was to be committed.'

'And what became of that desk,' I asked, participating in the conversation, and thus obeying my chief's express orders, 'when you heard the cry of "Murder!" followed by the revolver-shots?'

Old Jacques answered:

'We pushed it back against the wall here, close to where it is at the present moment, so as to be able to get at the door.'

I followed up my idea, to which, however, I attached only the importance of a mere supposition.

'Was the desk near enough to the door for a man, stooping low, to come out of the room, slip under the desk and leave unnoticed?'

'You are forgetting,' M. Stangerson said wearily, 'that my daughter had locked and bolted the door, that the door remained fastened, that we vainly tried to force it open from the very moment when the attack began, that we were at the door while the struggle between the criminal and my poor child was going on, that the noise of it reached us, and that we heard my daughter's stifled cries while she was being strangled by the very hands that have left their mark upon her throat.

Swift though the attack was, we were no less so, and rushed at once to the door which separated us from the tragedy!'

I rose from my seat and once more examined the door with the greatest care. Then I returned to my place with a discouraged look on my face.

'Imagine,' I said, 'that the lower panel of this door could be removed without the whole door necessarily being opened, and the problem would be solved. Unfortunately, this last hypothesis is untenable since close examination of the door reveals it to be a massive door made out of one piece of solid oak. That is plain to see, in spite of the damage done to it by those who broke it down.'

'Yes,' said Old Jacques, 'it is an old door taken from the chateau and fitted here. They don't make doors like that nowadays. Why, it needed this iron bar to get the better of it; and there were four of us, for Mme Bernier, like the good woman she is, joined us in our efforts. It is terrible to think that she and her husband are now prisoners!'

Old Jacques had no sooner uttered these words than the tears and wailing of the caretakers started afresh. I never saw more tearful prisoners; I was deeply disgusted (*sic*). Even if they were innocent, I could not understand how they could show so little self-control in the face of misfortune.

'Once more, enough of that snivelling!' cried M. de Marquet, 'and, in your own interests, tell us what you were doing under the window of the pavilion at the time your mistress was being attacked – for you were quite close to the pavilion when Old Jacques met you!'

'We were coming to the rescue,' they whined.

And, between two sobs, the woman burst out:

'Ah, if we only had the attacker, we should soon sort him out!'

Again it proved impossible to get out of them two consecutive, rational sentences. They kept denying their guilt, and declaring, by Heaven and all the saints, that they were in bed when they heard the sound of the revolver-shot.

'It was not one, but two shots that were fired! You see, you are lying! If you heard one, you would have heard the other.'

'Really, Monsieur, we only heard the second shot. We must have been asleep when the first shot was fired.'

'Two shots were fired, that's true enough,' said Old Jacques. 'I know that all the cartridges in my revolver were loaded and we found two spent cartridges and two bullets, and we heard two shots behind the door. Was not that so, Monsieur Stangerson?'

'Yes,' replied the professor, 'there were two revolver-shots. The first report was rather dull, but the second rang out loud and clear.'

'Why do you persist in lying?' cried M. de Marquet, turning to the caretakers. 'Do you think the police are as stupid as yourselves? Everything goes to prove that you were out of doors and near the pavilion at the moment of the tragedy. What were you doing there? You don't want to answer? Your silence proves your guilt. And, as for me,' he said, turning to M. Stangerson, 'I can only explain the fact that the criminal escaped if these two were his accomplices. As soon as the door was forced open, and while you, Monsieur Stangerson, were attending to your unfortunate child, the caretaker and his wife helped the attacker to escape. Hiding behind them, he reached the hall window and climbed out of it into the park. The caretaker closed the window after him, and fastened the shutters. After all, those shutters could not have closed and fastened themselves. That is the conclusion I have arrived at. If any of you has any other idea, let him state it now.'

M. Stangerson intervened:

'That's impossible! I do not believe in the guilt or the complicity of the caretakers, though I cannot understand what they were doing in the park at that late hour of the night. I say it was impossible, because Madame Bernier held the lamp and did not leave my side for a moment, because I, as soon as the door was forced open, threw myself on my knees beside my daughter, and it would have been impossible for anyone to leave or enter the room by the door without passing over her body and disturbing me. It would have been impossible, because Old Jacques and Bernier had but to cast a glance round the room and under the bed, as I did myself on entering, to see that there was no longer anyone in the room apart from my daughter, who was lying prostrate on the floor.'

'What is your view of the matter, Monsieur Darzac? You have not spoken yet,' said the judge.

M. Darzac replied that he had no opinion to express.

M. Dax, the Chief of the Sûreté, who, so far, had only listened and examined the place, at last deigned to open his lips:

'I think that, while we are waiting for the criminal to be arrested we have to discover the motive for the crime; that would advance matters a little.' Turning to M. Stangerson, he continued in that cold tone of voice which I regard as indicative of firm intelligence and strength of character: 'Was not Mlle Stangerson shortly to have been married?'

The professor looked sadly at M. Robert Darzac.

'Yes, to my friend here, whom I should have been happy to call my son, to M. Robert Darzac.'

'Mlle Stangerson is much better and is rapidly recovering from her injuries. The marriage is merely delayed, is it not, Monsieur?' insisted the Chief of the Sureté.

'I hope so.'

'What! Are you not sure?'

M. Stangerson did not answer. M. Robert Darzac appeared agitated, for I saw him playing nervously with his watch chain − nothing escaped me − M. Dax coughed, as did M. de Marquet when he was embarrassed.

'You will understand, Monsieur Stangerson,' he said, 'that, in so perplexing a case, we cannot afford to neglect anything. We must know everything, even the smallest and most trivial fact concerning the victim. The most insignificant detail may prove to be important information. What is it that makes you doubtful, now that we know that Mlle Stangerson is sure to recover, as to whether this marriage will take place? You said, "I hope so." That appears to me to imply a doubt. Why do you doubt it?'

M. Stangerson looked troubled.

'Yes, Monsieur,' he said at length, 'you are right; it is best that you should know a fact which, if I concealed it, might appear to be important. I am sure M. Darzac agrees with me.'

M. Darzac, whose pallor at that moment was altogether abnormal, made a sign that he agreed with the professor. I concluded that if he only answered by a sign, it was because he was unable to speak.

'I must tell you,' continued M. Stangerson, 'that my daughter has sworn never to leave me, and has held to her oath, in spite of all my prayers, for I have tried many times, as was my duty, to induce her to marry. We have known M. Robert Darzac for many years. M. Darzac loves my daughter. I believed at one time that she loved him, since I had the joy recently of hearing from her own lips that she at last consented to a marriage which I desired with all my heart. I am very old, Monsieur, and it was a blessing to know that when I am gone, she would have at her side, to love her and to continue our common labours, a man whom I love and esteem for his greatness of heart, and for his science. Now, Monsieur, two days before the crime, for some unknown reason, my daughter suddenly declared to me that she would not marry M. Robert Darzac.'

A deadly silence followed. It was a grave moment. M. Dax asked:

'Has Mlle Stangerson given you no explanation whatever? Has she not told you what her motive was?'

'She told me she was now too old to marry; that she had waited too long; that she had thought about it deeply; that she esteemed, indeed loved M. Darzac, but it was better that things should remain as they were. She would be happy to see the bonds which bind us both to M. Robert Darzac drawn closer, but on the understanding that there should never be any more talk of marriage.'

'That is very strange,' muttered M. Dax.

'Very strange!' echoed my chief.

M. Stangerson, with a pale and icy smile, added:

'You will certainly not find the motive for the crime there, Monsieur Dax.'

'The motive was clearly not theft,' said M. Dax impatiently.

'Oh, we're quite sure of that!' cried the examining judge.

At that moment, the door of the laboratory opened, and the officer in charge of the gendarmes entered, and handed a card to the examining judge. M. de Marquet read it and uttered an angry exclamation:

'What impudence!'

'What is it?' asked M. Dax.

'It is the card of a young reporter working for *L'Epoque* – Joseph Rouletabille by name – with these words written on it: "One of the motives of the crime was robbery"!'

The Chief of the Sûreté smiled.

'Aha, young Rouletabille! I've heard of him before. He is said to be rather ingenious. Let him come in, Monsieur.'

M. Joseph Rouletabille entered the laboratory, bowed to us, and waited until M. de Marquet had asked him to explain himself.

'Monsieur, you say that you know the motive of the crime. That motive, against all evidence, is, you think, robbery?'

'No, Monsieur, I do not say that robbery was the motive of the crime, and I do not believe it was.'

'Then what is the meaning of this card?'

'It means that *one of the motives* for the crime was robbery.'

'What leads you to think so?'

'This! If you will be good enough to accompany me.'

And the young man asked us to follow him into the hall, and we did so. He led us towards the washroom and asked my chief to kneel beside him. This washroom has a glass door, and when the door was open, the place was quite light. M. de Marquet and M. Rouletabille knelt down, and the young man pointed to a place on the tiles.

'The tiles here have not been washed by Old Jacques for some time,' he said, 'that can be seen by the layer of dust that covers them. Now, here you can see two large footprints and the black soot which everywhere accompanies the steps of the criminal. That soot, or ash, is nothing more than the charcoal dust that covers the path along which one has to come

82

through the forest directly from Epinay to Glandier. You know that at that place there is a small hamlet of charcoal-burners. Now, this is what the murderer must have done: he came in here during the afternoon, when there was no one in the pavilion, and carried out the robbery . . .'

'But what robbery? Where do you see any signs of robbery? What proof do you have that a robbery was committed?' we all asked at once.

'What led me to suppose a robbery,' the journalist continued, 'was . . .'

'Was this!' M. de Marquet broke in, still on his knees.

'Exactly,' said M. Joseph Rouletabille.

And my chief then explained that in the dust on the tiles was the clear impression of a heavy, rectangular parcel with a cord around it.

'You have been here before, then, Monsieur Rouletabille, though I gave strict orders to Old Jacques, who was left in charge of the pavilion, to allow no one to enter?'

'Don't scold Old Jacques. I came here with M. Robert Darzac.'

'Ah, indeed!' exclaimed M. de Marquet, none too pleased.

'When I saw the mark of the parcel by the side of the footprints I had no further doubts as to the robbery,' M. Rouletabille went on. 'The thief had not brought a parcel with him. He had obviously made up that parcel of stolen goods here and put it in this corner with the intention of taking it away when the moment came for him to make his escape. He had also placed his heavy boots beside the parcel; for, look, there are no indications of steps leading to the marks left by the boots, and the bootprints are side by side, like boots at rest and with no feet in them! That would account for the fact that the attacker, when he fled from the Yellow Room, left no trace of his steps either in the laboratory or in the hall. Having entered the Yellow Room in his boots, he took them off there, probably because he found them troublesome, or because he wished to make as little noise as possible. The marks made by him in going through the hall and the laboratory disappeared when Old Jacques washed the floor. Having taken off his boots, the attacker carried them from the door to the washroom and placed them there, for on the dust of the washroom tiles there is no trace of bare feet or stocking feet, nor of other boots. The man placed his boots beside the parcel, for the robbery had already been committed. The man then returned to the Yellow Room and slipped under the bed, where the mark of his body is perfectly visible on the floor, and even on the carpet, which has been slightly moved from its normal position and is badly creased. There are also bits of freshly broken straw which bear witness to the attacker's movements under the bed.'

'Yes, yes, we know all that,' said M. de Marquet.

'The return of the robber to his hiding place beneath the bed,' continued Rouletabille, 'proves that robbery was not his only motive. Don't tell me that he hid himself there because he saw through the hall window that M. and Mlle Stangerson were about to enter the pavilion. If his only purpose was flight, it would have been much easier for him to climb up to the attic and wait there for an opportunity to get away. No, no, he wanted to be in the Yellow Room.'

Here the Chief of the Sûreté intervened.

'That's not at all bad, young fellow, and I congratulate you, for if we do not yet know how the murderer succeeded in getting away, we can at least know how he got in and what he did — he committed a robbery. But what did he steal?'

'Some things of great value,' replied the young reporter.

At that moment, we heard a cry from the laboratory. We rushed there and found Professor Stangerson, his eyes wild, his limbs trembling, pointing to a sort of cabinet which he had opened and which we saw was empty.

At the same time, he sank into the large armchair near his desk and groaned.

'Once more I have been robbed!'

And large tears rolled down his cheeks.

'Please, do not say a word of this to my daughter. She would be more distressed than I am.' He heaved a deep sigh, and added, in a heartrending tone: 'After all, what does it matter as long as she lives?'

'She will live!' said M. Darzac, with deep emotion.

'And we will find the stolen objects,' said M. Dax. 'But what was in this cabinet?'

'Twenty years of my life,' replied the illustrious professor, 'or, rather, of our lives – the lives of my daughter and myself. Yes, our most precious documents, the most secret records of our experiments and researches for the last twenty years were in that cabinet. All the steps by which I arrived at the final proof of the destructibility of matter were there, carefully reported, labelled and filed, and illustrated with sketches and photographs – it was all there! The man who came wished to take everything from me – my daughter and my work, my heart and my soul.'

And the great Stangerson wept like a child.

We surrounded him in silence, deeply affected by his great distress. M. Robert Darzac tried in vain to hide his tears – a sight which, for a moment, almost made him sympathetic to me – in spite of the instinctive repulsion with which his peculiar attitude and strange anxieties had filled me.

M. Joseph Rouletabille, alone, as if his precious mission on earth did not permit him to dwell upon human suffering, had very calmly gone up to the empty cabinet, and addressing the Chief of the Sûreté, broke the respectful silence with which we received the great scientist's despair. He gave us some rather unnecessary explanations as to how he had been led to believe that a robbery had been committed, by the simultaneous discoveries he had made of tracks in the washroom and of the empty cabinet in the laboratory. He had only had a quick look at the latter room, but had at once been struck by the unusual shape of that cabinet, its solidity, the fact that it was made of iron – doubtless in order to be fireproof – clearly indicating that it was intended for the preservation of objects to which the highest value and importance were attached, and, above all, that the key of such a precious cabinet had been left in the lock. 'One does not generally have a safe and leave it open.' Then this little key, with its brass head and complicated design, had, it appeared, attracted M. Rouletabille's attention.

M. de Marquet seemed greatly perplexed, as if he did not know whether to be glad of the new direction given to the inquiry by the young reporter, or sorry that it had not been provided by himself. In our profession, when the general good is in question, we have to put up with these mortifications and trample our self-love under foot. M. de Marquet overcame his feelings, and thought it right to add his compliments to those M. Dax had paid the young reporter.

Rouletabille simply shrugged his shoulders and said:

'I've done very little. You will do well, Monsieur, to ask M. Stangerson who, ordinarily, had possession of that key.'

'My daughter,' replied the professor. 'It was always with her.'

'Ah, that changes things, and gives the lie to M. Rouletabille's theory,' said my chief. 'If that key was always with Mlle Stangerson, the murderer must that night have waited for her in her room in order to steal it from her, and the robbery could not have been committed until after the attack made on her life. But after the crime had been committed, there were four people in the laboratory! I can't make it out at all!'

And M. de Marquet repeated, with a desperate air, which must have been to him the acme of delight – for he was never so pleased as when unable to solve a mystery:

'I can't make it out at all.'

'The robbery,' said the reporter, 'could only have been committed before the attack upon Mlle Stangerson. I have special reasons to believe this. When the murderer entered the pavilion he was already in possession of the brass key.'

'That is impossible,' said M. Stangerson in a low voice.

'It is perfectly possible, Monsieur, and here is the proof.'

The youth drew from his pocket a copy of *L'Epoque* dated 21st October – I recall the fact that the crime was committed on the night of the 24th – and pointing to an advertisement, he read:

' "Yesterday, a small black satin bag was lost in the Magasins du Louvre. It contained, amongst other things, a small brass key. A handsome reward will be given to the person who found it. This person must write, Poste restante, Post Office 40, to this address: M.A.T.H.S.N." Do not these letters suggest the name of Mlle Stangerson?' continued the reporter. 'The brass key – is it not this key? I always read the advertisements. In my business, as in yours, Monsieur,' here he turned to my chief – 'one should always read the personal columns. In this advertisement in particular, I was very much struck by the mystery with which the woman who had lost the key – not a very compromising object – surrounded herself. She really cared about that key! She promised a handsome reward for its return! And I pondered over those six letters, M.A.T.H.S.N. The first four immediately indicated to me a Christian name. "Math," I thought, "that's obviously Mathilde". But I could make nothing of the last two letters. So I put the newspaper to one side and occupied myself with something else. Four days later, when the evening papers appeared with banner headlines announcing the attack on Mlle Mathilde Stangerson, the name Mathilde instantly brought back to me the letters in the advertisement. I had forgotten the two last letters, S.N. When I saw them again, I cried out: "Stangerson!" I jumped into a cab and rushed to post office no. 40, asking: "Do you have a letter addressed to M.A.T.H.S.N.?" The clerk replied, "No." And when I insisted, begged and entreated him to search again, he said: "Is this some kind of game, Monsieur? I did have a letter bearing the initials M.A.T.H.S.N., but I gave it to a lady who came for it three days ago. You come today to claim the same letter, and the day before yesterday another gentleman claimed it just as insistently. I've had enough of all this mystification!" I tried to question the clerk as to the two people who had already claimed the letter, but whether he wished to observe professional confidentiality – he may have thought he had already said too much – or was irritated by what he took to be a joke, he would not answer any of my questions.'

Rouletabille paused. We all remained silent. Each drew his own conclusions from the strange story of the letter in poste restante. It seemed, indeed, that we now held a solid thread, by the aid of which we should be able to guide ourselves through this extraordinary mystery.

M. Stangerson said:

'It seems certain that my daughter lost the key, and that she did not tell me of it in order to spare me anxiety, and that she begged whoever had found it to write poste-restante. She evidently feared that, by giving her address, inquiries would have resulted that would have apprised me of the loss of the key. It was quite logical, quite natural, for her to have taken that course, for I had already been robbed once before, Monsieur.'

'Where and when was that?' asked the Chief of the Sûreté.

'Oh, many years ago, in America, in Philadelphia. Some-body stole from my laboratory the notes for two inventions that might have made the fortune of a whole nation. Not only have I never discovered who the thief was, but I have never heard speak of the object of the robbery, doubtless because, in order to defeat the plans of the person who had despoiled me, I myself offered those two inventions to the public, thus ren-dering the theft valueless. From that time forth, I have been very suspicious, and I systematically lock myself in when I am at work. All the bars to these windows, the remoteness of this pavilion, this cabinet, which I had specially constructed, this lock, this unique key, all these are the result of fears brought on by sad experience.'

'Most interesting,' declared M. Dax.

And then M. Rouletabille asked about the satin bag. Neither M. Stangerson nor Old Jacques had seen it for several days; but a few hours later we were to learn from Mlle Stangerson herself that the bag had either been stolen from her, or else she had lost it, that things had occurred just as her father had stated. She had gone to post office no. 40 on 23rd October, and had received a letter which she declared was nothing but a vulgar joke, which she had immediately burned.

To return to our interrogation, or, rather, to our conversa-tion, I must state that the Chief of the Sûreté, having inquired of M. Stangerson how his daughter had gone to Paris on 20th

88

October – the day on which the bag was lost – we learned that she had gone there accompanied by M. Robert Darzac, who was not seen again at the chateau from that time to the day after the crime. The fact that M. Darzac was by her side in the Magasins du Louvre when the bag disappeared could not pass unnoticed, and, it must be said, strongly awakened our interest.

This conversation between judges, accused, victim, witnesses and journalist was coming to a close, when something truly theatrical occurred. The gendarmes came to announce that Frédéric Larsan asked to be admitted – a request that was at once complied with. The detective held in his hand a heavy pair of muddy boots, which he threw down on the floor of the laboratory.

'Here,' he said, 'are the boots worn by the attacker. Do you recognise them, Old Jacques?'

Old Jacques bent over them and, thunderstruck, recognised a pair of old boots which he had some time before thrown into a corner of his attic. He was so taken aback that he had to blow his nose to hide his agitation.

Then, pointing to the handkerchief in the old man's hand, Frédéric Larsan said:

'There's a handkerchief that bears an astonishingly close resemblance to the one found in the Yellow Room.'

'I know that well enough,' said Old Jacques, trembling. 'They are very much alike.'

'Finally,' Frédéric Larsan went on, 'the old beret, also found in the Yellow Room, might formerly have covered Old Jacques' head. All this, gentlemen, proves, I think, that the attacker wished to disguise his real identity. He did it in a very clumsy way, or so, at least, it appears to me, because we know for certain that Old Jacques is not the attacker, since he never left M. Stangerson's side. But suppose that M. Stangerson had not that night remained at his work quite so long, that, after saying goodnight to his daughter, he had gone back to the chateau and Mlle Stangerson had been attacked when there was no longer anybody in the laboratory, and when Old Jacques was sleeping in his attic. No one would then have doubted that the servant was the attacker. He owes his salvation, therefore, to the drama having taken place too soon, the attacker having, no doubt, assumed from the silence in the laboratory, that it was empty and that the moment for action had come. The man, who was so mysteriously to have let himself in here, and who took such pains to incriminate Old Jacques, was, there can be no doubt about it, someone who knew the house well. At what time did he actually let himself in? In the afternoon? During the evening? I could not say. One who was so familiar with the habits of the people in this pavilion could have entered the Yellow Room whenever he chose.'

'He could not have entered it when there were people in the laboratory!' said M. de Marquet.

'What do we know?' Larsan replied. 'There was the dinner in the laboratory, the coming and going of the servants in attendance. There was a chemical experiment being carried on between ten and eleven o'clock, and M. Stangerson, his daughter and Old Jacques were busy with the furnace in this corner of the fireplace. Who can say that the attacker – a man intimately connected with the house – did not take advantage of that moment to slip into the Yellow Room, having first removed his boots in the washroom?'

'It seems somewhat improbable,' said M. Stangerson.

'Granted, but it is not impossible. As to the escape, that's another thing. How did he escape? In the most natural way in the world.'

For a moment Frédéric Larsan paused. That moment seemed to us extremely long. We awaited his words with an eagerness that can only be imagined.

'I have not been in the Yellow Room,' Larsan went on, 'but I take it for granted that you have ascertained that one could only have left the room by way of the door. It is by the door, then, that the murderer made his exit. Since it cannot be otherwise, it must be so. He committed the crime and then left by the door. When? When it was easiest for him to effect his exit at the moment when the matter becomes least mysterious – so unmysterious, in fact, that there can be no other explanation. Let us consider the different "moments" that followed the crime. There is the first moment, when Stangerson and Old Jacques are close to the door, ready to bar the way. There is the second moment, during which Old Jacques is absent for a while, and M. Stangerson stands alone before the door. There is the third moment, when M. Stangerson is joined by the caretaker. There is the fourth moment, during which M. Stangerson, the caretaker, his wife and Old Jacques are all by the door. There is the fifth moment, during which the door was broken down, and the Yellow Room entered. The moment at which escape could most easily have taken place, the very moment when there was the smallest number of persons at the door. There is one moment when there is but one; that is the moment when M. Stangerson was alone at the door. Unless we believe Old Jacques to be guilty of withholding evidence – which I do not, for he would not have left the pavilion to go and examine the window of the Yellow Room if he had seen the door opening and the murderer come out – the door was opened in the presence of M. Stangerson alone, and the man escaped. Here we would have to say that M. Stangerson had powerful reasons for not arresting the attacker or causing him to be arrested, since he allowed him to reach the hall window and closed it after him! That done, as Old Jacques would soon return, and it was vital that he should find things as he had left them, Mlle Stangerson, though badly injured, had still strength enough – and, no doubt, in obedience her father's entreaties – to refasten the door of the Yellow Room, with both bolt and lock, before sinking, near to death, to the floor. We do not know who committed the crime. We do not know the wretch of whom M. and Mlle Stangerson are the victims, but there is no doubt that they do. This secret must be a terrible one for the father to have left his daughter to die behind the door which she shut upon herself, terrible indeed for him to have allowed the attacker to escape. But there is no other way in the world to explain how the attacker escaped from the Yellow Room!'

There was something awful about silence that followed this dramatic and brilliant explanation. We all of us felt for the illustrious professor, thus driven into a corner by the pitiless logic of Frédéric Larsan, and forced to confess the whole truth of his martyrdom, or to keep silent – an even clearer and more terrible admission. We saw this man – a very monument of sorrow – raise his head with a gesture so solemn that we bowed our heads to it, as at the sight of something sacred. He then pronounced these words, in a voice so loud that it seemed to exhaust him:

'I swear on the head of my suffering child that I never for an instant left the door of her room from the moment I heard her cry out for help, that that door was not opened while I was alone in the laboratory, and, finally, that when we entered the Yellow Room – my three servants and I – the attacker was no longer there. I swear I do not know who the attacker was!'

May I mention that, in spite of the solemnity of M. Stangerson's words, we did not believe his denial? Frédéric Larsan had shown us the truth, and we were not prepared to relinquish it so soon.

As M de Marquet declared that the conversation was at an end, and as we were about to leave the laboratory, Joseph Rouletabille approached M. Stangerson, took him by the hand with the greatest respect, and I heard him say:

'I believe you, Monsieur.'

CHAPTER XII

Frédéric Larsan's walking stick

It was not until six p.m. that I prepared to leave the chateau, taking with me the article hastily written by my friend in the little sitting-room which M. Robert Darzac had placed at our disposal. The reporter was to sleep at the chateau, availing himself of the inexplicable hospitality offered him by M. Robert Darzac, whom M. Stangerson, during those sad days, had left in charge of all domestic affairs. Nevertheless, Rouletabille insisted on accompanying me to the station at Epinay. As we crossed the park, he said to me:

'Frédéric really is a very able fellow and has not belied his reputation. You know how he came to find Old Jacques' boots? Near the spot where we noticed the elegant bootprints and the disappearance of the rough ones, there was a rect-angular hole, freshly made in the moist ground, indicating that a stone had been removed. Larsan searched for that stone without finding it; then it occurred to him that the stone could have been used by the attacker to sink the old boots in the lake. The idea was an excellent one, as the success of his search proves. That had escaped me, but it is fair to say that my mind was turned in another direction, for, given the extra-ordinary number of false trails left by the attacker, and the fact that the footprints corresponded with those of Old Jacques' boots – which I had established, without his suspecting it, from the floor of the Yellow Room – it had become perfectly clear to me that the attacker had sought to make suspicion fall on the old servant. That is precisely what made me say to Old Jacques that, since a beret had been found in the fateful room, it was bound to be similar to his. It further allowed me to give him a description of the stained handkerchief, which must be like the one I had seen him use. Up to that point, Larsan and I agree, but no further, and there is going to be a terrible duel between us, for, albeit in good faith, he is mistaken, and I have no way of proving that.'

At that moment, we were passing the back of the chateau. Night had fallen. A window on the first floor was partly open. A feeble light came from it, as well as some sounds that attracted our attention. We walked over to a door just under the window. In a low voice, Rouletabille explained to me that this window belonged to Mlle Stangerson's room. The sounds which had attracted our attention ceased, then started again for a while, and we heard the sound of stifled sobs. We were only able to catch these three words: 'My poor Robert!'

Rouletabille whispered in my ear: 'If only we knew what was being said in that room, my investigations would soon be over.'

He looked about him. The darkness of evening enveloped us; we could not see much beyond the narrow tree-edged lawn behind the chateau. The sobs had ceased.

'Since we cannot hear anything, we might at least try to see what is going on,' said Rouletabille.

And indicating to me to walk as quietly as possible, he led me across the path to the trunk of a tall birch tree, the white shape of which was visible in the darkness. This birch stood exactly in front of the window in which we were interested, its lower branches on a level with the first floor of the chateau. From the top of those branches, you would certainly be able to see what was going on in Mlle Stangerson's room. That was Rouletabille's idea, for, enjoining me to silence, he clasped the trunk with his vigorous arms and shinned up it. I soon lost sight of him amid the branches and a great silence ensued.

Above me, the light remained on in the open window and I saw no shadow move across it.

I listened, and presently, from above me, these words reached my ears:

'After you!'

'No, please, after you!'

Two people were talking right above my head, exchanging polite greetings! I was amazed, but still more so when two human forms slid quietly down the trunk to the ground. Rouletabille had climbed up alone and had returned as two!

'Good evening, M. Sainclair!'

It was Frédéric Larsan. The detective had already occupied the observation post, which my young friend had thought to be unoccupied. Neither took any notice of my astonishment, however. I assumed that they had witnessed some scene of tenderness and despair between Mlle Stangerson, lying on her bed, and M. Darzac, on his knees by her pillow. Already each appeared to have drawn different conclusions from what they had seen. It was easy to guess that the scene had strongly impressed the mind of Rouletabille in favour of M. Robert Darzac, while to the mind of Larsan it attested nothing but perfect hypocrisy, skilfully acted out by Mlle Stangerson's fiancé.

When we reached the park gate, Larsan stopped.

'My walking stick!' he cried. 'I left it down there, near the tree.'

And he left us, saying that he would rejoin us directly.

'Did you notice Frédéric Larsan's stick?' the young reporter asked me as soon as we were alone. 'It's quite a new one, which I have never before seen him use. He seems to take great care of it. He is never without it. Anyone would think he was afraid lest it should fall into the hands of strangers. I have never seen Frédéric Larsan with a walking stick until today. Where did he find it? It is odd that a man who has never before used a walking stick should, the day after the crime at Glandier, never move a step without one. On the day of our arrival at the chateau, as soon as he saw us, he put his watch in his pocket and picked up his stick, a gesture to which I was wrong, perhaps, not to have attached more importance.'

We were now out of the park. Rouletabille had grown silent. His thoughts were doubtless still dwelling on the subject of Frédéric Larsan's new walking stick. I had the proof of that when, as we drew near to Epinay, he said to me:

'Frédéric Larsan arrived at Glandier before me. He began his inquiry before me. He has had time to learn things and to find out things about which I know nothing. Where did he find that walking stick?'

Then he added: 'It is likely that his suspicions – no, more than suspicion, his reasoning – as to Robert Darzac's guilt have led him to lay his hands on something palpable. Can it have been that cane? Where the deuce can he have found it?'

At Epinay, as I had to wait twenty minutes for the train, we went into a small inn. Almost immediately, the door opened behind us, and Frédéric Larsan made his appearance, brandishing the famous walking stick.

'Found it!' he said gaily.

We all three sat down at a table. Rouletabille's eyes never left the cane. He was so absorbed that he did not notice a mysterious sign made by Larsan to a railway clerk, a very young man whose chin was adorned with a scrubby, blond beard. The young man rose, paid for his drink, and went out. I should not myself have attached any importance to that sign, if I had not been reminded of it some months later by the reappearance of the fellow at one of the most tragic points in this story. I then learned that the young man was an assistant of Larsan's, under orders to watch the movements of travellers at the station of Epinay-sur-Orge, for Larsan neglected nothing which he thought might be useful to him.

I again looked at Rouletabille.

'I say, Monsieur Fred,' he exclaimed, 'since when have you taken to using a walking stick?'

'It was a gift,' replied the detective.

'A recent one?' Rouletabille insisted.

'Yes, it was given to me in London.'

'Of course, you have just come from London, Monsieur Fred. May I have a look at your stick?'

'Why, certainly.'

Fred handed the stick to Rouletabille. It was a large yellow bamboo cane, with a curved handle and a gold mount.

Having examined it minutely, Rouletabille returned it to Larsan with a mocking look on his face, saying:

'How amusing! They made a present to you in London of a French walking stick.'

'Possibly,' said Fred imperturbably.

'Look at the mark here, in tiny letters: Cassette, 6A Opéra.'

'The French often have their laundry done in London,' said Fred, 'why should the English not buy their walking sticks in Paris?'

When Rouletabille had seen me into my carriage, he said to me:

'Remember the address!'

'Yes. Cassette, 6A Opera. Rely on me; you shall have word tomorrow morning.'

That evening, on reaching Paris, I saw M. Cassette, a dealer in walking sticks and umbrellas, and wrote to my friend:

'A man answering to the description of M. Robert Darzac – same height, slightly stooping, wearing a putty-coloured overcoat and a bowler hat – purchased a cane similar to the one in which we are interested, on the evening of the crime, at about eight o'clock. M. Cassette has not sold another such cane in the last two years. Fred's cane is new. It is clear that his is the one recently purchased at Cassette's. It was not he who purchased it, since he was in London at the time. Like you, I think that he must have found it somewhere in M. Robert Darzac's room. But if, as you say, the attacker was in the Yellow Room from five or even six o'clock, and as the tragedy did not take place until nearly midnight, the purchase of this stick provides M. Robert Darzac with an irrefutable alibi.'

CHAPTER XIII

'The vicarage has lost none of its charm nor the garden its brightness.'

A week after the events I have related, I received the following telegram at my home in Paris:

'Get the next train to Glandier. Bring revolvers. – Rouletabille.'

I had not heard anything about the progress of the mysterious affair for a week, apart from endless articles in the press and Rouletabille's brief notes in *L'Epoque*. Those notes had divulged the fact that old traces of human blood had been found on the cudgel, as well as Mlle Stangerson's blood; the old stains belonging to other crimes probably dating back years.

The affair caught the imagination of newspapers worldwide. No crime had so perplexed the general public. It appeared to me, however, that the judicial inquiry made very little progress, and I should have been more than happy to rejoin my friend at Glandier, had not the despatch contained the words: 'Bring revolvers.'

That worried me a great deal. If Rouletabille telegraphed to me to bring revolvers, it was because he foresaw that there would be occasion to use them. I confess it without shame, I am no hero. On the other hand, here was a friend, evidently in trouble, calling upon me to go to his aid. I did not hesitate for long and, after assuring myself that the only revolver I possessed was properly loaded, I hurried to Orleans station. On the way, I remembered that Rouletabille required not one, but two revolvers. I therefore went into a gunsmith's and bought an excellent weapon, which I decided to give to my friend.

I hoped to find him at the station at Epinay, but he was not there. However, a trap was waiting for me, and I soon reached Glandier. No one was at the gate, and it was only at the gateway to the chateau that I spotted Rouletabille. He greeted me in friendly fashion and embraced me, inquiring warmly after my state of my health.

When we were in the little sitting room which I have mentioned before. Rouletabille made me sit down and said:

'It's all going wrong.'

'What is?'

'Everything!'

He came nearer and whispered:

'Frédéric Larsan is working with all his might against M. Robert Darzac.'

This did not surprise me, since I had seen Mlle Stangerson's fiancé turn pale at the sight of his own footprints. However, I at once observed:

'What about that cane?'

'It is still in the hands of Frédéric Larsan, who never puts it down.'

'But does it not supply M. Darzac with an alibi?'

'Not at all. Under gentle questioning by me, M. Darzac denied having purchased a cane at Cassette's on that evening or on any other. Besides,' said Rouletabille, 'I won't swear to anything, because M. Darzac falls into such strange silences that one does not know exactly how to take what he says.'

'To the mind of Frédéric Larsan, this cane must appear to be a piece of damning evidence. But how? Given the time that it was bought, it could not have been in the possession of the attacker.'

'The time won't trouble Larsan. He is not obliged to adopt my system, which begins by introducing the attacker into the Yellow Room between five and six o'clock. Why should he not have got in there between ten and eleven o'clock at night? At that very time, M. and Mlle Stangerson, helped by Old Jacques, were engaged on an interesting chemical experiment in the part of the laboratory occupied by the furnaces. Larsan will say that the attacker slipped between them, however unlikely this may appear. He has already given the examining judge to understand as much. Larsan's idea is absurd when looked at closely, seeing that the criminal must have known that the Professor was presently going to leave the pavilion, and that it was necessary for him – the criminal – to put off acting until after the professor's departure. Why should he have risked crossing the laboratory while the professor was in it? And then, when could he have got into the Yellow Room?

'All these points have to be elucidated before Larsan's fanciful idea can be admitted. I am not going to waste my time over it, for I have an infallible system, which does not allow me to spend time over mere fantasy. Since I am obliged to keep silent, however, and since Larsan occasionally speaks, everything might, in the end, seem to point to M. Robert Darzac – were I not here,' added the young reporter proudly. 'For there is a lot of evidence stacked against M. Darzac, far more damning than the walking stick, which remains incomprehensible to me, all the more so since Larsan does not hesitate to let M. Darzac see him with that stick, which is supposedly Darzac's. I understand many things in Larsan's system, but not the business with the walking stick.'

'Is Larsan still at the chateau?'

'Yes, he hardly ever leaves it. He sleeps there, as I do, at the request of M. Stangerson, who has done for him what M. Robert Darzac has done for me. Accused by Frédéric Larsan of knowing the attacker and of having allowed him to escape, M. Stangerson is giving his accuser every help in arriving at the truth, just as M. Darzac is doing for me.'

'But you are persuaded of M. Darzac's innocence?'

'For a moment, I believed in the possibility of his guilt. That was when we arrived here for the first time. The moment has now come for me to tell you what happened between M. Darzac and me.'

Here Rouletabille stopped talking and asked if I had brought the weapons. I showed him the two revolvers. Having examined them, he said: 'Fine!' and handed them back to me.

'Will we need them?' I asked.

'Probably this evening. We shall spend the night here. You don't mind, do you?'

'Not at all,' I said with a grimace that made Rouletabille laugh.

'Come, now,' he said, 'this is no time for joking. Let us talk seriously. You remember the phrase which was the "Open Sesame" to this chateau mystery?'

'Yes,' I said, 'perfectly. "The vicarage has lost none of its charm nor the garden its brightness." It was that very phrase you found on the scorched piece of paper among the ashes in the laboratory.'

'Yes, at the bottom of the paper was the date: 23rd October. Remember that date, it is very important. I am now going to tell you about that curious phrase. On the evening before the crime – that is to say on the 23rd – M. and Mlle Stangerson went to a reception at the Elysée Palace. I know this, because I saw them there myself. I was there in my professional capacity, in order to interview one of the leading lights of the Academy of Philadelphia who was being entertained there that night. I had never before seen either M. or Mlle Stangerson. I was seated in the room adjoining the Ambassadors' Hall, and, tired of being jostled by all those people, I had fallen into a vague reverie, when near me I smelled the perfume of the "lady in black".

You will ask me what that means. You need know only that it is a perfume of which I have always been extremely fond, because it was worn by a lady who was very kind to me when I was a child. The lady who was wearing the perfume that evening was dressed all in white. She was wonderfully beautiful. I could not help getting up from my seat and following her. An old man held her arm under his, and, as they passed, I heard voices say, "It's Professor Stangerson and his daughter." That was how I found out who it was I was following.

They met M. Robert Darzac, whom I knew by sight. Professor Stangerson sat down in the great gallery with Mr Arthur William Rance, one of the American gentlemen and M. Darzac led Mlle Stangerson out into the conservatory. I was still following them. The weather was very mild that night; the doors to the garden were open. Mlle Stangerson threw a shawl over her shoulders, and I saw that it was she who begged M. Darzac to go with her into the garden. I followed further, intrigued by M. Darzac's obvious agitation. They slowly walked along the wall near the Avenue Marigny. I walked down the central avenue, parallel with them, and then crossed over in order to get closer to them. The night was dark, the grass deadened the sound of my steps. They had stopped under the flickering flame of a gaslight, and both appeared to be bending over a paper held by Mlle Stangerson, reading something which deeply interested them. I stopped, surrounded by darkness and silence.

Neither of them saw me, and I distinctly heard Mlle Stangerson repeating, as she was refolding the paper: "The vicarage has lost none of its charm nor the garden its brightness." It was said in a tone that was at once mocking and desperate, and was followed by such a nervous burst of laughter, that I think the phrase will never cease to sound in my ears. But yet another phrase was pronounced, this time by M. Darzac: "Shall I have to commit a crime, then, to win you?" He was in a singularly agitated state. He took Mlle Stangerson's hand and held it for a long time to his lips, and I thought from the way his shoulders were shaking, that he was weeping. Then they went away. When I returned to the great gallery,' Rouletabille continued, 'I saw no more of M. Darzac, whom I was not to see again until after the crime at Glandier. But I saw Mlle Stangerson, her father and the delegates from Philadelphia. Mlle Stangerson stood near Mr Arthur William Rance, who was talking with great animation, his eyes gleaming with a singular brightness. Mlle Stangerson, I thought, was not even listening to what he was saying, her face expressing total indifference. Mr Rance is a red-faced man, a whisky-drinker no doubt. When M. and Mlle Stangerson were gone, he went to the buffet, and never left it. I joined him there, and rendered him some little service in the midst of the pressing crowd. He thanked me and said he would be returning to America three days later, that is to say, on the 26th, the day after the crime. I talked with him about Philadelphia; he told me he had lived there for twenty-five years, and that it was there that he had known the illustrious Professor Stangerson and his daughter. Then he took to drinking champagne again, and I thought he would never leave off. I left him when he was very nearly drunk.

Such was my experience that evening. For some reason during the night, I couldn't help thinking of the Stangersons, and I leave you to imagine what effect the news of the attack on Mlle Stangerson had on me, the intensity with which I recalled the words pronounced by M. Robert Darzac: 'Shall I have to commit a crime, then, to win you?' It was not this phrase, however, that I repeated to him when we met here at Glandier. That phrase about the vicarage and the bright garden, which Mlle Stangerson had appeared to read from the piece of paper in her hand, sufficed to open to us the gate of the chateau. Did I think at the time that M. Darzac was the attacker? No, I do not believe I ever really thought so. At that moment, I did not have any serious idea or suspicion. I had so little evidence to go on. But I needed M. Darzac to prove to me at once that he had not been wounded in the hand.

When we were alone together, I told him how I had chanced to overhear part of his conversation with Mlle Stangerson in the garden of the Elysée Palace, and when I told him I had heard the words, "Shall I have to commit a crime, then, to win you?" he was greatly troubled, but certainly much less than he had been when hearing me repeat the phrase about the vicarage. What threw him into a state of real consternation was to learn from me that the day on which he was to meet Mlle Stangerson at the Elysée Palace, was the very day on which she had gone, during the afternoon, to post office no. 40, in search of the letter which was, perhaps, the one they read together that night in the garden of the Elysée Palace, which ended with the words, "The vicarage has lost none of its charm nor the garden its brightness." That supposition was confirmed by the discovery I made, as you remember, in one of the furnaces of the laboratory, of a fragment of that letter, dated 23rd October. The letter had been written and withdrawn from the post office on the same day.

There can be no doubt that, on returning from the Elysée Palace that night, Mlle Stangerson had tried to destroy that compromising piece of paper. It was in vain that M. Darzac denied that the letter had anything whatever to do with the crime. I told him that, in an affair as mysterious as this, he had no right to keep the incident of the letter from the police, an incident that I was personally convinced was of considerable importance, that the desperate tone in which Mlle Stangerson had pronounced the phrase about the vicarage, that his own tears, and the threat of a crime which he had expressed after the letter was read, left no room for doubt. M. Darzac became more and more agitated, and I determined to take advantage of the effect my words had produced on him.

"You were about to be married, Monsieur," I said negligently, not even looking at him, "and suddenly that marriage becomes impossible because of the author of that letter, since, as soon as you had read it, you spoke of a crime being needed if you were to win Mlle Stangerson. Therefore, there is someone between you and her, someone who forbids her to marry you, someone who would kill her — attempt to kill her — to prevent her from marrying!"

And I concluded this little speech with these words: "Now, Monsieur, you have only to give me the name of the attacker!"

I had, without realising it, pronounced words which were terrible to him, for, when I looked at him again, I saw that his face was contorted with anguish, his forehead was bathed in perspiration and terror lurked in his eyes.

"Monsieur," he said to me, "I am going to ask you something which may appear to be madness, but in exchange for which I would readily give my life. You must not tell the judge what you saw and heard in the garden of the Elysée Palace, nor anyone in the world. I swear to you that I am innocent, and I feel that you believe me, but I would rather pass for guilty than see the suspicions of the law fasten on that phrase 'The vicarage has lost nothing of its charm nor the garden its brightness.' The law must know nothing about that sentence. This affair belongs to you, Monsieur, I leave it in your hands; but forget that evening at the Elysée Palace. A hundred other roads are open to you that will lead to the discovery of the criminal. I will open them for you. I will help you. Do you wish to take up your quarters here? To take your meals and sleep here? To watch my actions, the actions of everyone here? You shall live at Glandier as if you owned it, Monsieur, but forget about that evening at the Elysée Palace!"

Rouletabille paused to take breath. I now understood M. Robert Darzac's extraordinary attitude towards my friend and the ease with which the young reporter had been able to settle in at the chateau. My curiosity could not fail to be excited by all I had heard. I asked Rouletabille to tell me more about the whole affair. What had happened at Glandier during the past week? Had not my friend told me that there was now circumstantial evidence against Darzac far more terrible than the walking stick found by Larsan?

'Everything seems to point to him,' my friend replied, 'and the situation is becoming exceedingly grave. M. Darzac does not appear to be much concerned about it. But he is wrong there! He cares only about Mlle Stangerson's health, which was improving daily until something occurred that is yet more mysterious than the mystery of the Yellow Room!'

'Impossible!' I cried. 'What could be more mysterious than that?'

'Let us first return to M. Darzac,' said Rouletabille, calming me. 'I was just telling you how everything seems to point to him. The elegant bootprints found by Frédéric Larsan appear to be his. The marks made by the bicycle may have been made by *his* bicycle. This point has been verified. Ever since he had that bicycle, M. Darzac has always left it at the chateau; why should he have taken it to Paris at that particular time? Was he to cease visiting the chateau? Did the breaking off of his engagement mean the end of his relationship with the Stangersons? Professor Stangerson, his daughter and M. Darzac himself declare that their relationship was to continue unchanged. What then?

Frédéric Larsan, however, believes that it was all over between M. Darzac and the Stangersons. M. Darzac did not return to Glandier from the day when he accompanied Mlle Stangerson to the Magasins du Louvre until the day after the crime. It must also be remembered that Mlle Stangerson lost her bag containing the brass key while she was in M. Darzac's company. From that day to the evening at the Elysée Palace, the Sorbonne professor and Mlle Stangerson did not see one another, but they might have written to one another. Mlle Stangerson went to post office no. 40 in search of a poste-restante letter, which Larsan believes to have been from Robert Darzac, for knowing, of course, nothing of what took place at the Elysée Palace, Larsan is led to believe that it was M. Darzac himself who stole the bag and the key in order to force Mlle Stangerson's consent, by getting possession of her father's most valuable papers – papers which would have been restored to him on condition that the marriage engagement was fulfilled.

All this would have been a very doubtful, and almost absurd, supposition, as Larsan himself admitted to me, but for, one other thing, far graver. In the first place, it is something which, so far, I have been unable to explain. It would seem that it was M. Darzac himself who, on the 24th, went to the post office and asked for the letter which Mlle Stangerson had called for and received on the previous day. The description of the man who made the application tallies in every respect with the appearance of M. Darzac, who, in answer to the questions put to him by the examining judge, denies that he went to the post office. I believe him, for, even admitting that the letter was written by him – which I don't believe to be the case – he knew that Mlle Stangerson had already called for and received it, since he had seen that very letter in her hands in the garden at the Elysée Palace. It was not him, then, who called at post office no. 40 on the 24th to ask for a letter which he knew was no longer there.

To me it seems clear that somebody strongly resembling him, and who is obviously the thief of the bag, demanded something in that letter which Mlle Stangerson declined to send to him. He must have been amazed at the failure of his demand, hence his appearance at the post office to find out whether his letter had been delivered to the person to whom it was addressed. Finding that, although it had been claimed, his request had not been granted, he became furious. What

106

was he asking for? No one but Mlle Stangerson knew this. Then, the next day, it was reported that she had been attacked during the night, and the following morning I discovered that the Professor had, at the same time, been robbed by means of the key referred to in the post-restante letter. It seems that the man who went to the post office to inquire for the letter is the attacker. Now Frédéric Larsan has argued that and the argument seems logical enough – only he applies it to M. Darzac. Needless to say, the examining judge, Larsan and myself have done our best to obtain from post office no. 40 precise details regarding the strange person who went there on 24th October. But nothing has been learned as to where he came from or where he went. We know nothing about him, beyond the description that makes him resemble M. Darzac – nothing.

I placed the following advertisement in all the leading newspapers: "A, handsome reward will be given to the coachman who drove a fare to post office no. 40 at about 10 a.m. on 24th October. Apply to the office of *L'Epoque* and ask for M. R." There has been no response. After all, the man may have walked to the post office, but as he was most likely in a hurry, there was a chance that he might have used a carriage. I have been pondering this problem night and day. Who is the man who so strongly resembles M. Darzac and who bought the cane which has fallen into the hands of Frédéric Larsan?

The most serious point of all is that M. Darzac, who, at the very same time that his double called at the post office, was due to deliver a lecture at the Sorbonne, did not deliver it. One of his friends replaced him. When I questioned him as to how he spent that time, he tells me that he went for a walk in the Bois de Boulogne! What do you think of this professor who gets another to do his work while he goes off to the Bois de Boulogne for a walk? Further, I must tell you that although M. Darzac says that he went for a walk on the morning of the 24th, he is totally unable to say what he did on the night of the 24th! When Frédéric Larsan asked him for information on this point, he quietly replied that it was no business of his how he spent his time in Paris. Fred then threatened him and declared that he would find out anyway.

All that seems to give some kind of basis to the great Fred's hypothesis, the more so if it could be established that Robert Darzac was in the Yellow Room thus corroborating the detective's explanation of how the attacker made his escape. M. Stangerson, in that case, would have allowed him to get away, in order to avoid a frightful scandal! It is that very hypothesis, which I believe to be altogether wrong, that is going to mislead Frédéric Larsan, something which would not displease me, were the life of an innocent person not at stake. Now, is that hypothesis really misleading Frédéric Larsan? That is the question, that is the question.'

'Perhaps he is right!' I exclaimed. 'Are you sure that M. Darzac is innocent? There seem to be an awful lot of unfortunate coincidences.'

'Coincidences,' my friend retorted, 'are the worst enemies of truth.'

'What does the examining judge think of the affair?'

'M. de Marquet is unwilling to charge M. Darzac in the absence of any direct evidence. Not only would public opinion be wholly against him, to say nothing of the University, but so would M. and Mlle Stangerson. Mlle Stangerson adores M. Robert Darzac. However little she saw of her attacker, it would be hard to make the public believe that she would not have recognised him if he had been the aggressor. We know that the Yellow Room was very dimly lit, but a nightlight, however dim, gives some light, remember. That, my friend, is how things stood when three days, or rather three nights ago, something incredible occurred.'

CHAPTER XIV

'Tonight I expect the attacker.'

'First of all,' said Rouletabille, 'I must show you over the chateau, to enable you to understand, or, rather, to persuade you that it is impossible to understand. I myself believe that I have found what everybody else is still searching for: how the attacker escaped from the Yellow Room entirely unaided, and without Mlle Stangerson having anything to do with it. But so long as I remain unsure of the identity of the attacker, I cannot say what my hypothesis is, only that I believe it to be correct, and, in any case, perfectly natural, that is to say, quite simple. As to what took place three nights ago in this chateau, for twenty-four hours it seemed absolutely inconceivable to me. And the hypothesis I draw from it is still so absurd that I would almost prefer the darkness of the inexplicable.'

The young reporter then invited me to go with him, and we walked round the chateau together. As we were passing by the tower, we met the Green Man, the gamekeeper, who did not greet us, but walked past us as if we did not exist. As on the day when I saw him for the first time, through the window of the Tower Inn, he had his gun slung across his back, his pipe in his mouth, his pince-nez on his nose.

'A queer customer!' muttered Rouletabille.

'Have you spoken to him?' I asked.

'Yes, but I can get nothing out of him. He answers only with growls, shrugs his shoulders and walks away. He lives in deep seclusion, never goes out without his gun, and only makes himself agreeable to women. He is handsome and well-groomed, and all the women for four leagues round are setting their caps at him. For the moment, he has eyes only for Madame Mathieu, whose husband is subsequently keeping an eagle eye upon her.'

After passing the tower, which stands at the far end of the left wing, we went back to the chateau. Pointing to a window which I recognised as one of the windows of Mlle Stangerson's apartments, Rouletabille said to me:

'If you had been here two nights ago, at one o'clock in the morning, you would have seen me at the top of a ladder preparing to enter the chateau by that window.'

As I expressed some astonishment at this piece of nocturnal gymnastics, he begged me to pay close attention to the exterior of the chateau, after which we went back into the building.

'I must now show you the first floor of the chateau – the right wing – which is where I am lodged,' said my friend.

In order to make quite clear the positions of the different rooms, I place before the reader a plan of the first floor of the right wing of the chateau, drawn by Rouletabille the day after the extraordinary phenomenon that I am about to recount in all its details.

Rouletabille motioned to me to follow him up a flight of stone stairs, which ended on the first floor in a landing. From this landing one could get to the right or left wing of the chateau by a gallery. This high, broad gallery extended the whole length of the building and faced north. The rooms, the windows of which faced south, opened on to that gallery. Professor Stangerson lived in the left wing of the building, Mlle Stangerson had her apartments in the right wing.

We entered the gallery to the right. A narrow carpet, laid on the waxed floor, muffled the sound of our footsteps. Rouletabille asked me in a low voice to walk quietly as we passed Mlle Stangerson's door. Her apartment comprised her bedroom, an anteroom, a small bathroom, a boudoir and a drawing room. One could pass from one to another of these rooms without having to go into the gallery. Only the drawing-room and the anteroom had doors that opened on to the gallery. The gallery continued straight to the eastern end of the building, where it was lit by a high window (window No. 2 on the plan). About two-thirds of the

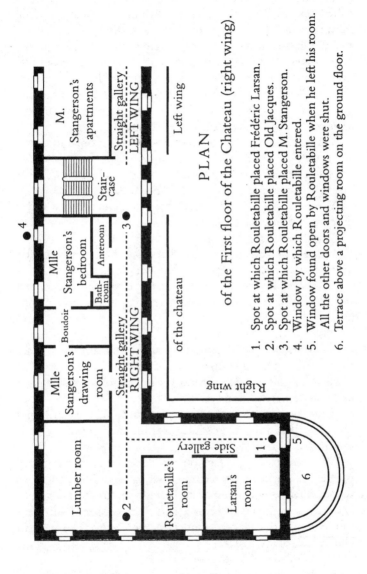

PLAN

of the First floor of the Chateau (right wing).

1. Spot at which Rouletabille placed Frédéric Larsan.
2. Spot at which Rouletabille placed Old Jacques.
3. Spot at which Rouletabille placed M. Stangerson.
4. Window by which Rouletabille entered.
5. Window found open by Rouletabille when he left his room.
   All the other doors and windows were shut.
6. Terrace above a projecting room on the ground floor.

way along, the gallery formed a right angle with another gallery that followed the right wing round.

To make all this quite clear, we shall call the gallery leading from the landing to the eastern window the 'straight gallery' and the gallery forming a right angle with it at the end, the 'side gallery'. It was at the point where those two galleries met that Rouletabille had his room, adjoining that of Frédéric Larsan. The doors of both those rooms opened on to the side gallery, whilst the doors of Mlle Stangerson's apartments opened into the straight gallery. (*See Plan.*)

Rouletabille pushed open the door of his room and closed and bolted it behind us.

I had not had time to glance around when he uttered a cry of surprise, and pointed to a pince-nez on a small table.

'What is that doing here?' he wondered. 'What's this pince-nez doing on my table?'

I could not tell him.

'Unless,' he said, 'unless it is what I have been searching for, unless it is a pince-nez for someone with long sight!'

He seized it eagerly, his fingers stroking the lenses, and then he looked at me, with a terrifying expression on his face.

'Ah!'

He repeated that exclamation again and again, as if his thoughts had suddenly turned his brain.

He rose and, putting a hand on my shoulder, he laughed like one demented, as he said:

'That pince-nez will drive me mad, for, scientifically speaking, the thing is possible, but, humanly speaking, it is impossible, or then again . . .'

We heard two light taps on the door. Rouletabille partly opened it. A head peered in. I recognised Mme Bernier, whom I had seen when she was being taken to the pavilion to answer the judge's questions, and I was astonished, for I thought that she was still under lock and key. The woman said, in a very low voice:

'It was in a crack in the floor!'

Rouletabille said 'Thank you' and the woman disappeared.

He again turned towards me, after having carefully bolted the door again. Then he uttered words which had no meaning to me, and as he spoke his eyes were wild.

'If the thing is scientifically possible, why should it not be humanly possible? But if it is humanly possible, the whole business is incredible!'

I interrupted his soliloquy.

'The caretakers are free, then?' I asked.

'Yes, I had them set free. I need trustworthy people about me. The woman is thoroughly devoted to me now, and the caretaker would give his life for me. And since this pince-nez has lenses made for a long-sighted person, I am going to need the help of people prepared to die for me!'

'Aha!' I said. 'You seem to be speaking in earnest. When is this likely to happen?'

'Tonight, for I forgot to tell you, my friend – *tonight I expect the attacker.*'

'What! You mean you expect the attacker tonight? You know who he is, then?'

'Possibly, but I would be mad to state categorically now that I know him, for the clue I have to the identity of the attacker points to such a frightening, monstrous answer that I very much hope I am mistaken. Oh, I hope so with all my heart!'

'How – since you did not know the attacker five minutes ago – can you say that you expect him tonight?'

'Because I know that he will come!'

At that moment, we heard someone walking in the gallery past our door. Rouletabille listened. The sound of footsteps died away in the distance.

'Is Frédéric Larsan in his room?' I asked, pointing to the dividing wall.

'No, he is not,' my friend answered. 'He went to Paris this morning, still on the scent of Darzac, who also went off to Paris. All that will turn out very badly. I foresee that within a week M. Darzac will be arrested. The worst of it is that everything seems to conspire against him – events, facts, people. Not an hour passes that does not bring new evidence against him. The examining judge is overwhelmed by it, and can see no other possible conclusion. I cannot blame him under the circumstances.'

'Yet Frédéric Larsan is not new to the game,' I said.

'I thought,' said Rouletabille, with a slightly contemptuous twist of the lips, 'I thought he was much cleverer than that. Of course, he is no fool. I had, indeed, a good deal of admiration for him, before I knew his methods, which are deplorable. He owes his reputation solely to his cunning, but he lacks philosophy; the mathematics behind his ideas is very poor indeed.'

I could not help smiling to hear this boy of eighteen talking like a lad of fifteen about a man of fifty who had shown himself to be the finest detective in Europe.

'You smile,' he said, 'but you're wrong! I swear to you that I will outdo him, and how! But I must make haste about it, for he has a colossal lead, given by M. Robert Darzac himself, and tonight that lead will be increased still more. Think of it! Every time the attacker comes to the chateau, by some strange fatality, M. Robert Darzac is away and flatly refuses to give any account of how he has spent his time.'

'What do you mean "Every time the attacker comes to the chateau"?' I cried. 'Has he returned, then?'

'Yes, on the night when the extraordinary phenomenon occurred.'

I was at last going to hear about that amazing phenomenon, which Rouletabille had mentioned several times during the last half hour, without giving me any explanation. But I had learned never to press Rouletabille, for he spoke only when the fancy took him or when he judged it to be useful, and cared much less about satisfying my curiosity than about making a complete summary of an important event in which he was interested.

At last, in short, rapid sentences, he apprised me of things so fantastic that, in truth, they made me feel as if I had lost the power of thought, and even common sense itself. I was utterly bewildered. Indeed, the events made possible by that still unknown science called hypnotism, for example, are no more explicable than the disappearance of an attacker precisely at the moment when four people had him in their grasp! And yet, if I had had Rouletabille's brain, I should, like him, have sensed some 'natural' explanation; for the most remarkable point about the mysteries of Glandier is undoubtedly the natural manner in which Rouletabille explained them. But who could have boasted then, and who, indeed, could boast today, of a brain like Rouletabille's! I have never seen such extraordinary bumps on any other forehead, with the exception, perhaps, of Frédéric Larsan's, although you had to look closely at the great detective to notice the bumps, whilst with Rouletabille they were immediately obvious.

Among the papers handed to me by the young reporter after the case was over, I have a notebook of his, in which there happens to be a complete account of the 'phenomenon of the disappearing attacker' and the thoughts to which it gave rise in my young friend's mind. It is preferable, I think, to give the reader that account rather than continue to reproduce my conversation with Rouletabille.

CHAPTER XV

The trap
(Extract from Joseph Rouletabille's notebook)

Last night (writes Rouletabille) – the night of 29th October
– I woke at about one o'clock in the morning. Was it sleep-
lessness or did I hear some noise outside? The cry of the Good
Lord's Beast rang out with fearful clarity at the other end of
the park. I rose and opened my window. Cold wind and rain;
thick darkness and silence. I closed the window. Again that
uncanny cry in the blue distance. I hastily slipped on a pair of
trousers and a coat. Outside, the weather was awful. No one
would turn even a cat out of doors on such a night. Who,
then, was imitating the cry of Mother Agenoux's cat so near
the chateau? I picked up a cudgel, the only weapon in my
possession, and, making not a sound, I opened my door.

I was now in the gallery, lit by a lamp. The flame flickered;
there was a draught, I could feel it. I turned round. Behind
me a window was open, the window at the far end of the side
gallery – where Larsan and I had our rooms. Those two
galleries formed a right angle. Who had left that window
open, or had it only just been opened? I went to the window,
and leaned out. Four feet below there was a sort of terrace
over the semi-circular projection of a room on the ground
floor. It would be easy to jump from the window on to the
terrace, and then drop into the main courtyard of the chateau.
Whoever came in that way evidently did not have a key to the
main door. But what made me imagine those nocturnal
gymnastics? An open window? It might have been left open
by a careless servant. I closed it again, smiling at the ease with
which I could construct a whole drama out of an open
window!

Again the cry of the Good Lord's Beast! Then silence. The

rain had ceased to beat against the window. Everyone in the chateau was asleep. I walked with infinite care across the carpet. On reaching the corner of the straight gallery I peered cautiously about me. There was another lamp lighting three armchairs and the pictures hanging on the wall. What was I doing there? Never had the chateau been quieter. Perfect silence reigned. What was that instinct urging me on to Mlle Stangerson's room? Why was a voice within me crying: 'Go to the door of Mlle Stangerson's room'? I looked down at the carpet I was walking on and I saw that my steps were being guided towards Mlle Stangerson's room by a series of footprints! Yes, there were muddy footprints leading straight to Mlle Stangerson's room! With a feeling of horror, I recognised those elegant bootprints instantly: they belonged to the attacker! He had come, then, on that abominable night. If you could get out of the gallery by way of the window, you could also get in.

The attacker was there, in the chateau, for there were no returning footprints. He had entered the chateau by the open window at the far end of the side gallery; he had passed Frédéric Larsan's door and mine, turned to the right into the straight gallery, and then into Mlle Stangerson's room. I was standing outside the door to her anteroom; it was half-open. I pushed it. I was in the anteroom. There, under the door of her room, I saw a line of light. I listened. Not a sound – not even that of breathing. Ah, if only I could know what was happening in the silence behind that door! I examined the door. I found that it was locked and that the key was on the inside. And to think that the attacker might be in there! He must be. Would he escape this time? Everything depended on me. It needed a cool head and, above all, no wrong moves! I must find a way of looking into that room. Should I enter it by Mlle Stangerson's drawing room? If I did that, I would have to cross her boudoir and the attacker would escape by the gallery door – the very door I was standing in front of.

No crime had yet been committed that night, for there was complete silence in the boudoir, where two servants, acting as nurses, were spending the night and would continue to do so until Mlle Stangerson was completely restored to health.

Since I was almost sure that the attacker was there, why not raise the alarm? The attacker might perhaps escape, but I might thus save Mlle Stangerson's life. What if that attacker were not an attacker? The door was opened to let him in – by whom? – and it had been locked again – by whom? For every night, Mlle Stangerson locked herself in her apartment with her nurses. Who turned the key of that room to let the attacker in? The nurses? Two faithful servants – the old chambermaid and her daughter Sylvia? That was very unlikely. Besides, they were sleeping in the boudoir and Mlle Stangerson – keenly aware, so M. Darzac told me, of the danger she was in – saw to her own safety, since she was able to move about her room, which I had not as yet seen her leave. This prudence on her part, which had so struck M. Darzac, had also given me food for thought. At the time of the crime in the Yellow Room, there can be no doubt that she expected the attacker. Was she expecting him again tonight? Who opened the door to the man in there? Was it she herself? She was bound to dread the coming of this attacker. What extraordinary reasons drove her to open the door to him? Ah, what would I not give to know!

There must have been some reason for the silence behind that door. My intervention might do more harm than good. How could I tell? My intervention might bring about another crime – I had no way of knowing. Ah, to see and to know, without breaking that silence!

I left the anteroom, turned to the left and went down the stairs. I was now in the entrance hall, and, as silently as possible, I made my way to the little room on the ground floor where Old Jacques had been sleeping since the attack took place in the pavilion.

I found him already dressed, his eyes wide open, almost wild. He did not seem surprised to see me. He told me that he had got up because he had heard both the cry of the Good Lord's Beast and footsteps outside, close to his window. He had looked through the window and seen a black phantom

118

pass by. I asked him whether he had a firearm. No, he no longer had one, not since the examining judge took his revolver from him. Together we went through a little back door into the park, and stole along by the side of the chateau to a point just below the window of Mlle Stangerson's room.

I placed Old Jacques by the wall, telling him to stay there. Then, taking advantage of a moment when the moon was hidden by a cloud, I walked to a place opposite the window, but remained outside the patch of light issuing forth from it – for the window was half-open. Why was it open? By way of a precaution? As a means of escape in the event of someone suddenly entering the room? Anyone jumping from that window would run the risk of breaking his neck! But the attacker might have a rope? He was sure to have thought of everything. Ah, if only I knew what was happening in that silent room! I returned to Old Jacques and whispered two words in his ear: 'A ladder!' I thought at first of the tree which, a week ago, I had used as a look-out, but I immediately saw that, given the angle at which the window was opened, I would be unable to see anything in the room. Besides, I wanted not only to be able to see, but to hear and to act.

Old Jacques was greatly agitated, almost trembling. He disappeared for a moment, then returned, without the ladder, but making frantic signs to me to rejoin him quickly. When I drew near, he gasped: 'Come with me!'

He led me round the chateau to the tower. Once there, he said:

'I went in search of my ladder in the lower room of the tower, which the gardener and I use to store lumber. The door was open and the ladder gone. When I came out, that's where I caught sight of it, in the moonlight.'

He was pointing to the other end of the chateau, to a ladder resting against the stone buttresses supporting the terrace, under the window which I had found open. The terrace had blocked my view of it. With that ladder, it would have been quite easy to climb into the side gallery on the first floor, and I no longer had any doubts that it had been used by the unknown man to gain entry.

We ran to the ladder but, the moment we reached it, Old Jacques drew my attention to the door of the little semi-circular room, situated beneath the terrace, at the far end of the right wing of the chateau. That door was ajar. Old Jacques pushed the door open a little further, and looked in.

'He's not here!' he whispered.

'Who is not there?'

'The gamekeeper!'

With his lips once more to my ear, he added:

'The gamekeeper has been staying in this room while they are repairing the tower!' And again he pointed to the half-open door, the ladder, the terrace and the window in the side gallery, which, a short while ago, I myself had closed.

What were my thoughts then? Did I have time to think? I felt more than I thought.

Evidently, if the gamekeeper was up there in the room – I say if, because at that moment, apart from the ladder and the fact that the gamekeeper's room was empty, I had no reason to suspect him – if he was there, he would have had to use the ladder to climb through that window; for, behind the room where he lives now is that of the butler and his wife -- the cook – and farther back, the kitchens, which would make it impossible for him to reach the front hall and the staircase. If it was the gamekeeper, it would have been easy for him to find some pretext to go into the gallery on the previous evening and fix the window so that he would only need to push it open from the outside and jump into the gallery. The fact of the unfastened window singularly narrowed the field in my search to discover the identity of the attacker. He must live in the house, or else have an accomplice, which I did not believe – unless – unless Mlle Stangerson herself saw that the window was not fastened on the inside. But then, what frightful secret would compel her to remove the obstacles separating her from her attacker?

I seized the ladder and we went round to the back of the chateau. The window of Mlle Stangerson's room was still ajar; the curtains were drawn, but not completely, allowing a bright stream of light to flood out on to the path at our feet. I placed my ladder beneath the window. I was almost sure that I made no noise. And, while Old Jacques remained at the foot of the ladder, I climbed slowly up, my stout stick in my hand. I held my breath. I lifted my feet and placed them on the rungs with the utmost care. The heavens opened in a fresh downpour. That was lucky! I wouldn't be heard at all!

Suddenly I heard the sinister cry of the Good Lord's Beast. I stopped climbing. It seemed to me to have come from somewhere behind me, only a few yards away. What if the cry were a signal! What if some accomplice had seen me on my ladder! Perhaps this cry would call the attacker to the window! Perhaps . . .

Heavens! The man was at the window! I sensed him above me. I could hear him breathing. And I could not look at him; the least movement of my head and I would be lost! He was gone. He saw nothing. I felt rather than heard him, moving on tiptoe about the room, and I climbed up a few more rungs. My head was on a level with the windowsill; I peered over it to see between the two curtains.

A man was there, seated at Mlle Stangerson's little desk. He was writing. He had his back to me.

A bewildering fact! Mlle Stangerson was not there! Her bed had not been slept in! Where, then, was she sleeping? Doubtless in the next room, with her nurses.

But who was this man, sitting writing at this desk as if he were at home? Were it not for the footprints of the attacker on the carpet in the gallery, the open window and the ladder beneath that window, I might have been persuaded that this man had a perfect right to be there, for reasons I did not yet know. But there was no doubt that this mysterious person was the man of the Yellow Room, the man who made the terrible attempt on Mlle Stangerson's life, the man she dared not denounce. Ah, if only I could see his face! If I could surprise him, capture him!

If I had sprung into the room at that moment, he would have escaped through the anteroom, or by the door on the right, which opened onto the boudoir. Then he would have run through the drawing room into the gallery, and I would have lost him. Now, I had him; another five minutes and he would be as much mine as a caged bird! What was he doing there alone in Mlle Stangerson's room? Who was he writing to? I went back down the ladder and placed the ladder on the ground. Old Jacques followed me. We went back into the chateau. I sent Old Jacques to wake M. Stangerson. He was to wait for me in the Professor's room and tell him nothing until I got there. I would go and wake Frédéric Larsan. That was most annoying; I would have liked to have worked out everything by myself and arrested the attacker under the very nose of the sleeping Larsan! But Jacques and M. Stangerson are old men, and I might not be strong enough. Larsan is used to dealing with ruffians, able to wrestle with them and throw them to the ground, then spring to his feet afterwards with the villains in handcuffs. Larsan opened the door of his room. His eyes were puffy with sleep; he was tempted to send me away with a flea in my ear, for he did not believe in my 'cub reporter's fancies'. I had to assure him that the man was there.

'That's very strange,' he says. 'I thought I left him this afternoon in Paris!'

He got dressed quickly and armed himself with a revolver. We stole quietly into the gallery.

'Where is he?' Larsan asked.

'In Mlle Stangerson's room.'

'And Mlle Stangerson?'

'She is not in her room.'

'Let's go there now.'

'Don't! At the first sign of danger, he will escape! He has three possible exits – the door, the window and the boudoir where the nurses are sleeping!'

'I'll shoot him.'

'And what if you miss him, what if you only succeed in wounding him? He'll escape again! Besides, he is certainly armed! No, let me arrange this and I'll take full responsibility!'

'As you like,' he replied, with fairly good grace.

Then, after satisfying myself that all the windows in the two galleries were secured, I placed Frédéric Larsan at the end of the side gallery, in front of the window which I had found open and had closed again.

'On no account,' I said to Fred, 'must you stir from this spot until I call you. It is quite possible that the man will return to this window and try to escape through it when he is pursued, for this is how he made his entrance and prepared for his flight. You have a dangerous post.'

'Where will you be?' asked Fred.

'I shall burst into the room and drive him towards you.'

'Take my revolver,' said Fred, 'and I'll take your stick.'

'Thanks,' I said, 'you're a good fellow!'

I took it from him. I was going to be alone with the man who was writing in the room and was very glad to have the revolver.

I left Fred, having posted him at the window (No. 5 on the plan), and went, still as quietly as possible, to M. Stangerson's apartment in the left wing of the chateau. I found him with Old Jacques, who had faithfully obeyed my instructions, confining himself to telling his master to dress as quickly as possible. In a few words, I explained to M. Stangerson what was happening. He too armed himself with a revolver, followed me, and all three of us hurried into the gallery. All this took about ten minutes. The Professor wanted to round on the attacker at once and kill him. I convinced him that, in his desire to shoot him, he must not miss and allow him to escape.

When I had sworn to him that his daughter was not in the room and was in no danger, he got a grip on himself and let me direct the whole affair. I told M. Stangerson and Old Jacques that they should only come to me if I called out to them, or if I fired my revolver, and I told Old Jacques to station himself by the window at the far end of the straight gallery (No. 2 on the plan). I chose that position for Jacques because I imagined that the attacker would flee down the gallery towards the window which he had left open, and seeing, from the corner of the two galleries, that the window was guarded by Larsan, would run instead along the straight gallery. There he would encounter Old Jacques, who would prevent him jumping out of the window into the park. Under that window there was a sort of buttress, while all the other windows in the galleries were at such a height above the ditches surrounding the chateau that it would be almost impossible to jump from them without breaking your neck. All the doors and windows, including those in the lumber room at the end of the straight gallery – as I had rapidly assured myself – were firmly shut.

Having thus indicated to Old Jacques the post he had to occupy, and having seen him take up his position, I placed M. Stangerson on the landing at the top of the stairs, not far from the door of his daughter's anteroom. Everything led me to suppose that when I came upon the attacker in the room, he would escape by way of the anteroom rather than through the boudoir where the women were, the door of which must have been locked by Mlle Stangerson herself if, as I thought, she had taken refuge in the boudoir in order to avoid the attacker whom she knew would visit her. In any case, the man had to return to the gallery, where people were waiting for him at every possible exit.

On reaching the gallery, he would see M. Stangerson on his left. He would veer to the right towards the side gallery, his planned escape route. At the intersection of the two galleries he would see, as I have explained, Frédéric Larsan to his left at the end of the side gallery and, opposite him, Old Jacques at the end of the straight gallery. M. Stangerson and myself would run behind him. He would be ours! He could no longer escape us!

The plan I had formed seemed to me the best, the surest and the simplest of plans. It would, no doubt, have been simpler still had one of us been placed behind the door of Mlle Stangerson's boudoir, which opened on to her bedroom. We would then have been in a position to guard the two doors of the room the man was actually in; but we could only enter the boudoir by way of the drawing room, the door of which had been locked on the inside by Mlle Stangerson. It was out of the question. But even if I had had access to the boudoir I would have kept to my original plan, because any other plan of attack would have separated us when the moment came to grapple with the man. My plan, however, brought us all together for the attack at a spot which I had selected with almost mathematical precision – the intersection of the two galleries.

Having thus positioned my men I again went out of the chateau, hurried to my ladder and, placing it once more against the wall under the window of Mlle Stangerson's room, I climbed up, revolver in hand.

CHAPTER XVI

*The strange phenomenon of the dissociation of matter
(Extract from Joseph Rouletabille's notebook, contd.)*

I was again standing at the windowsill and peering above it. I
prepared myself to look between the curtains and was anxious
to know which way the attacker would be facing. I hoped he
would have his back turned towards me, that he would still be
seated at the desk writing! But perhaps he was no longer
there? Yet, how could he have fled? After all, I had his ladder? I
mustered every ounce of coolness and self-control. I peered
further over. He was there! I could see his monstrous back,
distorted by the shadow cast by the candle. He was no longer
writing and the candle was not on the desk. It was on the floor
now and he was bending over it. A strange position, which
served my purpose.

I breathed again. I climbed a few more rungs. I was at the
top of the ladder. With my left hand I took hold of the rail
running round the sill. I gripped my revolver between my
teeth. My right hand was now on the rail too. One jump and I
would be on the window ledge. I hoped the ladder would
hold firm, but alas, I was obliged to press down heavily to raise
myself up and hardly had my feet left the top rung than the
ladder swayed beneath me. It grated on the wall and fell, but
my knees were already on the stone ledge and with a lightning
movement I pulled myself over.

The attacker, though, was quicker still. He had heard the
noise of the ladder against the wall. I saw the man's monstrous
back rise suddenly. He turned. I saw his face. Or did I? The
candle on the floor only lit his legs. Above his waist there was
nothing but shadow and darkness. I saw a man with long hair
and a beard, a man with mad-looking eyes, a pale face, framed
by large whiskers; they were red whiskers – at least, I think so,

for it was very difficult to see anything properly, and besides, I only got a glimpse of him. I did not know the man. That was the main impression I received from that face in the dim light in which I saw it. I did not know the face, or, at least, I did not recognise it.

Ah! Then was the moment for rapid action! I had to be the wind, the hurricane, lightning itself! But alas there were a few necessary movements to be made, and whilst I was making them – my knees on the window ledge, my feet on the ground – the man, who had seen me at the window, had jumped to his feet and rushed, as I foresaw he would, to the door of the anteroom, had had time to open it and flee. But I was already behind him, revolver in hand, shouting 'Help!'

I had darted like an arrow across the room, but I had time to notice that there was a letter on the table. I almost overtook the man in the anteroom, for it took him a second or so to open the door and go out into the gallery. He slammed the door on me. But my feet had wings and I was in the gallery only a few feet behind him. As I guessed he would, he had fled along the gallery to his right, the route he had prepared for his flight. 'Jacques! Larsan! Help!' I cried.

He could not escape us! I gave a shout of joy, a savage yell of victory. The man reached the intersection of the two galleries barely two seconds before M. Stangerson and I, and the meeting which I had calculated and prepared for – the fatal encounter that must inevitably take place at that spot – occurred. We all met at that crossroads: Stangerson and I coming from one end of the straight gallery, Old Jacques coming from the other end of the same gallery, and Frédéric Larsan coming from the side gallery. But the man was not there!

We looked at each other stupefied, terrified, in the face of this impossibility, of this unreality. The man was not there!

'Where is he? Where is he?' we all asked at the same time.

'He could not have escaped!' I cried, in a fit of temper, for I felt more angry than terrified.

'I actually touched him!' Frédéric Larsan exclaimed.

'He was here! I felt his breath on my face!' cried Old Jacques.

'We touched him!' M. Stangerson and I repeated.

And once more we all repeated, like madmen: 'Where is he? Where is he? Where is he?'

We raced madly along the two galleries; we checked doors and windows. They were closed – hermetically sealed. No one could have opened them, since we found them all shut. Besides, would not the opening of a door or window by this man whom we were hunting, without our having perceived it, have been even more inexplicable still than his disappearance?

'Where is he? Where is he?' He could not have escaped through a door or a window or by any other means. He could not have passed through our bodies.

I confess that, at that moment, I felt done for. For the gallery was brightly lit and there were no traps or secret doors in the walls, no possible hiding-places. We moved the armchairs and looked behind the pictures. Nothing! We would have looked inside the flower pots had there been any.

When this mystery, thanks to Rouletabille, was explained, in a perfectly natural way, by the help alone of the young man's prodigious logic, we were forced to realise that the attacker had not got away either through a window, a door, or by the stairs.

CHAPTER XVII

The mysterious gallery
(Extract from Joseph Rouletabille's notebook, contd.)

Mlle Mathilde Stangerson appeared at the door of her ante-room. We were standing near her door, in the gallery, where the incredible phenomenon had just happened. There are moments when one feels one's brain, as it were, gradually melting away. A bullet in the head, a fractured skull, the seat of logic crushed, reason shattered – all that is, no doubt, comparable to the sensation that was exhausting, nay, draining me.

Luckily, Mlle Stangerson appeared. I saw her, and that was a diversion from my chaotic state of mind. I breathed in the perfume of the lady in black. Dear lady in black, whom I shall never see again! Ten years of my life – half my life even – I would gladly give to see her again! Alas, I only ever encounter – and that very rarely – her perfume, or a similar perfume which reminds me of the past, which takes me back to the little visitors' room in the school of my youth! [When he wrote this, Rouletabille was eighteen years of age, yet he spoke of his youth! I have reproduced his narrative exactly as it stands, but I wish to warn the reader that the episode concerning the 'perfume of the lady in black' has nothing to do with the Mystery of the Yellow Room. It is not my fault if, in the document I am transcribing, Rouletabille refers to certain other memories.]

It was that sharp reminder of that dearest of perfumes which made me go to this lady, dressed entirely in white, and so pale – so pale, so beautiful – standing near the mysterious gallery. Her beautiful golden hair, gathered up at the nape of her neck, revealed the red star on her temple, the wound which had nearly caused her death. At the start of this affair, I imagined that on the night of the mystery of the Yellow Room, Mlle Stangerson had worn her hair parted in the middle. But before I had been in the Yellow Room, how could I have reasoned otherwise? Then, after the mysterious occurrence in the gallery, I no longer reasoned. I stood there, stupefied, before the pale, lovely apparition of Mlle Stangerson. She was clad in a white dressing gown. She could have been mistaken for a gentle ghost. Her father took her in his arms and kissed her tenderly as if he were recovering his lost child. She had been in danger, and he might easily have lost her again. He dared not question her. He led her back into her room. We followed them, for we wanted to understand what had happened. The door of the boudoir stood open. The terrified faces of the two nurses were turned towards us. Mlle Stangerson asked what all the fuss was about.

'It's all very simple,' she said. Very simple, indeed! She said that she had decided to sleep that night not in her room, but in the boudoir with the nurses. She locked the door of the boudoir herself. Ever since the night of the attack she had been subject to sudden fears. What could be more natural?

But why should she, that particular night when 'he' was due to arrive, by mere chance, have decided to shut herself in with the two women? Why would she not accept her father's offer to sleep in her drawing room? Why was the letter which, a few moments before, I saw on the table in that room no longer there? Anyone capable of understanding all this will doubtless say: 'Mlle Stangerson knew that her attacker was coming – she could not prevent his coming again – and she warned no one because the attacker had to remain unknown – above all, unknown to her father, unknown to all but to M. Robert Darzac.' Yes, M. Darzac must know him now – perhaps knew him before. One need only recall the phrase in the Elysée Palace garden: 'Shall I have to commit a crime, then, to win you?' Who would that crime be committed against, if not against the obstacle – that is, against the attacker? One should always remember the words of Darzac in answer to my question: 'Would it displease you if I discovered the identity of the attacker?' 'I would kill him with my own hands!' And I replied: 'You have not answered my question.' Which was true. Indeed, M. Darzac knows the attacker so well that, whilst wishing to kill him himself, he fears my discovering him. There are only two reasons why he assisted me in my inquiries: firstly, because I forced him to do it, and, secondly, because she would be better guarded.

I was in the room – in her room. I looked at her and I looked at the place where the letter had been moments before. She had picked it up. The letter was obviously for her – obviously. Ah, how she trembled! She trembled at the fantastic story told her by her father of the presence of the criminal in her room, and of the chase. But it was evident that she was not wholly satisfied by the assurances given her, until she was told that the attacker, by some incomprehensible means, by magic, had managed to escape.

Then there was silence. What a silence! We were all standing there, looking at her – her father, Larsan, Old Jacques and I. What thoughts were being silently woven about her? After the mysterious incident in the gallery, after the amazing yet real presence of the attacker in her room, it seemed to me that all our thoughts might be expressed in these words to her: 'You know the the solution to the mystery, explain it to us and we can save you, perhaps!' Oh, how I longed to save her – from herself and from that other person! I could not help but weep as I watched her. Yes, my eyes filled with tears at the sight of such misery, so fearfully concealed.

There she was – the woman with the same perfume as the lady in black. At last, I saw her in her room, in that room where she would never allow me to enter, in that room where she would remain ever silent. Since that fateful hour in the Yellow Room, we have all hovered about this silent, invisible woman in order to learn what she knows. Our desire, our will to know, must be yet another torment to her. Perhaps if we did discover the nature of her mystery, that would be the signal for an even more terrible tragedy to take place? It might bring with it her death? Yet she nearly died and we knew nothing – or, rather, there are some of us who knew nothing But I – if I knew who it was, I should know all. Who? Who?

Since I do not know, I must remain silent out of pity for her. For there is no doubt that she knows how he escaped from the Yellow Room, and yet keeps her secret. Why should I speak? When I know who it is, I will speak to him – to him!

She looked at us, as if from afar, as if we were not in the room. M. Stangerson broke the silence. He declared that henceforth he would not leave his daughter's apartments. In vain she tried to oppose this; M. Stangerson firmly held to his purpose. He would install himself there, that very night, he said. Then, solely concerned with his daughter's health, he reproached her for having left her bed; he fell to talking to her as if she were a little child; he smiled at her; he barely knew what he was saying or doing. The illustrious professor was losing his mind. We were all more or less in the same state of mental collapse. Suddenly, Mlle Stangerson said: 'Father, father!' in such an intensely tender and concerned voice, that he burst into a fit of sobbing. Old Jacques blew his nose and Frédéric Larsan was obliged to turn away to hide his emotion. As for me, I thought nothing – I was unable to feel. I felt thoroughly disgusted with myself.

It was the first time that Frédéric Larsan had found himself face to face with Mlle Stangerson since the attack in the Yellow Room. Like me, he had insisted on being allowed to question the unfortunate lady, but he had not been received, anymore than I had. To him, as to me, the same answer had always been given: Mlle Stangerson was too weak to see us; the interrogation by the judge had worn her out quite enough as it was, etc. There was a clear intent not to assist us in our researches, which did not surprise me, but it astonished Frédéric Larsan. It is true that he and I had a totally different conception of the crime.

They wept. And I kept repeating to myself: 'Save her, save her in spite of herself, without compromising her, without allowing him to speak! Who is 'he'? Who is the attacker? Arrest him and silence him once and for all!' But M. Darzac has made it clear that, to silence him, the man must be killed! That is the logical conclusion to be drawn from Darzac's words. Now, did I have the right to kill Mlle Stangerson's attacker? No, but let him only give me the chance! If only to see whether he really is a creature of flesh and blood, if only to see his dead body, since we cannot take him alive!

Ah, how could I make that woman, who did not even look at us, who was so consumed by her fear and by her father's distress, understand that I was capable of doing anything to save her? Yes, yes, I would once more apply my reason and I would work wonders!

I moved towards her. I would speak to her. I would entreat her to have confidence in me; I would, in a few words, make her understand – she and I alone – that I knew how the attacker had escaped from the Yellow Room, *that I had guessed the reasons for her secrecy*, and that I pitied her with all my heart. But she was already gesturing to us, begging us to leave her alone. She was weary; she needed immediate rest. M. Stangerson asked us to go back to our rooms, thanked us, dismissed us. Frédéric Larsan and I bowed to him and, followed by Old Jacques, we returned to the gallery. I heard Larsan murmur: 'Strange, very strange!' He beckoned to me to enter his room. On the threshold, he turned to Old Jacques and asked:

'You clearly saw the man, did you not?'

'Saw him? I should think I did! He had a big red beard and red hair.'

'That's how he appeared to me,' I said.

'And to me also,' said Larsan.

The great Fred and I were left alone then, talking in his room. We discussed the matter for an hour, turning it this way and that. From the questions he asked me, from the explanations he gave, it was clear to me that, despite the evidence of his eyes, of my eyes, of everybody's eyes, he is persuaded that the man disappeared along some secret passage in the chateau.

'For he knows the chateau well,' Larsan said, 'he knows it very well indeed.'

'He is a rather tall man, well built.'

'He is as tall as he wants to be,' he murmured.

'I understand,' I said. 'But how do you account for his red hair and beard?'

'Too much beard and too much hair – they are false,' Fred explained.

'That's easily said. You are always thinking of Robert Darzac. Can you not free yourself from that idea? I am certain Darzac is innocent.'

'So much the better. I hope he is. But everything conspires to condemn him. You've noticed the marks on the carpet? Come and have a look at them.'

'I have seen them. They are the prints left by the elegant boots, the same as were found by the shore of the lake.'

'Can you deny that they are those of Robert Darzac?'

'No, but one might be mistaken.'

'Have you noticed that those footprints only go in one direction – to Mlle Stangerson's room – but do not return thence? When the man came out of the room, pursued by us all, he left no footprints behind him!'

'The man might have been in her room for hours, and the mud on his boots had time to dry. Then he sped along on tiptoe! We saw him running, but we did not hear the sound of his steps.'

Suddenly I broke off that useless chatter, devoid of logic and unworthy of us. I made a sign to Larsan to listen.

'There, below, someone is shutting a door!'

I got up. Larsan followed me. We went down to the ground floor. We stepped outside. I led Larsan to the little semi-circular room under the terrace, beneath the window of the side gallery. I pointed to the door, now closed, but which a short while ago had had a line of light beneath it.

'The gamekeeper!' Fred exclaimed.

'Come on!' I whispered.

Having decided – I know not why – to believe that the Green Man was the culprit, I went to the door and rapped smartly on it.

Certain readers may think that this return to the game-keeper's door was rather belated, that our first duty, having found that the attacker had escaped us in the gallery, was to search everywhere else, around the chateau, and in the park.

All I can say is that the attacker had disappeared from the

gallery in such a fantastic way that we really thought he was no longer anywhere! He had eluded us when all our hands were outstretched to seize him – when he was almost within our grasp. We had no grounds for hoping that we could clear up the mystery of the night and the park. Besides, the disappearance of the man had almost maddened us.

As soon as I rapped at the door, it was opened and the gamekeeper quietly asked us what we wanted. He was undressed and ready to go to bed. The bed had not yet been disturbed.

We went in.

'Not yet gone to bed?' I said.

'No,' he replied bluntly. 'I've been making a round of the park and the woods. I only just got back and I'm tired.'

'Look here,' I said, 'a little while ago there was a ladder close by this window.'

'What ladder? I didn't see any ladder! Goodnight, gentlemen!'

And he simply bustled us out of the room. When we were outside, I looked at Larsan. He was inscrutable.

'Well?' I said.

'Well?' he repeated.

'Does this not give you some new ideas?'

There was no mistaking his ill humour. As we went back into the castle, I heard him mutter:

'It would be strange, very strange indeed, for me to be so very wrong.'

And these words he said, or so I thought, to me rather than to himself. Then he added:

'In any case, we shall soon know what to think. Dawn will bring with it the light.'

CHAPTER XVIII

Rouletabille draws a circle between the two bumps
on his forehead
(Extract from Joseph Rouletabille's notebook, contd.)

We parted outside our rooms with a melancholy handshake. I was glad to have awakened some suspicion of error in that original mind – extremely intelligent, but entirely unmethodical. I did not go to bed. I awaited the coming of daylight, and then went down to the front of the chateau. I walked around it and examined all the footprints coming to it or leaving it. But they were so mixed and confused that I could make nothing of them. Here I should say that I do not as a rule attach overmuch importance to the external signs of a crime.

That method, which consists in tracking down the criminal from his footprints, is altogether primitive. There are so many identical footprints. One may use them as an indication, but they can never be considered as absolute proof. However that may be, in my troubled state of mind I went into the deserted main courtyard, and looked at all the footprints I could find there, looking for some clue to what had happened in the gallery.

I must apply my reason! Desperate, I sat down upon a stone. What had I been doing for the last hour if not the most elementary work of the most ordinary detective? I had been looking for some mistake, like any cheap inspector, for some footprints that would make me say and think what they wanted me to say and think.

I felt that I was even more absurd – lower down the intelligence scale – than those detectives imagined by modern novelists, men who have acquired their methods from reading the stories of Edgar Allan Poe or Conan Doyle. Ah, storybook-detectives, who erect mountains of nonsense out of one footprint in the sand, or out of the impression of a hand on a wall! Their methods lead them to have innocent persons convicted and you, Larsan, are, after all, just another of those detectives!

You have been able to convince the judge, the Chief of the Sûreté himself – everybody. You need one final piece of evidence. Fool! You still do not have the very first! The evidence supplied by the senses only is no proof at all. I too am bent over superficial clues, but only to demand that they come within the circle drawn by my reason. This circle has often been very small indeed. But, however small, it was also immense, for it contained nothing but the truth. Yes, yes, external signs have never been anything to me but servants – they were never my masters. That is why, my dear Frédéric Larsan, I shall triumph over your error and your 'instinctive' methods.

How stupid, how weak of me! There I was, bending over the ground, searching the mud for footprints. All this because, during the night, an event took place in the gallery that apparently refused to fit within the circle drawn by my reason!

Come, lift up your head, Rouletabille, my friend; that event must fit – you know it! Well, lift up your head, press your two hands to the bumps on your forehead, and remember that when you traced that circle – drawing a geometrical figure upon your brain, as on a sheet of paper – you began to apply your reason.

Now, go on. Go back to the mysterious gallery, leaning on your reason as Frédéric Larsan leans upon his cane, and you will soon have proved that the great Fred is nothing but a fool.

Joseph Rouletabille
30th October, Noon.

As I thought, so I acted. My brain burning, I returned to the gallery, and suddenly, without finding anything more than

137

I had seen last night, my reason pointed out to me something so extraordinary that I still have to cling on to it in order to save myself from falling.

Ah, I shall need strength now to discover the external clues that are about to fit – that must fit – the circle, larger now, which I have drawn here, between the two bumps on my forehead.

> Joseph Rouletabille.
> 30th October, Midnight.

CHAPTER XIX

Rouletabille invites me to lunch at the Tower Inn

It was not until much later that Rouletabille handed me the notebook, in which he set down the story of the mysterious phenomenon in the gallery on the morning after that enigmatic night.

The day I rejoined him at Glandier in his room, he told me, in detail, everything that the reader now knows – including what he had done during the few hours he had spent in Paris that week, where he learned nothing that could be of any use to him.

The events in the mysterious gallery had occurred on the night of 29th October, that is to say, three days before my return to the chateau. It was on 2nd November, then, that I went back to Glandier, summoned by my friend's telegram and bringing the two revolvers with me.

I was in Rouletabille's room, and he had just finished his account of events.

All the time he was speaking, he kept stroking the pince-nez which he had found on the table, and I understood, by the pleasure he took in this, that they must be one of those external signs destined to be placed in the circle drawn by his reason. I was no longer surprised by his unique way of expressing himself, but one often needed to understand his thinking before one could understand the words he used, and that was not always easy.

When he had finished his story, Rouletabille asked me what I thought of it. I replied that his question greatly embarrassed me. He then begged me to try applying my reason to the problem.

'Well,' I said, 'it seems to me that the starting-point of my argument would be this: There can be no doubt that, at a certain moment, the attacker whom you pursued *was* in the gallery . . .'

I paused.

'Having made such a brilliant beginning, why continue!' he exclaimed. 'Come, make a little effort!'

'I'll try. Since he was in the gallery, and disappeared from it without passing through any door or window, he must have got away through some other opening.'

Joseph Rouletabille looked at me pityingly, smiling vaguely, and did not hesitate to tell me that I reasoned like a child – or like Frédéric Larsan.

For Rouletabille's feelings for the great Fred alternated between admiration and contempt. Sometimes he would cry out: 'He really is clever!' sometimes, he would growl: 'What a fool!' And I noticed that his opinion depended on whether the discoveries made by Frédéric Larsan tallied with his reasoning, or contradicted it. That was one of the weak points in this strange young man's otherwise noble character.

We got up and he led me into the park. Just as we went into the main courtyard and were making for the gate, the sound of shutters being thrown open made us turn our heads, and we saw at a window of the first floor of the chateau the red, clean-shaven face of a man I did not know.

'Hello,' muttered Rouletabille, 'it's Arthur Rance!'

He dropped his head, quickened his pace and I heard him mutter: 'Was he in the chateau last night? What has he come here for?'

When we had gone some distance from the castle, I asked my friend who this Arthur Rance was, and how he had come to know him. He reminded me that Mr Arthur William Rance was the American from Philadelphia, with whom he had so freely clinked glasses at the reception at the Elysée Palace.

'But was he not to have left France almost immediately?' I asked.

'He was. That's why I am so surprised to find him not only still in France, but at Glandier of all places! He did not arrive this morning and he did not arrive last night; he must have arrived before dinner, then! Why did the caretakers not inform me?'

I remarked to my friend, with reference to the caretakers, that he had not yet told me what he had done to have them set at liberty.

It so happened that we were close to their lodge. Bernier and his wife were standing at the door watching us approach. My friend asked them at what time Arthur Rance had arrived. They said that they did not know he was in the chateau. He must have called on the previous evening, but they had not had to open the gate for him, because Mr Rance usually got off at St-Michel station and walked up to the chateau through the forest. He reached the park via the grotto of Ste-Geneviève, and climbed over the gate into the park.

As the caretakers spoke, I saw Rouletabille's face cloud over with a look of discontent, doubtless with himself. Evidently, he was rather vexed that, having so minutely studied the people and things at Glandier, he had only just learned that Arthur Rance was a frequent visitor to the chateau.

Much annoyed, he demanded an explanation.

'You say that Mr Arthur Rance often comes here? When did he last come?'

'We couldn't say exactly,' replied Bernier, 'seeing that we were in prison; besides, he doesn't go through the gate when he leaves either.'

'Do you know when he first came here?'

'Oh, yes, Monsieur, nine years ago!'

'He was in France nine years ago, then?' said Rouletabille. 'But how often has he been to Glandier in recent weeks?'

'Three times.'

'When did he come last, as far as you know?'

'About a week before the attack took place in the Yellow Room.'

This time Rouletabille asked the woman:

'It was in a crack in the floor?'

'In a crack in the floor,' she replied.

'Thanks,' said Rouletabille. 'Prepare yourselves for

141

tonight.' He pronounced those words with a finger on his lips, commanding discretion and silence.

We left the park and walked towards the Tower Inn.

'Do you often come and eat at this inn?' I asked.

'Sometimes.'

'But you take your meals at the chateau?'

'Yes, Larsan and I have our meals served sometimes in my room, sometimes in his.'

'M. Stangerson has never invited you to his table?'

'Never.'

'Does your presence in the chateau displease him?'

'I don't know. In any case, he does not act as if we were in his way.'

'He does not question you?'

'Never. His mind is still in turmoil; he has not yet got over the astounding events that took place in the Yellow Room. Remember, he was behind the door when his daughter was being attacked. He broke down the door and found no attacker. That would be enough to upset anybody's mental balance. The professor is convinced that since he did not discover anything then, there is still less reason why we should discover anything now. But he has made it a duty, ever since Larsan's words about him, not to oppose what he calls our 'vain illusions'.'

Rouletabille was now once more lost in thought. At last, he remembered I was there, and told me how he had had the two caretakers freed.

'Recently,' he said, 'I went to M. Stangerson, taking with me a piece of paper, on which I asked him to write the following words: 'I promise that, whatever they may confess, I will keep my two faithful servants, Bernier and his wife, in my service' and to sign this paper. I explained to the professor that, if he signed this, I would be able to make the caretakers speak out; I also said that I was convinced that they had had nothing to do with the crime. He had thought so himself from the first. The judge presented the signed document to the Berniers. They talked and they said what I knew they would say as soon as they were sure they would not lose their

142

positions. They confessed to poaching on M. Stangerson's estate; they admitted that they had been out poaching on the night of the crime and happened to be near the pavilion at the moment when the attempt was made on Mlle Stangerson's life. The few rabbits they secured by poaching they sold to the landlord of the Tower Inn, who served them to his customers or sent them to Paris. That was the truth, and I had guessed it from the first. Do you remember what I said on entering the inn the first time? 'From now on we shall have to eat red meat!' I heard those words the very morning we arrived at the park gate and you heard them too, but you did not attach any importance to them. You recollect that, just as we reached that gate, we stopped to look at a man who was running along beside the wall constantly consulting his watch. That man was Frédéric Larsan, who was already at work. Now, behind us, the landlord of the Tower Inn was standing on the steps of the inn and saying to somebody inside: 'From now on we shall have to eat red meat.' Why that 'now'? When one is, as I am, in search of the most mysterious of truths, one cannot afford to allow anything to escape one. You have to find out the meaning of everything. We had arrived in an out-of-the-way place which had been thrown into turmoil by a crime. Logic led me to consider every word spoken about me as being a possible reference to the events of the day. 'Now' meant to me 'since the crime'. From the very beginning of my inquiry, therefore, I sought to find a connection between that phrase and the drama. We had lunch at the Tower Inn. I bluntly repeated the words, and saw, by Mathieu's look of surprise and concern, that I had not exaggerated the importance of the phrase.

I had, at the time, learned that the caretakers had been placed under arrest. Mathieu spoke of them as true friends. A very simple association of ideas formed in my mind, and I thought, 'Now that the caretakers are arrested, we shall have to eat red meat!' No more caretakers, no more game. How was I led to this precise idea of game? Very simply. The hatred expressed by Mathieu for M. Stangerson's gamekeeper, a hatred which, he suggested, was shared by the caretakers, led me gently to the idea of poaching. Now, since the caretakers could not have been in bed at the moment of the drama – which was perfectly obvious – why were they abroad that night? To take part in the drama? I was not disposed to think so, for I already thought, for reasons which I shall tell you later, that the attacker had no accomplice, and that all this drama is a mystery between Mlle Stangerson and the attacker, that the caretakers had nothing to do with.

As far as the caretakers were concerned, the poaching idea explained everything. Admitting it, in principle, I searched for proof in their lodge, which, as you know, I entered. I found there, under their bed, some snares and brass wire. 'I have it!' I thought. 'These things explain why the Berniers were out at night in the park.' I was not therefore astonished at their dogged silence before the judge, even when accused of being accomplices in the crime. They did not want to confess they had been poaching. Poaching would save them from the court, but it would lose them their jobs; and as they were perfectly sure of their innocence in regard to the crime, they hoped that it would soon be solved and that their poaching would continue to go unsuspected. There would always be time for them to speak, before it was too late. I hastened their confession by the promise signed by M. Stangerson, a document which I handed to them myself. They gave all the necessary proofs and were set at liberty, and conceived for me a sense of deep gratitude. Why did I not have them released sooner? Because I was not sure that they were guilty of nothing more serious than poaching. I wanted to study the ground. As the days went by, I became more and more convinced. The day after the mysterious events in the gallery, as I had need of reliable people, I decided to bind the Berniers to me by having them released at once from their captivity.'

I looked at Rouletabille and once more I could not but be astonished at the simplicity of the reasoning which had led him to the truth in this matter of the suspected complicity of the caretakers. Certainly it was a small matter, but I sincerely believed that very soon the young man would explain to us, with the same simplicity, the fantastic mystery of the Yellow Room, and that of the gallery.

We reached the Tower Inn and walked in.

This time we did not see the landlord, but were received with a pleasant smile by the hostess.

'How's Mathieu?' asked Rouletabille.

'Not much better, Monsieur, not much better; he is still in bed.'

She spoke in a soft voice. Everything about her was expressive of a gentle nature. She was a truly beautiful woman, a touch indolent, with large, tender, caressing eyes. Mathieu must have been proud to have such a wife. But what of her? Was she happy with her crabbed, rheumatic husband? The scene we had once witnessed did not lead us to believe that she could be; yet there was something in her general attitude that was not suggestive of despair. She vanished into the kitchen to prepare our luncheon, leaving on the table a bottle of excellent cider. Rouletabille poured it out for us into earthenware mugs, filled his pipe, and quietly explained why he had sent for me and asked for the revolvers.

'Yes,' he said, following with a dreamy eye the clouds of smoke he was puffing out, 'yes, my dear friend, I expect the attacker tonight.'

There was a brief silence, which I took care not to interrupt, and then Rouletabille went on:

'Last night, just as I was going to bed, M. Robert Darzac knocked at the door of my room. I opened it and he confided to me that next morning – that is to say, today – he had to go to Paris. The reason which made this journey necessary was both pressing – since it was impossible for him not to go – and mysterious – since it was impossible for him to reveal to me the object of that journey. 'I go,' he said, 'and yet I would give my life not to leave Mlle Stangerson at this moment.' He did not hide from me the fact that he believed her to be still in danger. 'If something happened in the course of the coming night,' he added, 'I should not be greatly surprised. Yet I have no option but to leave. I cannot be back at Glandier before the day after tomorrow, in the morning.''

'I asked him to give me some kind of explanation, and this is all he said: The idea that Mlle Stangerson was still in grave danger had come to him solely because the attacks seemed to coincide with his absences. On the night of the mysterious incident in the gallery, he had been obliged to be away from Glandier; on the night of the attack in the Yellow Room he had been unable to be at the chateau and, in fact, we knew he was not there. At least, we know it officially, from his own statements. That M. Darzac, knowing this, should again absent himself today, must mean that he is obeying some will stronger than his own. That is what I thought, and I said as much to him. He replied: 'Perhaps.' I asked him whether that will stronger than his own was that of Mlle Stangerson. He gave me his word that it was not, and that his decision to go to Paris had been taken without any instructions from her.

In short, he repeated that his belief in the possibility of a fresh attack being made on her was based wholly on the extraordinary coincidence which he had noticed, and which the judge himself had mentioned to him. 'If anything happened to Mlle Stangerson,' he said, 'it would be terrible for her and terrible for me; for her, because she would once more be on the brink of death; for me, because I had been unable to defend her and afterwards would be forced to say where I had spent the night. Now I quite understand the suspicions that weigh upon me. Both the judge and Frédéric Larsan – the latter shadowed me the last time I went to Paris, and I had the Devil's own job to get rid of him – are all but convinced of my guilt.' 'Why do you not just tell us the name of the attacker, since you know it?' I cried. M. Darzac appeared extremely troubled by my question, and replied to me in a hesitant tone:

'I – know the name of the attacker? Who could have told it to me?'

I replied at once: 'Mlle Stangerson.'

Then he turned so pale that I thought he was going to faint, and I saw that I had struck home: *both Mlle Stangerson and he knew the name of the attacker.* When he had recovered himself, he said to me:

'I shall leave you now, Monsieur. I have had the opportunity, in talking to you, to appreciate your exceptional intelligence and your unequalled ingenuity. I have a service to ask of you. I am perhaps wrong to fear that an attack will occur during the coming night, but, since one must act with foresight, I rely on you to make such an attack impossible. Take all the necessary steps to guard Mlle Stangerson. Watch her room like a good guard dog. Do not sleep. The man we live in dread of is prodigiously cunning; his cunning has probably never been equalled in this world. That very cunning will save Mlle Stangerson if you keep watch, for he will know you are watching. And, knowing that, he will not venture to attempt anything.'

'Have you spoken of all this to M. Stangerson?'

'No.'

'Why not?'

'Because I do not want M. Stangerson to say to me, as you did to me just now, "You know the name of the attacker!" If you are surprised when I say: "The attacker may come tonight," you can readily imagine how amazed M. Stangerson would be if I said the same to him. I have told you all this, Monsieur Rouletabille, because I have great confidence in you. I know that you do not suspect me.'

The poor man was speaking as best he could, in fits and starts. He was suffering. I pitied him, the more so because I felt sure that he would rather die than tell me who the attacker was, just as Mlle Stangerson would rather allow herself to be murdered than denounce the man who had disappeared from the Yellow Room and from the gallery. That man must have some terrible hold over her or over them both, and they must dread most of all M. Stangerson finding out that his daughter was in the power of her attacker.

I promised M. Darzac to watch throughout the night. He insisted that I should create an impassable barrier around Mlle Stangerson's room, the boudoir where the nurses were sleeping, and the drawing room where, ever since the events in the mysterious gallery, M. Stangerson had slept – in short, a barrier about the whole of her apartments.

I realised that M. Darzac was asking me not only to make it impossible for the man to reach Mlle Stangerson's room, but to make that clear to the man himself, who would then disappear without a trace. That was how I understood his final words to me: 'When I am gone, you may speak to M. Stangerson of your suspicions about tonight, as well as Old Jacques, Frédéric Larsan and everyone in the chateau, and in that way organise a watch which everyone will assume to be entirely your idea.'

The unfortunate man went off, not knowing quite what he was saying. He could tell from my silence and the way that I looked at him that I had guessed three-quarters of his secret. He must have been at his wits' end to have come to me at such a moment, and to abandon Mlle Stangerson, when he felt so sure that another attack was imminent.

When he had gone, I thought the whole matter over. I realised that I must be more cunning than cunning itself, so that the man, if he should go to Mlle Stangerson's room during the night, would not for a second suspect that his coming was expected. Yes, that was the idea: to prevent him from entering, even if I had to shoot him, but to allow him to go far enough, so that, dead or alive, we would see his face clearly. For he must be got rid of. Mlle Stangerson must be freed from this renewed danger of attack!

Yes, my friend, I must see the fellow's face distinctly, so as to bring it within the circle which I have drawn with my reason.'

At that moment, the hostess reappeared, bearing the traditional omelette savoyard. Rouletabille joked with her a little, and she took it with the most delightful good humour.

'She is much more cheerful when Mathieu is confined to his bed with rheumatism than when he is up and about,' Rouletabille remarked softly.

When he had finished eating his omelette, and we were again alone, Rouletabille went on:

'When I sent you my telegram first thing this morning, I had only M. Darzac's word that the attacker might come tonight; now I can tell you that he will *certainly* come. I expect him.'

'What makes you so sure? Is it that . . .'

Rouletabille interrupted me:

'Don't, old boy, you're sure to make some silly remark; I know what you want to say.' Then he added: 'I have been sure that he would come since half-past ten this morning, that is to say, since before your arrival and, consequently, before we saw Arthur William Rance at the window in the main courtyard.'

'Really!' I said. 'But tell me, why since half-past ten?'

'Because at half-past ten I had proof that Mlle Stangerson was taking great pains to allow the attacker to enter her room tonight as Robert Darzac was taking to prevent it!'

'Is that possible?' I exclaimed. Then I whispered: 'But did you not tell me that Mlle Stangerson adores M. Darzac?'

'I did and it is the truth.'

'Then don't you think it strange . . .'

'Everything in this affair is strange, my friend, but take my word for it, the strangeness you know about is nothing to the strangeness that awaits you!'

'One would have to admit, then,' I said, 'that Mlle Stangerson and her attacker know each other, that they write to one another . . .'

'Admit it, my friend, admit it! You risk nothing. I have told you about the letter left on the table by the attacker on the night of the events in the gallery, the letter that disappeared into Mlle Stangerson's pocket. We must assume that in that letter the attacker ordered her to grant him a meeting and that, as soon as he was sure of Darzac's absence, he made it known to her that the meeting must be tonight?'

My friend laughed to himself. There were times when I wondered whether he was not laughing at me!

The door of the inn opened. Rouletabille was on his feet so suddenly that one might have thought he had been ejected from his seat by an electric charge.

'Mr Arthur Rance!' he exclaimed.

The American stood before us, making a low bow.

CHAPTER XX

Mlle Stangerson acts

'You recognise me, Monsieur?' asked Rouletabille.

'Of course,' replied Arthur Rance. 'And I have come down from my room to shake hands with you.'

The American held out his hand. Rouletabille shook it and introduced us, then invited Mr Rance to share our luncheon.

'No, thanks, I'm lunching with M. Stangerson.'

'Arthur Rance speaks our language perfectly, almost without accent,' Rouletabille said. 'I did not expect to have the pleasure of seeing you again, Monsieur. Were you not to have left our country a few days after the reception at the Elysée Palace?'

My friend and I, apparently indifferent to this passing conversation, lent an attentive ear to every word spoken by the American.

The man's red face, his heavy eyelids, certain nervous twitchings, were all proofs of his addiction to drink. How did this sorry specimen of humanity come to be the guest of M. Stangerson, and even his friend?

A few days later, I was to learn from Frédéric Larsan, who, like ourselves, had been surprised to find the American at the chateau, that Mr Arthur Rance had only been a drunkard for about the last fifteen years, that is to say, only since the departure of the professor and his daughter from Philadelphia. At the time when the Stangersons lived in the United States they had been on very intimate terms with Arthur Rance, who was one of the most distinguished phrenologists in the New World. Thanks to new experiments, he had made considerable advances in the science of Gail and Lavater. The warmth with which Mr Rance was received at Glandier can be explained by the fact that he had one day rendered a great service to Mlle Stangerson, by rescuing her from great danger. and putting his own life at risk, when the horses pulling her carriage bolted. It was even probable that the outcome of that incident had been a momentary friendly alliance between him and the professor's daughter, but nothing could lead one to suspect that love had in any way entered into their friendship.

Where had Frédéric Larsan picked up this information? He did not tell me, but he appeared to be pretty sure of his facts.

Had we known all this when Arthur Rance came to join us at the Tower Inn, his presence at the castle would not have been such a puzzle to us, but they would certainly have increased our interest in this new personage. The American must then have been about forty-five years of age. He answered Rouletabille's question in a perfectly natural tone of voice.

'When I heard of the attempt on her life, I put off my return to the States; I wished to assure myself that Mlle Stangerson had not been mortally injured and I shall not leave until she is quite well again.'

Arthur Rance then took the lead in the conversation, withholding answers to some of Rouletabille's questions, but giving us, without our inviting him to do so, his personal ideas on the subject of the attack, ideas which, as far as I could make out, were not far from Frédéric Larsan's. He did not name him, but one did not need to be very clever to know what he really thought. He told us that he knew what efforts young Rouletabille was making to unravel the tangled skein of the Yellow Room mystery. He explained that M. Stangerson had told him all about the events in the gallery. While listening to Mr Rance, one constantly had the impression that he was thinking of Robert Darzac. Several times he expressed regret that M. Darzac was absent from the chateau when those dramatic events occurred and his meaning was perfectly clear. Finally, he expressed the opinion that M. Darzac had been clever, indeed inspired, to install Rouletabille in the chateau, since he, M. Joseph Rouletabille, was bound, sooner or later, to learn the identity of the attacker! These last words were spoken with obvious irony. Then he rose, bowed to us, and left the inn.

Rouletabille watched him through the window, and said:

'A most singular person!'

I asked:

'Do you think he'll spend the night at Glandier?'

To my amazement the young reporter replied that that was a matter of total indifference to him!

I passed on to the question of our programme for the afternoon. I need say only that Rouletabille took me to the grotto of Ste-Geneviève and that he affected to speak of anything but what was uppermost in his mind. In this way, evening came. I was astonished not to see him make any of the preparations I had expected him to make. I said as much when night fell and we were together in the room. He replied that his arrangements were already made, and that this time the attacker could not escape him.

When I expressed some doubt, reminding him of the man's disappearance in the gallery, and saying that the same thing might occur again, he replied that he hoped it would, that, in fact, that was exactly what he wanted to happen that night. I did not insist, knowing from experience how pointless and tactless any insistence would have been. He told me, however, that from early morning, thanks to him and the caretakers, the chateau had been watched in such a manner that no one could approach it without his being informed, and that if no one came from outside, he was perfectly happy about the persons inside the castle.

It was then half-past six by the watch he drew from his waistcoat pocket. He rose, made a sign to me to follow him, and, without taking any further precautions, without trying to deaden the sound of his footsteps, without enjoining me to silence, he led me through the gallery. We reached the straight gallery and went along it to the landing, which we crossed. We then continued our way along the same gallery, but in the left wing, past Professor Stangerson's apartment.

At the far end of that gallery, before we reached the tower, there was a room which was then occupied by Arthur Rance. We knew that, because we had seen the American at the window of that room, which looked on to the main court-yard. The door of that room faced on to the gallery at the end of the left wing. It faced the east window at the far end of the straight gallery (in the right wing) where Rouletabille had placed Old Jacques on that famous night, and commanded an uninterrupted view of the straight gallery from end to end of the chateau – left wing, landing and right wing. Naturally, one could not see the side gallery in the right wing from there.

'That side gallery,' said Rouletabille, 'I reserve for myself. When I ask you to do so, you will come here and do what I ask you to do.'

And he made me get inside a little dark triangular cupboard built in a corner of the wall, to the left of the door of Arthur Rance's room. From this recess I could see everything that took place in front of Arthur Rance's door, and I was able to watch that door as well. The door of the cupboard, which was to be my place of observation, was fitted with a glass window. It was quite light in the gallery, where all the lamps ware burning. It was quite dark in the cupboard, which thus formed a fitting post for a spy.

We returned along the gallery. As we reached the door of Mlle Stangerson's apartments it opened, pushed by the butler, who was serving at the dinner table – for the last three days, M. Stangerson had dined with his daughter in her drawing room – and, since the door remained ajar, we distinctly saw Mlle Stangerson – taking advantage of the butler's absence and of the fact that her father was stooping to pick up some-thing he had dropped on the floor – pour the contents of a phial into his glass.

CHAPTER XXI

On watch

This act, which staggered me, did not appear greatly to affect Rouletabille. We returned to his room and, not even mentioning the scene we had just witnessed, he gave me his final instructions for the night. After dinner, I was to go and hide in the cupboard, and wait there as long as was necessary.

'If you see him before I do,' he explained, 'you must let me know. You will see him sooner than I shall if the man reaches the straight gallery by another way than by the side gallery, since you will have a view down the whole length of the straight gallery, while I shall only command a view of the side gallery. To warn me, you will merely have to undo the cord holding back the curtain of the window nearest to the cupboard. The curtain will fall and immediately, since all the lamps in the gallery are lit, that will create a square of shadow where previously there was a square of light. To do this, you need only reach out from the cupboard, for the curtain is within easy reach. I will be in the side gallery. From there you can see all the squares of light in the straight gallery through the window. When your square disappears, I will understand.'

'And then?'

'Then you will see me appear at the end of the side gallery.'

'What am I to do then?'

'You will immediately come towards me, keeping behind the man, but I shall already be upon him and will have seen whether his face fits within my circle.'

'The circle that you have drawn with your reason?' I added with a smile.

'Why do you smile? It is quite unnecessary! Enjoy these few remaining moments of relaxation, for I swear to you that a few moments hence you will have no reason to laugh!'

'And if the man escapes?' I asked.

'So much the better!' said Rouletabille phlegmatically. 'I don't want to capture him. He may take himself off down the stairs and into the entrance hall on the ground floor, before you even reach the landing, since you are at the far end of the gallery. I will let him go after I have seen his face. That's all I want. Afterwards I shall arrange matters in such a way that the man ceases to exist for Mlle Stangerson, even though he continues to live. If I took him alive, Mlle Stangerson and M. Darzac would, perhaps, never forgive me. And I wish to keep their respect; they have noble hearts.

When I saw Mlle Stangerson pour a sleeping-draught into her father's glass so that he will not be awoken tonight by the conversation she is going to have with her attacker, you may imagine how pleased she would be if I brought the man from the Yellow Room and the mysterious gallery to her father! It is perhaps very fortunate that on that night in the gallery the man vanished as if by magic. I understood as much when I saw the radiant look of relief that lit up Mlle Stangerson's face as soon as she learned that he had escaped. I have come to understand that, in order to save the unfortunate lady, it is less important to capture the man than to keep his mouth shut, by whatever means possible. But to kill a man — to kill a man! That's no trifle! Besides, it is no business of mine, unless the man makes it impossible for me to deal with him otherwise. On the other hand, to compel him to silence with no help or information from the lady is a task that involves me guessing everything with nothing to go on. Fortunately, my friend, I have guessed — or, rather, I have reasoned out — his identity and I only ask of the man who is coming tonight to show me his face, so that it may fit . . .'

'Into your mental circle?'

'Exactly! And his face will not surprise me.'

'But I thought you saw his face on the night when you sprang into the room?'

'Only vaguely. The candle was on the floor and what with his long beard.'

'Will he not be wearing the beard this evening?'

'I think I can say for certain that he will. But the gallery is well lit and now I know – or, at least, my brain knows – and my eyes will see.'

'If it is just a matter of seeing him and allowing him to escape, why are we armed?'

'Because, if the man from the Yellow Room and the mysterious gallery knows that I know, he is capable of anything. Then we shall have to defend ourselves!'

'And you are sure he will come tonight?'

'I am positive! At half-past ten this morning, Mlle Stangerson managed, in the cleverest way possible, to make sure that her nurses are not there tonight. She gave them a day's leave on some plausible pretext, and has asked to have only her father to watch over her while they are away. He is to sleep in the boudoir and has accepted his new duty with grateful joy. The coincidence of M. Darzac's departure (after what he said to me), and the exceptional precautions Mlle Stangerson took to make sure she would be alone leave no room for doubt. The coming of the attacker, which Darzac dreads, Mlle Stangerson is herself preparing for.'

'That's terrible!'

'Yes.'

'And what we saw her do was to send her father to sleep?'

'Yes.'

'In short, for tonight's business, there are just the two of us?'

'Four. The Berniers will keep watch. It is better so, though I think their watch will be of little use beforehand. But Bernier may be useful to me afterwards if there is any killing.'

'You think, then, that there may be?'

'Yes, if *he* wishes it.'

'Why did you not warn Old Jacques? Are you not using him today.'

'No!' replied Rouletabille in a sharp voice.

I remained silent for a while; then, desirous of getting to the bottom of what was in Rouletabille's mind, I asked him point-blank:

'Why not tell Arthur Rance? He may be of great assistance to us.'

'Look here!' said Rouletabille angrily. 'Do you want to let everybody into Mlle Stangerson's secrets? Let us go and have dinner; it is time. This evening we dine with Larsan in his room, unless he is still hot on the heels of M. Darzac! He sticks to him like a leech. But, never mind! If he is not there now, I am quite sure he will be there tonight. I'm going to beat that fellow at his own game.'

At that moment, we heard a noise in the next room.

'It must be Frédéric Larsan,' said my friend.

'I forgot to ask you,' I said. 'When we are with the detective I assume we won't make the slightest reference to tonight's activities. Is that the idea?'

'It goes without saying. We are working alone tonight, entirely for our own sakes.'

'And all the glory will be for us . . .'

Rouletabille laughed and replied:

'Just so!'

We dined with Frédéric Larsan in his room. He told us that he had only just arrived and invited us to sit at the table. The dinner passed most congenially and I realised that Rouletabille's and Larsan's cheerfulness was due to their certainty that each held the solution to the mystery.

Rouletabille told the great Frédéric that I had come on my own account to see him, and that he had kept me there to help him write the article that he had to finish that night for *L'Epoque*. I was going back to Paris, he said, by the eleven o'clock train, taking his copy with me. It was to be a sort of *feuilleton*, in which he recounted the principal events of the mystery of Glandier. Larsan smiled at this explanation, like a man who is not deceived, but refrains out of politeness from expressing the least opinion with regard to things which do not concern him.

Choosing their words and even their intonation carefully, Larsan and Rouletabille conversed at length on the subject of Mr Arthur Rance's presence at the chateau, of his past in America, about which they both wished they knew more details, at least so far as his relations with the Stangersons were concerned. At one moment, Larsan, who seemed to me to be unwell, said with an effort:

'I think, Monsieur Rouletabille, that we do not have much left to do now at Glandier, and that we shall not sleep here many more nights.'

'That is what I think too, Monsieur Frédéric.'

'You think, then, my friend, that the whole affair is over.'

'I do indeed. I believe that we have nothing more to find out,' Rouletabille retorted.

'Do you know who the attacker is?'

'And you?'

'I do.'

'So do I,' said Rouletabille.

'Can it be the same person . . .'

'I don't think so, not unless you have changed your mind,' said the young reporter, interrupting Larsan. And he added with great emphasis:

'Monsieur Darzac is an honest man!'

'I believe the contrary to be true!'

'So it's a fight between you and me, then?'

'Are you sure of that?' asked Larsan.

'Yes, a fight. *And I shall beat you*, Monsieur Frédéric Larsan!'

'Youth never has any doubts about anything,' said the great Frédéric in conclusion, laughing and holding out his hand to me.

Rouletabille repeated like an echo:

'Never.'

Suddenly Larsan, who had risen to bid us goodnight, pressed both his hands to his chest and staggered. He had to lean on Rouletabille to save himself from falling; he had grown extremely pale.

'Good heavens!' he cried. 'What is the matter with me? Can I have been poisoned?'

He looked at us with wild eyes. In vain we questioned him; he did not answer us. He had sunk into an armchair, and we could not get a word out of him. We were extremely anxious, both on his account and on our own, for we ourselves had

158

partaken of all the dishes Frédéric Larsan had eaten. At last, the pain seemed to ease, but his heavy head had fallen back, and his eyes were tightly closed. Rouletabille stooped over him and listened to his heart.

When he rose, my friend's face was as calm as it had been agitated only a minute before. He said:

'He is asleep.'

He led me to his room, after having closed the door of Larsan's room.

'Was it the sleeping-draught?' I asked. 'Does Mlle Stangerson want to send everyone to sleep tonight?'

'Perhaps,' replied Rouletabille, who was thinking about something else.

'But what about us?' I exclaimed. 'How do we know that we have not been dosed with the same sleeping-draught?'

'Do you feel indisposed?' Rouletabille asked, with perfect self-control.

'Not in the least.'

'Do you feel at all sleepy?'

'Well, then, my friend, have one of these excellent cigars.'

And he handed me a choice Havana which M. Darzac had given him, while he lit his pipe – his eternal pipe!

We remained in his room until ten o'clock without another word being spoken by either of us. Sunk in an arm-chair, Rouletabille smoked. At ten o'clock he took off his boots and made a sign to me to do the same. When we were in our stocking feet, he said – so quietly that I guessed rather than heard the word he uttered:

'Revolver!'

I drew my revolver from my coat-pocket.

'Cock it!' he whispered.

I did as he ordered.

Then he moved towards the door of the room and opened it with infinite care, so as not to make any noise. We were now in the side gallery. Rouletabille made another sign to me. I understood that I was to take up my position in the cupboard.

When I was some distance from him, he rejoined me and embraced me. Then I saw him, with the same care, return to his room. Astonished by his embrace and somewhat troubled by it, I arrived at the straight gallery without any difficulty, and crossed the landing to the cupboard.

Before entering it, I examined the cord of the curtain. I found I had merely to touch the cord with one finger for the curtain to fall shut and thus create the square of shadow – the signal we had agreed upon. The sound of footsteps made me stop outside the door of Arthur Rance's room. He was not yet in bed, then. But what was he doing in the chateau at all, since he had not dined with M. Stangerson and his daughter? At least, I had not noticed him at the table with them when we saw Mlle Stangerson emptying the phial into her father's glass.

I withdrew into the dark cupboard. I was perfectly comfortable in there. I could see down the whole length of the gallery. Clearly nothing whatever could happen there without my seeing it. But what was going to happen? Something, perhaps, of the gravest import. Again I thought of Rouletabille's embrace. People do not embrace their friends like that except on great occasions or when they are in great danger. Was I in great danger, then?

My hand closed on the butt of my revolver, and I waited. I am no hero, but I am no coward either.

I waited for about an hour. During that interval I noticed nothing unusual.

My friend had told me that probably nothing would occur before midnight or one o'clock in the morning. It was scarcely half-past eleven, however, when I heard the door of Arthur Rance's room open. I heard the slight creaking it made as it turned on its hinges. It was as if it had been pushed open from inside with the greatest stealth. The door remained open for what seemed like a very long minute. Since the door opened outwards, I could not see what was happening in the room or behind the door.

At that moment, I noticed a strange noise coming from the park, repeated three times. The third time the mewing was so strange and sharp that I recalled what I had heard said about the cry of the Good Lord's Beast. Since the cry had accompanied every one of the attacks at Glandier, I could not help but shudder.

Directly afterwards, I saw a man emerge from the room, closing the door after him. I did not recognise him at first, for he had his back to me and was stooping over a rather large parcel. Having closed the door and picked up the parcel, he turned towards the cupboard, and then I saw who he was. The man coming out of Arthur Rance's room was the gamekeeper – the Green Man. As the cry of the Good Lord's Beast sounded for the fourth time, he put down his parcel in the gallery and went to the second window along from the cupboard. I did not move, afraid I might betray my presence.

He rested his head against the panes and peered out into the park. He remained in that position for half a minute. The night was lit at intervals by the moon, which would disappear suddenly behind heavy clouds. The Green Man raised his arms twice, making signs which I did not understand; then, leaving the window, he again took up the parcel and walked along the gallery to the landing.

Rouletabille had said to me: 'The moment you see anything, undo the cord on the curtain.' I was certainly seeing something! Was this what Rouletabille expected? That was not my business; I had only to do what I had been told. I unfastened the cord. My heart was beating as if it would burst. The man reached the landing, but, to my amazement, just as I expected him to continue his way along the gallery, I saw him go down the stairs leading to the entrance hall.

What was I to do? I looked wildly at the heavy curtains which had now dropped before the window. The signal had been given and yet I did not see Rouletabille appear at the end of the side gallery. Nothing happened. No one came. I was greatly perplexed. Half an hour passed, which seemed an age to me. What was I to do now, even if I saw anything else unusual? The signal had been given and I could not give it a second time. On the other hand, to venture into the gallery at that moment might upset all Rouletabille's plans. After all, I had done nothing wrong, and if anything unexpected did happen, he could only blame himself for it. Unable to warn him further of anything untoward, I took the risk. I left the cupboard, and, still in my stocking feet, still listening intently, I made my way towards the side gallery.

No one was there. I went to the door of Rouletabille's room and listened. I could hear nothing. I knocked gently. There was no answer. I turned the doorknob and went into the room.

Rouletabille lay full-length on the floor.

CHAPTER XXII

The strange wound

With unspeakable anxiety I bent over the reporter, and rejoiced to find that he was merely sleeping. It was the same unnatural and profound sleep that had overcome Frédéric Larsan. My friend, too, had fallen victim to the sleeping-draught which had been mixed in our food. How was it that I had not met with a similar fate? I realised that the narcotic must have been put in our wine, for I never drink during meals. I shook Rouletabille hard, but could not get him to open his eyes.

This sleep of his was, no doubt, the work of Mlle Stangerson.

She had obviously thought that she had even more to fear from the watchfulness of this young man who foresaw every-thing, who knew everything, than from her father: I recalled that the butler, when serving us, had recommended an excel-lent Chablis, which had most likely come from the table of the professor and his daughter.

More than a quarter of an hour passed. In these extreme circumstances, I decided to resort to strong measures: I threw a pitcher of cold water over Rouletabille's head. At last, he opened his eyes – his poor, dull eyes, lifeless and sightless. I slapped his cheeks smartly and helped him up. I felt him stiffen in my arms and heard him murmur: 'Go on, but don't make a noise.' I pinched and shook him again, and at length he was able to stand up. We were saved!

'They drugged me" he said. 'Ah, but how I fought against sleep. I struggled. But it is over now. Don't leave me!'

He had no sooner uttered those words than we heard a terrible scream that rang through the chateau.

'Great heavens!' Rouletabille roared. 'We shall be too late!'

He tried to rush to the door, but he was still dazed and fell against the wall. I was already in the gallery, revolver in hand, dashing towards Mlle Stangerson's room. The moment I arrived at the point where the side gallery and the straight gallery met, I saw a man escaping from her apartment. In a few strides, he reached the landing.

I was not the master of my actions. I fired. The report made a deafening noise, but the man continued his flight down the stairs. I ran after him, shouting: 'Stop, stop, or I'll kill you!' As I rushed after him down the stairs, I came face to face with Arthur Rance, coming from the gallery in the left wing of the chateau, shouting: 'What is it? What is it?' We reached the foot of the stairs almost at the same time. The window of the hall was open. We distinctly saw the flying form of a man. Instinctively, we fired our revolvers in his direction. He was no more than ten paces ahead of us. He staggered and we thought he was going to fall. Already we had sprung out of the window, but the man dashed suddenly away with renewed vigour. I was in my socks and the American was barefoot. We could not hope to overtake the man if our revolvers failed to reach him. We fired our last cartridges at him, but he still sped on. However, he was racing down the right side of the main courtyard towards the far end of the right wing of the castle. He would not be able to escape, for in that corner, surrounded by ditches and huge gates, there was only the door of the little room occupied by the gamekeeper.

The man, though evidently wounded by our bullets, was only twenty yards ahead of us. Suddenly a window above our heads in the gallery behind us opened, and we heard the voice of Rouletabille calling desperately:

'Shoot, Bernier, shoot!'

And the night, at that moment bright with moonlight, grew brighter still with a sudden flash of lightning.

By its light, we saw Bernier standing with his gun at the door of the Tower.

He had taken good aim. The shadow dropped, but because it had reached the far end of the right wing, it had dropped behind the building, that is to say, we saw it fall, but it only sank to the ground on the other side of the wall, which we could not see. Bernier, Arthur Rance and myself reached that spot twenty seconds later. The shadow was lying dead at our feet.

Evidently awakened from his lethargic sleep by the cries and the shouting, Larsan opened the window of his room and called to us, as Arthur Rance had done:

'What is it? What is it?'

We were bending over the shadow, the mysterious dead form of the man. Rouletabille, now wholly awake, joined us at that moment and I cried out to him:

'He is dead, he is dead!'

'So much the better,' he replied. 'Take him into the entrance hall.' But, as if he had second thoughts, he added: 'No, no, let us take him to the gamekeeper's room.'

Rouletabille knocked at the door. No one answered, which, naturally enough, caused me no surprise.

'He's obviously not there, otherwise he would have answered,' said the reporter. 'Let's carry the man into the hall.'

Since we had reached the dead man, dense clouds had covered the moon and the night had become so dark that we could not make out his features. And yet we were anxious to know who he was. Old Jacques, who joined us then, helped us to transport the body to the hall of the chateau. There we laid it on the bottom step of the stairs. On the way, I had felt the warm blood from the man's wounds dripping on to my hands.

Old Jacques ran to the kitchen and returned with a lantern. He held it close to the face of the dead man and we recognised the gamekeeper, whom the landlord of the Tower Inn had called the Green Man and who, an hour earlier, I had seen coming out of Arthur Rance's room carrying a parcel. But what I had seen I could only report to Rouletabille when we were alone, as I did a few minutes later.

I must mention the amazement, the cruel and overwhelming disappointment shown by both Rouletabille and Frédéric

Larsan, who had joined us in the hall. They both fell upon the body. They looked at the dead face, at the green clothes, and they repeated:

'Impossible! It's impossible!'

Rouletabille even exclaimed:

'It's enough to send one mad, to make one give up altogether!'

Old Jacques was almost hysterical and kept uttering strange lamentations. He declared that there had been some mistake, that the gamekeeper could not possibly be his mistress' attacker. We had to order him to keep quiet. Had his own son been slain he could not have been more griefstricken and I explained his exaggerated feelings by his fear lest it should be thought that he rejoiced in this dramatic death. For everyone knew how Old Jacques had detested the gamekeeper. I noticed that, while all the rest of us were more or less undressed, barefoot, or in our stocking feet, Old Jacques was fully dressed.

Rouletabille, meanwhile, had not left the body. Kneeling on the flagstones of the hall, lit by Old Jacques' lantern, he was loosening the gamekeeper's clothing. He laid bare the man's chest. It was still bleeding.

Suddenly, snatching the lantern from Old Jacques, Rouletabille held it quite close to the gaping wound. Then he rose and said in a singular tone, with a touch of bitter irony:

'This man, whom you think you killed with the bullets of your revolvers and guns, died from a knife-wound in the heart!'

I thought once more that Rouletabille had gone mad, and in my turn bent over the corpse. I was then able to satisfy myself that the body bore no trace of a bullet-wound, and that the only wound was one inflicted by a sharp blade in the region of the heart.

CHAPTER XXIII

The double trail

I had not yet recovered from the bewilderment into which this discovery had plunged me, when my young friend touched me on the shoulder and said:

'Follow me.'

'Where?'

'To my room.'

'What are you going to do there?'

'Think.'

He closed the door behind us, offered me a seat, sat down opposite me, and, of course, lit his pipe.

I watched him thinking and then I dropped asleep. When I woke, it was daylight. My watch showed eight o'clock. Rouletabille was no longer in the room; his armchair was empty. I rose and was beginning to stretch my limbs, when the door opened and my friend entered. I saw at a glance that he had not wasted his time while I had been sleeping.

'Mlle Stangerson?' I asked at once.

'Her condition, though extremely alarming, is not hopeless.'

'Is it long since you left this room?'

'I went out at dawn.'

'You have been working?'

'I have indeed.'

'And what have you discovered?'

'A double set of footprints – most remarkable – which *might* have perplexed me.'

'But they no longer do?'

'No.'

'Do those footprints explain anything to you?'

'They do.'

'Concerning the gamekeeper's wounds.'

'Yes. They seem far less strange to me now. I discovered this morning, whilst walking round the chateau, two distinct sets of footprints side by side, made at the same time last night. I say "at the same time", as if those two people had been walking together. This double set of footprints left all the other footprints in the centre of the main courtyard and went in the direction of the oak grove. I was leaving the main courtyard, following the tracks, when I was joined by Frédéric Larsan, who immediately became interested in my work, for this double track was really worth sticking to. I saw there the double footprints I saw in the Yellow Room – those made by rough, hobnailed boots and those made by the elegant boots. But whilst in the Yellow Room, the rough bootprints only joined the elegant ones near the lake and subsequently disappeared – which led Larsan and me to the conclusion that the two tracks belonged to one and the same person, who had simply changed boots – in the present case, however, both the rough and the elegant bootprints coexist and travel together. This, of course, upset my former conclusions. Larsan seemed to have the same problem, and so we examined those footprints over and over again with the greatest care. I took the paper cut-outs from my pocket-book. The first was the one I had taken from the impressions made by Old Jacques' rough boots, found by Frédéric in the lake. It fitted perfectly over one of the rough prints we saw. The second paper pattern was that of the elegant bootmarks. It too fitted the corresponding tracks, but there was a slight difference in the toe of one boot. We could not say from this comparison that the footprints were those of the same person, neither could we swear to the contrary, for the unknown man might not have worn the same boots.

Still following the course of the two sets of footprints, Larsan and I were led out of the oak grove, and found ourselves at the same place on the edge of the lake as on our first search. But this time the footprints did not stop there, for the two sets, still together, followed the little path leading to the high road to Epinay. There we came upon a part of the road which had been recently macadamised, and on which, in consequence, it was impossible to see anything. So we returned to the chateau, without exchanging a word.

On reaching the main courtyard we separated, but, since our thoughts had travelled in the same direction, we met again at the door of Old Jacques' room. We found the old servant in bed and noticed at once that his clothes, which had been taken off and thrown over a chair, were in a lamentable state, and that his boots – the soles of which matched the bootprints exactly – were plastered with mud. He had certainly not got his boots in that state and his clothes drenched while helping to carry the gamekeeper's body from the end of the main courtyard to the hall, or going to the kitchen to fetch a lantern, since, at the time, it was not raining.

We questioned him. He began by telling us that he had gone to bed immediately after the arrival of the doctor, whom the butler had been sent to fetch; but we so pressed him, so clearly proved that he was lying, that he finally confessed he had been away from the chateau. Naturally, we asked his reason. He said that he had had a headache and needed to get some fresh air, but that he had not gone further than the oak-grove. We then described to him the road he had taken as well as if we had seen him walking along it ourselves. The old man sat up and began to tremble.

'You were not alone!' cried Larsan.

'You saw him then?' gasped Old Jacques.

'Who?' I asked.

'The black phantom!'

Old Jacques then told us that for several nights he had seen the 'black phantom.' It appeared in the park at the stroke of midnight and glided through the trees with incredible ease. Twice, Old Jacques had seen the phantom through his window by the light of the moon; he had risen and gone in search of the strange apparition. The night before last he had very nearly overtaken it, but it had vanished at the corner of the tower. Finally, he said that last night, having left the chateau, with his mind troubled by the idea of a new crime that had been committed, he had suddenly seen the black phantom

issue forth from somewhere in the middle of the main courtyard. He had followed it, cautiously at first; he had passed by
the oak grove and reached the road to Epinay. There the
phantom had suddenly disappeared.

'You did not see its face?' Larsan inquired.

'No, I saw nothing but the black veils.'

'And after what had happened in the gallery, you did not
seize it by the throat?'

'I couldn't. I was too terrified! I barely had strength enough
to follow it.'

'*You did not follow*, Old Jacques,' I said, in a threatening tone,
'you went with the phantom as far as the road to Epinay. You
walked arm-in-arm with the phantom!'

'No!' he cried. 'It started pouring with rain – I turned
back! I don't know what became of the black phantom!'

But his eyes were turned away from me as he spoke.

We left him. When we were outside, I said to Larsan, in a
meaning tone, looking him full in the face to find out what
was going on in his mind:

'An accomplice?'

Larsan raised his arm and said:

'How can one tell? Can one be sure of anything in such a
case? Twenty-four hours ago, I would have sworn that there
was no accomplice!'

And he left me, saying that he was going to Epinay.

When Rouletabille had finished this account, I asked him:

'Well, what do you conclude from all that? As for me, I
cannot see a way forward at all, I cannot grasp anything. In
short, what do you know?'

'Everything!' he exclaimed. 'Everything!'

I had never seen him look so happy. He rose and shook
hands with me.

'Then explain to me . . .' I began.

'Let us go and ask for news of Mlle Stangerson,' he said
abruptly.

CHAPTER XXIV

Rouletabille knows the two halves of the attacker

Mlle Stangerson had been nearly murdered for the second time. Unfortunately, the injuries she received in this second attack were worse than those she had sustained in the first. After the three wounds made in her breast by the attacker's knife on that tragic night, she hovered for a long time between life and death, and when, at last, life proved the stronger, and there was hope that she would escape her terrible fate, it was found that while she gradually recovered her senses, she did not recover her reason. The least reference to the horrible tragedy made her delirious, and it is no exaggeration to say that the arrest of M. Darzac, which took place at the Chateau du Glandier the day after the discovery of the gamekeeper's body, deepened still further the mental abyss into which we saw that fine intelligence disappear.

M. Robert Darzac arrived at the chateau at about half-past nine. I saw him hurrying through the park, his hair and his clothes in disorder, entirely covered with mud, and altogether in a fearful state. His face was deathly pale. Rouletabille and I were looking out of the window in the gallery. M. Darzac saw us and uttered a cry of despair:

'I am too late!'

Rouletabille cried:

'She is alive!'

A minute later, M. Darzac entered Mlle Stangerson's room, and, through the door, we heard him sobbing.

'Fate!' groaned Rouletabille, by my side. 'What infernal gods are behind this family's misfortunes? If I had not been sent to sleep, I would have saved Mlle Stangerson from the man, and silenced him for ever – and the gamekeeper would not have been killed.'

M. Darzac came to us bathed in tears. Rouletabille told him everything, and how he had provided for Mlle Stangerson's safety as well as his, Darzac's; how he would have succeeded in sending the man away for ever after having seen his face; and how his plan had been drowned in blood, owing to the sleeping-draught.

'Ah! If only you had had complete confidence in me!' said the young man in a low voice. 'If only you had told Mlle Stangerson to have confidence in me! But here everyone distrusts everyone else; the daughter distrusts her father, and even her own fiancé. While you were telling me to do all I could to prevent the attacker from reaching her, she was preparing everything so that she would be attacked! And I arrived too late – half asleep – almost dragging myself to the room where only the sight of the unfortunate lady, bathed in her own blood, thoroughly awoke me.'

At M. Darzac's request, Rouletabille described the scene. Leaning against the wall to save himself from falling, while we were in the main courtyard pursuing the attacker, he had made his way towards the victim's room. The doors of the anteroom being open, he went in. Mlle Stangerson lay unconscious, thrown half across the desk, with her eyes closed. Her dressing-gown was red with blood, which was gushing forth from her breast. It seemed to Rouletabille, still under the influence of the sleeping-draught, that he was in the middle of some hideous nightmare.

He went back out into the gallery, opened the window, shouted to us, ordered us to kill the man, and then returned to the room. Presently, he crossed the deserted boudoir, entered the drawing room, the door of which was ajar, shook M. Stangerson, who was lying on the sofa, and woke him up, just as I had previously woken Rouletabille himself. The Professor sat up, wild-eyed, and let himself be led by Rouletabille into the room, where, seeing his daughter, he uttered a heart-rending cry. Ah, Rouletabille was awake by then! Together they carried the victim to her bed.

Then Rouletabille rejoined us, desperate for information. Before leaving the room, he stopped near the desk. On the floor there was a parcel, an enormous parcel. How did that parcel come to be there by the desk? The wrapping was loose. Rouletabille knelt down; the parcel contained papers, documents, photographs, all bundled together. He scanned them:

'New Differential Condensing Electroscope.' 'Fundamental Properties of the Intermediary Substance between Ponderable Matter and Imponderable Ether.' What mystery was this, what astounding irony of fate could make somebody, at the very moment when his child is being slain, restore to M. Stangerson those useless papers, which he would merely hurl into the fire the next day?

On the morning following that horrible night, we saw M. de Marquet reappear, with his registrar and his gendarmes. We were all interrogated, except, naturally, Mlle Stangerson, who was in a state bordering on coma. Rouletabille and I, after having conferred together, said what we had mutually agreed to say. I took good care not to mention the sleeping-draught and my presence in the cupboard. In short, we kept to ourselves everything that could lead to a suspicion that we had expected the events, also anything that might suggest that Mlle Stangerson had expected the attacker. The unfortunate woman was perhaps about to pay with her life for the mystery with which she surrounded her attackers. It was not our business to render such a sacrifice useless.

To my amazement, Arthur William Rance coolly told everyone that he had seen the gamekeeper for the last time at about eleven o'clock in the evening. He had come, he said, to fetch his bag, which he was to take to St- Michel station early next morning, and they talked together until late about poachers, game and shooting. Arthur Rance was, in fact, to have left the castle in the morning and intended to walk, according to his custom, to the station. He had therefore taken advantage of an early errand the gamekeeper had to make to the village in order to get rid of his luggage.

M. Stangerson confirmed all this and added that he had not had the pleasure of having Arthur Rance at his table because his friend had taken leave of himself and his daughter at about five o'clock. Mr Arthur Rance had merely had tea served to him in his own room, saying that he was slightly indisposed.

Bernier, the caretaker, in accordance with Rouletabille's instructions, reported that he had been required by the gamekeeper himself that night to give chase to poachers (the gamekeeper could not contradict him); that the meeting place was the oak grove, and that, when the gamekeeper did not appear, he had gone in search of him. He had nearly reached the Tower, having gone through the small door into the main courtyard, when he saw a man fleeing as fast as he could along the opposite side, towards the right wing of the chateau. At the same moment, shots rang out; Rouletabille had appeared at one of the gallery windows. Rouletabille saw Bernier, and ordered him to fire the gun he was carrying. He had done so and believed that he had not only injured, but killed the man, until Rouletabille, on unbuttoning the man's clothing, had found that he had been killed, not by a bullet, but by a knife-wound. Bernier added that he could understand nothing about this whole fantastic affair, since, if the body they had found was not that of the man we had all fired at, the fugitive must needs be somewhere else.

Thus spoke Bernier; but the judge reminded him that, where we were standing, in the corner of the court, it was very dark, since we had been unable to recognise the gamekeeper until we had carried his body into the entrance hall of the chateau, and a lantern had been brought.

To this, Bernier retorted that if they had not been able to see the other body, dead or alive, they would have trodden on it, considering the very small size of the courtyard. 'Also, there were five of us in that restricted space – not including the dead man – and it would have been strange if the other body had escaped us! The only door that opened on to the court-yard there was that of the gamekeeper's room and that was closed. The key to it had been found in the Green Man's pocket.'

However, as this argument of Bernier's – which, at first sight, appeared logical – led to the conclusion that we had shot dead a man who had died from a stab wound in the heart, the judge did not spend much time over it. It was evident to all of us that he was convinced that we had missed the man we were pursuing, and that we had come upon a body that had nothing to do with our affair. For him, the corpse of the gamekeeper was a different affair altogether. He wished to prove it at once. It is possible that this new affair tallied with the idea he had formed concerning the life of the game-keeper, his acquaintances and his recent dalliance with the wife of the landlord of the Tower Inn. It also coincided with reports made to him concerning the threats uttered against the Green Man by Mathieu. For, at one o'clock in the after-noon, Mathieu, in spite of his rheumatic pains and his wife's protestations, was arrested and taken under escort to Corbeil. Nothing compromising, however, had been discovered at his home. But his threats, made on the previous day, in the pres-ence of some waggoners, who repeated them, compromised him more than if the knife used to kill the Green Man had been found under his bed.

Though harried by many events, as terrible as they were inexplicable, our amazement only increased when Frédéric Larsan returned to the chateau, which he had left after seeing the judge. He was accompanied by a railway clerk.

At that moment, Rouletabille and I were in the hall with Arthur Rance, arguing about the guilt or innocence of Mathieu, or, rather, Mr Rance and I were talking, for Rouletabille seemed to have gone off in some distant dream, paying scarcely any attention to what we were saying.

The judge and the registrar were in the small green draw-ing room, into which Robert Darzac had taken us when we arrived for the first time at Glandier. Old Jacques had been sent for by the judge, and had just come into the room. M. Darzac was upstairs in Mlle Stangerson's room with M. Stangerson and the doctors. Frédéric Larsan entered the hall with the railway clerk. Rouletabille and I immediately recognised this clerk by his scrubby blond beard.

'It's the station clerk from Epinay-sur-Orge!' I exclaimed.

And I looked at Larsan, who replied, smiling:

'The booking clerk.'

Larsan had himself announced to the judge by the gendarme on duty at the drawing-room door. Old Jacques came out, and Frédéric Larsan and the clerk were led in. About ten minutes passed. Rouletabille was very impatient. The door of the drawing-room was again opened; the judge called to the gendarme, who entered the room and presently came out, went upstairs, and, after a minute or two, came down again. He then opened the drawing room door, and, without closing it behind him, said to the judge:

'Monsieur Robert Darzac will not come.'

'What, he'll not come?' cried M. de Marquet.

'He says he cannot leave Mlle Stangerson in her present state.'

'Very well,' said M. de Marquet, 'since he will not come to us, we will go to him.'

M. de Marquet and the gendarme mounted the stairs. He made a sign to Larsan and the booking clerk to follow him. Rouletabille and I completed the procession.

On reaching the door of Mlle Stangerson's room, the judge knocked at it. A chambermaid appeared. It was Sylvia, a little damsel with sad features and untidy hair.

'Is M. Stangerson there?' asked M. de Marquet.

'Yes, Monsieur.'

'Tell him that I wish to speak with him.'

The professor came to us. He was weeping. It was indeed painful to watch him.

'What do you want now?' he asked the judge. 'May I not, at such a moment, be left in peace, Monsieur?'

'Monsieur,' said the judge, 'it is absolutely vital that I speak with M. Robert Darzac at once. Can you not encourage him to leave Mlle Stangerson's room? Otherwise, I shall be compelled to enter it in the name of the law.'

The professor made no reply. He looked at the judge, at the gendarme, at all who were present, as a condemned man might look at his executioners, and went back into the room.

M. Robert Darzac immediately came out. He was already very pale and wan, but when he saw the booking clerk standing behind Larsan, his face became yet more anguished. His eyes were wild and he gave a deep, hollow groan.

We all noticed the tragic expression on that troubled face, and could not but exclaim in pity. We felt that something important was happening, something that would decide the fate of Robert Darzac. Frédéric Larsan alone had a radiant face, showing the triumphant joy of a dog that has at last seized his prey.

The judge said to M. Darzac, pointing to the young booking clerk:

'Do you recognise this gentleman?'

'I do,' said M. Darzac. 'He is a clerk at the station of Epinay-sur-Orge.'

'This young man,' continued M. de Marquet, 'declares that you stepped out of a train at Epinay-sur-Orge . . .'

'Last night,' said M. Darzac, completing the sentence, 'at half-past ten. It is true.'

There was a silence.

'Monsieur Darzac,' the judge went on in a tone of deep emotion, 'Monsieur Darzac, what were you doing last night at Epinay-sur-Orge, at a very short distance from the place where an attempt was made on Mlle Stangerson's life?'

M. Darzac remained silent. He did not lower his head, but he closed his eyes, either to hide his sorrow, or for fear that something of his secret might be read in them.

'Monsieur Darzac,' the judge insisted, 'can you tell me how you spent last night?'

Darzac reopened his eyes. He seemed to have recovered all his self-control.

'No, Monsieur.'

'Think carefully, Monsieur, for if you persist in your strange refusal, I shall be forced to hold you against your will. *Monsieur Robert Darzac, in the name of the law, I arrest you!*'

The judge had no sooner pronounced these words than I saw Rouletabille move quickly towards M. Darzac. He was obviously going to speak, but M. Darzac stopped him with a gesture. Besides, the gendarme had already approached his prisoner. At that moment, a despairing cry rang through the room:

'Robert! Robert!'

We all recognised the voice of Mlle Stangerson, and we all shuddered at that sorrowful sound. Larsan himself turned pale this time. As to M. Darzac, he had flown back into the room in response to the pathetic cry.

The judge, the gendarme and Larsan followed close behind. Rouletabille and I remained on the threshold. The scene was heartbreaking! Mlle Stangerson, whose face had the pallor of death, had sat up in bed, despite the two doctors and her father. She held out trembling arms to Robert Darzac, on whom Larsan and the gendarme had laid hands. Her eyes were wide open. She saw, she understood. Her mouth seemed to utter a word – a word that expired on her bloodless lips – a word which no one heard – and suddenly she fell back in a swoon.

The gendarme hastily led M. Darzac out of the room. Larsan went to fetch a carriage and we stayed in the hall. Everyone was greatly affected. M. de Marquet had tears in his eyes. Rouletabille took advantage of the general emotion to say to M. Darzac:

'Will you defend yourself?'

'No,' replied the prisoner.

'Then I will defend you, Monsieur.'

'You cannot,' said the unfortunate man, with a faint smile. 'You cannot do what neither Mlle Stangerson nor I have managed to do.'

'I will do it!' And Rouletabille's voice was strangely calm and confident. He went on: 'I will do it, Monsieur Robert Darzac, because I know more than you do!'

'Nonsense!' murmured Darzac, almost angrily.

'Oh, don't worry! I will find out only what is necessary to save you!'

'If you want my gratitude, young man, I would rather that you found out nothing at all!'

Rouletabille shook his head, and went very close to M. Darzac.

'Listen to what I am doing to say,' he whispered, 'and trust me. You know only the name of the attacker and Mlle Stangerson only knows one half of him; *but I know his two halves* – I know him altogether!'

Robert Darzac's wide eyes clearly showed that he had not understood a word of what Rouletabille had said to him.

The carriage arrived at that moment, driven by Frédéric Larsan himself. Darzac and the gendarme got in, Larsan remained on the box. The prisoner was taken to Corbeil.

CHAPTER XXV

Rouletabille goes on a journey

That same evening, Rouletabille and I left Glandier. We were very glad to do so, and there was nothing to detain us there. I declared that I gave up any attempt to solve the mystery, and Rouletabille told me that he had nothing more to learn at Glandier, because Glandier had taught him everything.

We reached Paris about eight o'clock, dined rapidly, and then, weary, we separated, agreeing to meet next morning at my lodgings.

At the appointed time, Rouletabille entered my room. He was dressed in a suit of English tweed, had an overcoat over his arm, a cap on his head and a bag in his hand. He told me he was going on a journey.

'How long will you be away?' I asked.

'A month or two,' he said. 'It depends.'

I did not venture to question him further.

'Do you know,' he said, 'what the word was that Mlle Stangerson uttered before she fainted, with her eyes fixed on M. Darzac?'

'No, no one heard it.'

'I beg your pardon,' replied Rouletabille, 'I heard it. She said "Speak".'

'And will M. Robert Darzac speak?'

'Never!'

I would have liked to prolong our interview, but he warmly shook my hand, wished me goodbye, and I only had time to ask him:

'You do not fear that, during your absence, fresh attempts will be made on Mlle Stangerson's life?'

'I fear nothing of the sort, now that M. Darzac is in prison,' he replied.

Having spoken these strange words, Rouletabille left me.

I would not see him again until M. Robert Darzac's trial, when my young friend reappeared *to explain the inexplicable.*

CHAPTER XXVI

In which Joseph Rouletabille is impatiently awaited

On 15th January, *L'Epoque* published the following sensational article on its front page:

'The jury of Seine-et-Oise are today called upon to decide one of the most mysterious cases in the annals of the law. No case has ever presented so many obscure, inexplicable points. And yet, the prosecution has not hesitated to place in the dock a man who is respected and beloved by all who know him: a young scholar, one of our most promising scientists, in fact, a man whose whole existence has been devoted to study and who has always been a model of probity.

When Paris heard that M. Robert Darzac had been arrested, there was a universal cry of protest. The entire Sorbonne, outraged by the action taken by the judge, proclaimed their faith in the innocence of Mlle Stangerson's fiancé. M. Stangerson himself loudly attested to the error into which the law had fallen. No one doubts that, if the victim could speak, she would claim from the twelve jurors of Seine-et-Oise the man whom she desires to make her husband, and whom the prosecution would send to the scaffold. It is to be hoped, therefore, that, at an early date, Mlle Stangerson will recover her reason, which has been momentarily overthrown by the terrible events at Glandier. Must she, then, be doomed to lose her reason, and forever, by hearing that the man she loves has perished, has died at the hands of the executioner? This question we ask of the members of the jury, and we propose to deal with them this very day.

We have decided not to allow twelve worthy men to commit an abominable judicial error. We know that terrible coincidences, suspicious clues, the enigma of how M. Darzac spent his time, the total absence of an alibi, must all have led the judges to their conclusions, for, having vainly searched elsewhere for the truth, they are resolved to find it in M. Darzac's guilt. The charges are, apparently, so overwhelming that a detective as well-informed, intelligent and successful as M. Frédéric Larsan, may well be excused for having been blinded by them. Hitherto everything has gone against M. Robert Darzac during the judge's inquiry. Today we are going to defend him before the jury and we shall solve the whole mystery of Glandier, *for we are in possession of the truth*!

We have not spoken out sooner, because the interests of the cause we seek to defend demanded that we should wait.

Our readers have probably not forgotten the private inquiries, of which we published an account, relating to the left foot found in Rue Oberkampf, the famous robbery at the Banque de Crédit Universelle, and the case of the theft of the gold ingots from the Paris Mint. In all those cases we were enabled to discover the truth, even before the wonderful ingenuity of Frédéric Larsan revealed it. Those inquiries were made by our youngest reporter, Joseph Rouletabille, a youth of eighteen years of age, who, tomorrow, will be famous. When the first attack at Glandier took place, our young reporter went there, had all doors opened to him, and settled down in the chateau from which all other representatives of the press had been excluded. Side by side with Frédéric Larsan, he sought the truth; horrified, he realised the complete and dangerous error into which the celebrated detective was being drawn. In vain, he tried to draw Larsan away from the false trail he was following; the great Frédéric would not be taught a lesson by this "cub reporter". We know where Larsan's error has led M. Robert Darzac.

Now France must know, the entire world must know, that, on the same evening that M. Darzac was arrested, young Rouletabille came into our Editor's office and said to him: "I am going on a journey. I cannot tell you how long I shall be away; perhaps one month, two months, three months – I may never return! Here is a letter. If I am not back by the day on which M. Robert Darzac is due to appear before the judge, open this letter in court, after all the witnesses have been heard. Arrange this matter with M. Darzac's counsel, for M. Robert Darzac is innocent. This letter contains the name of the attacker. I will not add the proof, for I am now going in search of it; but the envelope contains, at least, an irrefutable explanation of the man's guilt."

Our reporter departed. For a long time we had no news of him, but a week ago, a stranger called upon our Editor and said: "Act in accordance with the instructions of Joseph Rouletabille, if it becomes necessary to do so. The truth is in the letter." This gentleman would not give his name.

This day, 15th January, is the day of the trial. Joseph Rouletabille has not returned, and perhaps we shall never see him again. It is quite possible that Joseph Rouletabille has given his life for the sake of his professional duty! We shall know how to avenge him.

This afternoon, our Editor will be at the court at Versailles with the letter — the letter containing the name of the attacker.'

At the head of the article was a portrait of Rouletabille.

Parisians who flocked that day to the court at Versailles, to the trial of what was known as the 'Mystery of the Yellow Room', will certainly not have forgotten the extraordinary and tumultuous crowds at Gare Saint Lazare. The article in *L'Epoque* had aroused everyone, excited universal curiosity and fuelled people's passion for debate. Blows were exchanged between the partisans of Joseph Rouletabille and the fanatical supporters of Frédéric Larsan, for, strange though it may seem, the excitement of the people arose less from the thought that an innocent man might be sentenced to death than from the interest they took in the different theories about the Mystery of the Yellow Room. Each had his own explanation, to which he held fast. Those who explained the crime as Frédéric Larsan did, would not admit any doubts as to the perspicacity of that popular detective; and all the others who had different solutions naturally claimed that they must be identical with that of Joseph Rouletabille, with which they were not yet acquainted.

With copies of *L'Epoque* in their hands, the 'Larsans' and the 'Rouletabilles' argued and jostled one another on the steps of the court at Versailles, and even in the court itself! An unusually large number of police had been assembled to cope with the enormous crowd.

Those who could not gain admission hung around the building until evening, hungry for news, welcoming the most fantastic rumours.

In the court, the trial proceeded under the direction of M. de Rocoux, a judge with all the usual prejudices of lawyers, but thoroughly honest. The names of the witnesses had been called out. I was one of them; others were those who, from far or near, had been connected with the mystery of Glandier: M. Stangerson, who looked ten years older and was unrecognisable; Larsan; Mr Arthur William Rance, his face as red as ever; Old Jacques; Mathieu, the innkeeper, who was brought into court handcuffed between two gendarmes; Mme Mathieu, in tears; the Berniers; the two nurses; the butler; all the chateau servants; the clerk from post office no. 40; the booking clerk from Epinay; several friends of M. and Mlle Stangerson; and all the witnesses for M. Darzac, the accused. I had the good fortune to be amongst the earliest witnesses called; this allowed me to be present at nearly the whole of the subsequent proceedings.

I need hardly say that the place was packed. Lawyers were sitting on the very steps of the court and, behind the prosecutors in their red robes, were representatives from other courts. M. Robert Darzac appeared in the dock between two gendarmes, so calm, tall and handsome that a murmur of admiration rather than of compassion greeted him. He immediately bent forward towards his counsel, Maître Henri Robert, who, assisted by his chief secretary, Maître André Hesse, then at the beginning of his career, was already engaged in examining the documents and notes before him.

Many expected Professor Stangerson to go over to the accused and shake hands with him, but the names of the witnesses were called out and they left the court, with no sensational incidents.

At the moment when the jurors took their seats, it was noticed that they appeared to be deeply interested in a rapid conversation which the Editor of *L'Epoque* was having with Maître Henri Robert. The former then took his place on one of the front seats reserved for the public. Some were surprised that he did not follow the other witnesses to their allotted room.

The reading of the indictment took place, as usual, without incident. I shall not here report the lengthy cross-examination to which M. Darzac was subjected. He answered the questions promptly in a most natural manner, but, at the same time, with great reserve. Everything he said seemed utterly reasonable; everything he withheld appeared to tell terribly against him, even in the estimation of those who believed him to be innocent. His silence on certain points – of which the reader is aware – told against him, and it seemed that his silence would be his undoing. He resisted all the entreaties of the judge and of the representatives of the Public Prosecutor. He was told that to remain silent in such circumstances would mean capital punishment.

'Very well, then,' he said, 'I must die! But I am innocent!' With the immense skill on which his reputation has been built, Maître Henri Robert – M. Darzac's counsel – taking advantage of the incident, tried to show the nobility of his client's character, by the very fact of his silence, alluding to the sense of moral duty of which only heroic natures are capable. The eminent barrister only succeeded, however, in strengthening still further the confidence of those who knew M. Darzac, but the others remained unmoved. The hearing was suspended and, a little later, the witnesses were called in turn. Rouletabille had not yet arrived. Every time a door opened, all eyes turned first towards it and then towards the Editor of *L'Epoque*, who remained impassive. At last he was seen to feel in his pocket and draw from it a letter. A loud murmur followed this movement.

I do not intend to report here everything that happened at the trial. I have given enough facts to make any fresh description of the events that occurred at Glandier and of the obscurity surrounding them unnecessary. I am anxious to come to the really dramatic moment of that memorable day.

It occurred when the trial was resumed, when Maître Henri Robert was questioning Mathieu, who, standing in the witness box between two gendarmes, was defending himself against the charge of murdering the Green Man. His wife was called and confronted with him. Bursting into tears, she confessed that she had been infatuated with the gamekeeper, and that her husband had suspected it; but she again affirmed that he had nothing to do with the murder of her lover. Maître Henri Robert thereupon asked the court to hear Frédéric Larsan on the matter.

'In a short conversation which I had with Frédéric Larsan during the recess,' the famous counsel declared, 'he has given me to understand that the death of the gamekeeper may be explained other than by the intervention of Mathieu. It will be interesting to know the views of Frédéric Larsan.'

Frédéric Larsan was brought in. He explained himself very clearly.

'I see no need,' he said, 'for the intervention of Mathieu in all this. I have told M. de Marquet so. But the murderous threats of this man evidently compromised him in the eyes of the judge. To me it appears that the attacks on Mlle Stangerson and on the gamekeeper are one and the same affair. Mlle Stangerson's attacker, fleeing through the main courtyard, was fired upon; it was thought that he had been struck, that he was killed, but, in fact, he only stumbled, just as he disappeared behind the corner of the right wing of the chateau. There the criminal encountered the gamekeeper, who, no doubt, tried to grapple with him. The attacker still had in his hand the knife with which he had stabbed Mlle Stangerson; he stabbed the gamekeeper in the heart and the gamekeeper fell dead on the spot.'

This very simple explanation appeared very plausible, more so than many of those who were interested in the mysteries of Glandier had thought.

The President then asked:

'What became of the attacker?'

'He evidently hid himself in a dark corner at the end of the courtyard and, after the departure of the people carrying the body to the chateau, he was able to disappear quietly.'

At that moment, from the back of the public gallery, a youthful voice was raised. In the midst of the general hubbub, it was heard to say:

'*I agree with Frédéric Larsan as to the stabbing of the gamekeeper, but I disagree as to the manner in which the attacker escaped from the end of the courtyard.*'

Everyone turned round. The ushers sprang towards the speaker and commanded silence. The judge angrily asked who had dared to speak, and ordered the immediate expulsion of the intruder. But the same clear voice was heard again:

'*It is I, Monsieur le Président – I – Joseph Rouletabille!*'

CHAPTER XXVII

In which Rouletabille appears in all his glory

There was a terrible commotion. People fainted. No more heed was given to the majesty of the Law. All was wild confusion. Everyone wanted to see Joseph Rouletabille. The judge announced that he would have the court cleared, but no one heard him. Meanwhile, Rouletabille leapt over the balustrade separating him from the seated public, made unsparing use of his elbows and reached his Editor, who embraced him warmly. He took his letter from the Editor's hands, put it in his pocket, and made his way, jostled and jostling, to the witness box. His face was bright with joy; his head was truly a red ball, made brighter still by the fiery gleam of his two large, round eyes. Rouletabille was wearing the same suit that I had seen him wear on the day of his departure, but the state it was in! The same cap was on his head and the same overcoat over his arm. He said:

'I beg your pardon, Monsieur le Président! The steamer was late! I have only just arrived from America! I am Joseph Rouletabille!'

There was a roar of laughter. Everyone was glad of the lad's arrival. It seemed as if a great weight had been lifted from everyone's conscience. Everyone breathed more freely, for everyone felt certain that he really had brought the truth with him and that he was now going to make it known.

But the judge was furious.

'So, you are Joseph Rouletabille, are you?' he replied. 'Well, young man, I must teach you what comes of contempt of court. For the present, while the Court will consider your case, I shall hold you in detention according to my discretionary powers.'

'But, Monsieur le Président, I *want* to be at the Court's

disposal. That is the very thing I am asking. That is what I have come here for – to place myself at the disposal of the Law. If my entrance has been a trifle noisy, I humbly apologise to the court. I beg you to believe, Monsieur le Président, that no one has a greater respect for the Law than I have. But I entered in the only way I could.'

And he began to laugh and everyone laughed with him.

'Take him away!' the judge ordered.

But Maître Henri Robert intervened. He began by excusing the young man, who, he said, was driven by the best intentions in the world. He persuaded the judge that it would be difficult to pass over the evidence of a witness who had lived at Glandier during the whole of that mysterious week; above all, of a witness who claimed he could prove the innocence of the accused and make known the name of the attacker.

'You are going to tell us the name of the attacker?' the judge asked, wavering but sceptical.

'That's all I have come for, Monsieur le Président,' said Rouletabille.

People were about to applaud, but the energetic shushing of the court attendants restored silence.

'Joseph Rouletabille,' said Maître Henri Robert, 'has not been subpoenaed as a witness, but I hope that M. le Président, according to his discretionary powers, will be kind enough to examine him.'

'Very well,' the judge replied. 'We'll question him. But first let us proceed by order.'

The counsel for the prosecution stood up.

'It would perhaps be better,' he remarked, 'if this young man told us the name of the person he believes to be the attacker.'

The judge agreed with an ironical remark.

'If the prosecuting counsel attaches some importance to the evidence of M. Joseph Rouletabille, I see no reason why this witness should not tell us the name of the attacker.'

The silence was complete. You could have heard a pin drop.

Rouletabille remained silent and looked sympathetically

190

across at M. Robert Darzac, who, for the first time since the beginning of the trial, seemed perturbed and deeply anxious.

'Well,' cried the judge, 'we are ready to hear you. We are waiting for the name of the attacker.'

Rouletabille very calmly felt in his waistcoat-pocket, drew a large watch from it, and, having looked at the time, replied:

'Monsieur le Président, I cannot tell you the name of the attacker before half-past six. We have four solid hours ahead of us.'

The judge seemed delighted. Maître Henri Robert and Maître André Hesse were much annoyed.

The judge said:

'This little joke has gone on long enough. You may retire, Monsieur, to the witnesses' room. You are detained by the court.'

Rouletabille protested.

'I assure you, Monsieur le Président,' he cried, in his sharp, clear voice, 'that when I tell you the name of the attacker you will understand why I could not tell it to you before half-past six. Take my word for it – the word of Joseph Rouletabille. But, meanwhile, I can explain the murder of the gamekeeper. M. Frédéric Larsan, who has seen me at work at Glandier, can tell you with what care I have studied this whole affair. Although I disagree with him, and declare that, by having M. Robert Darzac arrested, he charges an innocent man, M. Larsan does not doubt my good faith, and realises the importance of my discoveries, which have often corroborated his own.'

Frédéric Larsan then said:

'Monsieur le Président, it will be interesting to hear M. Joseph Rouletabille, the more so as we do not agree.'

As the judge remained silent, Frédéric Larsan continued:

'We agree, M. Rouletabille and I, as to the stabbing of the gamekeeper by Mlle Stangerson's attacker, but, since we do not agree as to how the attacker escaped from the courtyard, it would be interesting to know how M. Rouletabille explains that escape.'

'It certainly would be,' said my friend.

There was general laughter. The judge instantly declared that, if this were repeated, he would not hesitate to carry out his threat and have the court cleared.

'Really,' added the judge, in conclusion, 'in a case like this I see nothing to provoke laughter.'

'Nor do I,' said Rouletabille.

People in front of me stuffed their handkerchiefs in their mouths to suppress further merriment.

'Now, young man,' said the judge, 'you have heard what M. Frédéric Larsan has just said. How, in your view, did the attacker escape from the courtyard?'

Rouletabille looked at Mme Mathieu, who smiled sadly at him.

'Since Mme Mathieu,' he said, 'has frankly admitted her weakness, and has not concealed the fact of her admiration for the gamekeeper, I am free to tell you that she often met him at the Tower. Mme Mathieu would come to the chateau at night, wrapped in a large black shawl, which disguised her, and made her look like a dark phantom, which sometimes gave Old Jacques some uneasy nights. She had learned to imitate the sinister cry of a cat belonging to one Mother Agenoux, an old sorceress who lives in Ste- Geneviéve-des-Bois. When the gamekeeper heard this cry, he would at once leave the tower, and go and open the little gate for Mme Mathieu. When the repairs to the tower were underway, their conversations took place in the room at the far end of the right wing of the chateau, which was separated from the butler's apartment by only a thin partition.

Mme Mathieu had left the gamekeeper in perfect health before the dramatic events in the courtyard. She and her admirer left the tower together. I only learnt these details, Monsieur le Président, by an examination I made of the foot-prints in the main courtyard the next morning. Bernier, the caretaker, whom I had placed with his gun on watch behind the tower, as I will allow him to explain for himself, could not see what was going on in the main courtyard. He did not get there until a little later on, summoned by the revolver shots. He in turn fired his gun.

In the darkness and silence of the main courtyard Mme Mathieu bade the gamekeeper goodnight. She walked to the open gate and he returned to his room at the far end of the right wing. He had nearly reached the door when shots rang out; he turned back anxiously. He had nearly reached the corner when a shadow rushed at him and stabbed him in the heart. His body was immediately picked up by people who believed they had found the attacker, but who were, in fact, bearing away the murder victim.

Meanwhile, what was Mme Mathieu doing? Surprised by the revolver shots and by the people rushing into the main courtyard, she made herself as small as she could in the darkness. The main courtyard is very large, and, finding herself near the gate, she might easily have left unseen. But she did not leave; she remained there and saw the body carried away. In an agony of mind that may readily be imagined, urged on by a sense of tragic foreboding, she walked to the hall of the chateau, and saw on the stairs, lit by Old Jacques' lantern, the body of the gamekeeper. She saw this and fled.

Old Jacques must have seen her, for he followed the black phantom that had caused him so many sleepless nights. That very night, before the crime took place, he had been woken by the cries of the Good Lord's Beast, and had, through his window, seen the black phantom. He had quickly pulled on his clothes, which explains why he arrived fully dressed in the hall when we brought the body there. Doubtless he had that night tried to get a closer look at the phantom. He recognised her; Jacques is an old friend of Mme Mathieu. She probably confessed to him her infatuation for the gamekeeper, and besought him to protect her at that difficult moment. Her condition after seeing the dead body of her admirer must have been pitiable. Old Jacques took pity on Mme Mathieu, and accompanied her through the oak grove out of the park and beyond the lake to the road to Epinay. From there she had but a little way to go to reach her home.

Old Jacques returned to the chateau, and, seeing how important it was for Mme Mathieu that her presence at the chateau should remain unknown, he did his utmost to hide from us this dramatic episode in a night already filled with terrible incident.

I need not ask Mme Mathieu or Old Jacques to confirm these explanations. I know that things occurred as I have related them. I will simply appeal to the memory of M. Larsan, who, no doubt, already understands how I learned all this, for he saw me the next morning bent over the double trail, the footprints of Old Jacques and of Mme Mathieu.'

Rouletabille turned to the innkeeper's wife and bowed to her, saying:

'Madame's footprints bear a strange resemblance to the elegant footprints of the attacker.'

Mme Mathieu trembled and gazed at the young reporter with a look of eager curiosity. What was he saying? What did he mean?

'Madame,' Rouletabille went on, 'has an elegant foot, long and rather large for a woman. Its imprint, but for the pointed toe, is similar to that of the attacker.'

There was a stirring in the audience; with a gesture Rouletabille put a stop to it.

'I hasten to say,' he continued, 'that all this is of little importance, and that a detective who would build up a whole system on such superficial clues as these, without recourse to a general idea to support them, would be heading straight for a terrible miscarriage of justice. M. Robert Darzac also has the same feet as the attacker, yet he is not the attacker either.'

These words created a great sensation.

The judge asked Mme Mathieu:

'Is that how things happened that night, Madame?'

'Yes, Monsieur le Président,' she replied. 'It's almost as if M. Rouletabille had been there with us.'

'You saw the attacker escaping to the far end of the right wing, Madame?'

'Yes, just as, a minute later, I saw people carrying away the body of the gamekeeper.'

'But what became of the attacker? You remained alone in the main courtyard, so it would be quite natural for you to have seen him there. He did not know you were there, and the moment had come for him to escape.'

'I saw nothing, Monsieur le Président,' said Mme Mathieu. 'At that moment, the night became very dark.'

'So it is up to M. Rouletabille,' said the judge, 'to explain to us how the attacker made his escape?'

'Certainly!' the young man replied, with such confidence than even the judge could not refrain from smiling.

Rouletabille continued:

'The attacker could not have escaped by ordinary means from the end of the courtyard without being seen by us. If we had not *seen* him, we would have *touched* him. The area there is very small, a tiny square surrounded by ditches and high iron railings. The attacker would have had to tread on us – or we on him.'

'Then, since the man was trapped in that narrow square, tell us how it was that you did not find him there. I have been asking you this question for the last half hour!'

Rouletabille once more took his watch from his waistcoat pocket, observed the time, and said in a quiet tone:

'Monsieur le Président, you may ask me that for another three hours and thirty minutes, but I shall not be able to answer you before half-past six!'

This time the murmurs were neither hostile nor disappointed. The audience were beginning to believe in Rouletabille. They were amused by his self-assurance, and by his daring to fix a time for the judge, as if he were making an appointment to meet a colleague.

As for the judge, after wondering whether he ought to be angry, he decided to be amused by the slender youth, as was everyone else.

Rouletabille was clearly a decent chap, and the judge was already beginning to like the young man. Besides, Rouletabille had so clearly defined the part played by Mme Mathieu in the affair, and had explained every one of her actions that night so clearly, that M. de Rocoux felt compelled to take him almost seriously.

'As you please, Monsieur Rouletabille,' he said at last, 'but I don't want to see you again before half-past six!'

Rouletabille bowed to the judge and made his way to the witnesses' room.

He looked for me but did not see me. I quietly made my way through the crowd, and left the court almost at the same time as Rouletabille. He greeted me effusively and jubilantly shook both my hands. I said to him:

'I won't ask, you, my friend, what you have been doing in America. No doubt you would say to me what you said to the judge – that you cannot tell me anything before half-past six.'

'No, no, my dear Sainclair, no! I am going to tell you at once why I went to America, because you are a friend. I went to America in search of the name of the attacker's other half!'

'Really! The name of his other half?'

'Exactly. When we left Glandier for the last time, I knew the two halves of the attacker, and the name of one of his halves. It was the name of the other half that I went to America to discover.'

We were entering the witnesses' room at that moment. They crowded about Rouletabille greeting him warmly. The reporter was friendly to all, except Arthur Rance, to whom he was markedly cool.

Frédéric Larsan entered the room. Rouletabille went up to him and shook his hand. Rouletabille must have felt perfectly sure that he had got the better of the great detective Larsan, who, equally sure of himself, smiled, and, in his turn, asked what he had been doing in America. Then my friend, in a charming way, took him by the arm, and told him several anecdotes about his trip. After a while, they moved away, deep in conversation about more serious matters and I discreetly left them. Moreover, I was anxious to return to the court, where the examination of witnesses was continuing. I resumed my seat and realised at once that the public felt very little interest in what was then going on, and were impatiently awaiting the hour of half-past six.

Half-past six at last!

. Joseph Rouletabille was again brought in. It would be impossible to describe the excitement with which the crowd watched him as he walked to the witness box. Everyone present held their breath. Robert Darzac rose to his feet; he was as pale as death.

The judge said gravely:

'I will not compel you to take the oath, Monsieur,, since you have not been officially summoned. But I hope there is no need to explain to you the great importance of what you are about to say in this court.'

And he added as a warning:

'The great importance of your words – *to you*, if not to others!'

Rouletabille, who was not in the least perturbed, looked him in the eye and replied:

'Yes, Monsieur.'

'Now then,' said the judge, 'we were speaking a little while ago of the small courtyard where the attacker sought refuge, and you promised to tell us at half-past six both how he managed to escape and his name. It is twenty-five minutes to seven, Monsieur Rouletabille, and we have learned nothing from you yet.'

'Quite so, Monsieur!' began my friend, in the midst of a solemn silence. 'I told you that the far end of the courtyard was closed off, and that it was impossible for the attacker to escape from there without being seen by the people looking for him. That is the exact truth. When we were there in that courtyard, the attacker was there with us!'

'And you did not see him! That's exactly what the prosecution says.'

'We all saw him, Monsieur le Président!' cried Rouletabille.

'And you did not arrest him!'

'I was the only one who knew he was the attacker. It was important to me that he should not be arrested just then. Moreover, I had no proof, only my personal belief. Yes, my reason alone proved to me that the attacker was there and that we were looking at him. I have taken my time in bringing irrefutable proof to this court, but it is a proof which, I am sure, will satisfy everybody!'

'Speak out, Monsieur, speak out, then! Tell us the name of the attacker!'

'You will find it amongst the names of those who were in that courtyard,' replied Rouletabille, who did not appear to be in the slightest hurry.

The public began to grow impatient.

'The name, give us the name,' several voices murmured.

'I am delaying this deposition of mine a little, Monsieur le Président, because I have certain reasons for doing so.'

'The name! The name!' the crowd repeated.

'Silence!' cried the usher.

The judge said:

'You must tell us the name at once, Monsieur. Those who were in the courtyard were, first of all, the dead gamekeeper. Was *he* the attacker?'

'No, Monsieur.'

'Old Jacques?'

'No, Monsieur.'

'The caretaker, Bernier?'

'No, Monsieur.'

'Mr Arthur William Rance then? The only other people present were Arthur William Rance and yourself. You are not the attacker, are you?'

'No, Monsieur.'

'Then you accuse Mr Arthur William Rance?'

'No, Monsieur.'

'I no longer understand you! What are you leading up to? There was no one else in that courtyard.'

'I beg your pardon, Monsieur. There was no one else in the courtyard, but there was someone above it, someone leaning out of his window above the courtyard.'

'Frédéric Larsan!' cried the judge.

'FRÉDÉRIC LARSAN!' replied Rouletabille in thundering tones.

There was a general outcry expressing amazement, indignation, scepticism and, in some cases, enthusiasm for the youth who was bold enough to make such an extraordinary accusation. The judge did not attempt to quell the uproar. When it had subsided under the energetic shushing of those who wished, impatiently, to know more, Robert Darzac was distinctly heard to murmur:

'That's impossible! He's mad!'

The judge spoke:

'You dare to accuse Frédéric Larsan, Monsieur! See what an impression your accusation has made! M. Robert Darzac himself calls you a madman! If you are not mad, you must have proof.'

'Proof, Monsieur? You want proof? Well, I am going to give you one to begin with!' cried the piercing voice of Rouletabille. 'Call Frédéric Larsan!'

'Usher!' cried the judge. 'Call Frédéric Larsan!'

The usher hurried to the door of the witnesses' room, opened it and disappeared. The little door remained open; the eyes of all were turned towards it. The man reappeared and advanced to the centre of the court.

'Monsieur le Président,' he said, 'Frédéric Larsan is not there. He left at about four o'clock and has not been seen since.'

'My proof – there you have it!' Rouletabille shouted triumphantly.

'Explain yourself – what proof?' asked the judge.

'My irrefutable proof,' said the young reporter. 'Don't you see it in Larsan's flight? I can swear to you that he will not return! You will see no more of Frédéric Larsan!'

'If you are not mocking the Law, Monsieur, why did you not take advantage of his presence with you in this court to accuse him, face to face? At least he would have been able to answer you!'

'What answer *could* be more complete than this, Monsieur le Président? He does not answer me! He will never answer me! I accuse Frédéric Larsan of being the attacker and he runs away! You consider that to be no answer, Monsieur?'

'We refuse to believe . . . we cannot believe that Larsan, as you say, has fled! Why should he? He did not know that you were going to accuse him!'

'Oh yes he did, Monsieur, he did know, since I told him so myself, not so very long ago!'

'You did that! You believe that Larsan is the attacker, and you gave him the means of escaping?'

'Yes, Monsieur le Président, I did,' replied Rouletabille proudly. 'I have nothing to do with the Law, neither am I a member of the police. I am merely a journalist, and it is not my business to get people arrested. I serve truth in my own way – that is *my* business. You, the judges, are here to protect society as best you can, and that is *your* business. If you are just, Monsieur le Président – and you are – you will find that I am right. Did I not tell you, a short time ago, that you would understand why I could not pronounce the name of the attacker before half-past six. I had calculated the time necessary to warn Frédéric Larsan and allow him to take the 4.17 train to Paris and safety. One hour to reach Paris, an hour and a quarter to enable him to destroy all trace of his arrival there – that brought us to half-past six! You will not find Frédéric Larsan.' Rouletabille fixed his eyes on M. Darzac. 'Larsan is too cunning. He is a man who has always escaped you, and whom you have long pursued, always in vain. If he is not quite as clever as I am, he is cleverer than all the police on earth. The man who four years ago managed to join the detective squad and, in that capacity, become famous as Frédéric Larsan, is famous, much more famous, for other reasons and under another name, which is also well known to you. Frédéric Larsan, Monsieur le Président, is *Ballmeyer!*'

'Ballmeyer!' cried the judge.

'Ballmeyer!' Robert Darzac exclaimed, springing to his feet. 'Ballmeyer! It was true then!'

'Aha! You do not think me mad now, M. Darzac!' said Rouletabille.

Cries of 'Ballmeyer! Ballmeyer! Ballmeyer!' were all that was heard in the court.

The judge suspended the hearing.

One can readily imagine the excitement and uproar that reigned during this interval in the proceedings. The public had quite enough to think and talk about. Ballmeyer! Everyone thought the young man a marvel! Ballmeyer! He had been reported dead a few weeks before. Ballmeyer, then, had escaped death, as all his life he had escaped the police. Do I need to recount here Ballmeyer's doings? For twenty years they have filled the law reports and the newspapers and though some of my readers may have forgotten the mystery of the Yellow Room, the name of Ballmeyer will certainly not have passed from their memory.

Ballmeyer was the classic society swindler. He was a 'perfect gentleman'. There was no one more skilled at sleight-of-hand than he. There was no more terrible and audacious thug. Received in the best society, admitted to the membership of the most exclusive clubs, he had robbed families of their honour and punters of their money with a mastery never surpassed. On certain difficult occasions he had not hesitated to make use of the knife and the cudgel. As a matter of fact, he never hesitated, and he was capable of anything. Having fallen into the hands of the Law, he escaped on the morning of his trial by throwing pepper in the eyes of the guards who were taking him to court. It became known later on that, on the day of his escape, while the best detectives were after him, he was – having made no attempt at a disguise – quietly sitting in one of the stalls at the Théâtre Français watching the first performance of a new play!

Afterwards, he left France to 'work' in America, and the Ohio state police one day laid hands on that extraordinary bandit. But the next day he escaped again. His story would fill a whole book. This was the man who had become Frédéric Larsan! And it was this boy, Rouletabille, who had learned all that! It was this youngster who, although he knew Ballmeyer's past, had once more allowed him to laugh at the world by giving him the means of escape!

In this respect, I could not but admire Rouletabille, for I knew that his purpose was to serve both M. Robert Darzac and Mlle Stangerson by freeing them from Larsan, without allowing him to speak.

The crowd had not yet recovered from the amazement

caused by the young reporter's revelations, and I had already heard some of the most excited amongst them saying: 'If the attacker was Frédéric Larsan, that still doesn't explain how he got out of the Yellow Room,' when the hearing was resumed.

Rouletabille was immediately called to the witness box, and his examination – for he had to submit to an interrogation rather than make a deposition – was resumed.

'You have told us,' said the judge, 'that it was impossible to escape from the courtyard. I agree. I will even agree that, since Frédéric Larsan was leaning out of the window above you, he was still, in a sense, in the courtyard. But how did he get out of the courtyard and up to that window?'

'I said that he did not escape by ordinary means,' Rouletabille replied. 'He must, consequently, have done so by extraordinary means. For the courtyard was closed off only in the ordinary sense, whilst the Yellow Room was completely sealed off. It was possible to climb up the wall in the courtyard – something that was impossible in the Yellow Room; one could then spring on to the terrace, and from there – while we were bending over the body of the gamekeeper – gain access to the gallery by the window just above it. Larsan, having done that, had merely to open the window and speak to us. All that was mere child's play to an acrobat of Ballmeyer's ability. And here, Monsieur le Président, you have the proof.'

Rouletabille then drew from his pocket a small packet, which he opened and produced a strong peg.

'Here, Monsieur le Président,' he said, 'is a peg which fits perfectly into a small hole still to be seen in the cornice supporting the terrace. Larsan, who foresaw everything, and thought of all possible means of flight to or from his room – a necessary precaution when one is playing the little game he played – had previously fixed this peg into the stone. One foot on the stone post at the corner of the chateau, the other foot on this peg, one hand on the cornice above the gamekeeper's door, the other on the terrace, and Frédéric Larsan vanishes into the air – all the more easily because he is extremely nimble and quick, and, furthermore, because that evening he was not under the influence of a sleeping-draught as he had wanted us to believe.

We dined with him, Monsieur le Président, and during dessert he pretended to feel suddenly sleepy, for he himself wanted to appear to have been drugged, so that the next day no one would be surprised that I too should have been given the same opiate whilst dining with him. Since we had shared the same fate, he would not be suspected. For I, Monsieur le Président, was sent into the deepest of sleeps, and by Larsan himself! If I had not been in that condition, Larsan would not have been able to enter Mlle Stangerson's room that night and the crime would not have been committed.'

A groan was heard. It came from M. Darzac, who could not control his grief.

'You can understand,' added Rouletabille, 'that the fact of my room being next to his was particularly annoying to Larsan that night, for he knew, or, at least, he may have suspected, that I would be watching. Naturally, he did not for a moment believe that I suspected him, but I might discover him just at the moment when he was leaving his own room to go to Mlle Stangerson's. That night he waited until I was asleep and my friend Sainclair was busy in my room trying to awaken me, before going to Mlle Stangerson's room.

Ten minutes later, Mlle Stangerson was being attacked and was screaming.'

The judge then asked:

'How did you come to suspect Larsan!'

'My reason told me it was him, Monsieur le Président, and so I kept my eye on him. But he is a terribly smart fellow and I had not foreseen the sleeping-draught trick. And whilst my reason pointed him out to me, I required visible proof. I wanted, as it were, to see that proof with my own eyes, having seen it with the right end of my reason.'

'What do you mean by "the right end of your reason"?'

'Well, Monsieur le Président, reason has two ends – a right one and a wrong one. There is only one on which you can safely rely and that is the right one. You recognise it by the fact

203

that nothing can make it give way or break, whatever you do or whatever you say. The day after the mysterious incident in the gallery, when I was still on the lowest of mental planes amongst those who don't know how to use their reason, whilst I was bending over the ground examining those deceptive superficial clues, I suddenly looked up, and, leaning on the right end of my reason, I walked up to the gallery.

There I satisfied myself that the attacker whom we were all pursuing could not, on that occasion, have left the gallery either by ordinary or extraordinary means. Then with the right end of my reason I drew a circle around the problem. Around this circle, I mentally wrote these bright words: "Since the attacker cannot be outside the circle, he must be within it!" Who, then, did I see within my circle? The right end of my reason showed me that, besides the attacker, who must necessarily find himself within it, there were Old Jacques, M. Stangerson, Frédéric Larsan and myself. That is, five people including the attacker. Now when I searched within the circle – or, if you prefer it, in the gallery – I found only four people. That demonstrated that the fifth person could not have fled, could not have got out of the circle. In other words, I had within the circle one person who was really two, that is to say, a being who, in addition to being himself was also the attacker. Why had I not realised that before? Simply because the idea that a man might be two men had not occurred to me.

With which of the four people enclosed within my circle had the attacker been able to double up, without my having noticed it? Obviously not the people whom I saw independently of the attacker. Thus in the gallery I had seen *at one and the same time* M. Stangerson and the attacker, Old Jacques and the attacker, and myself and the attacker. The attacker, therefore, could not be either M. Stangerson, Old Jacques, or myself. Did I see Frédéric Larsan and the attacker at the same time? No! Two seconds passed, during which I lost sight of the attacker, for, as I have noted in my papers, he arrived two seconds before M. Stangerson, Old Jacques and myself at the point where the two galleries meet. Those two seconds were enough for Larsan to run into the side gallery, snatch off his false beard, turn round and rush towards us as if, like us, he were in pursuit of the attacker. Ballmeyer has done far more difficult things than that. As you see, it was child's play for him to disguise himself in such a way that he appeared at one time with a red beard to Mlle Stangerson and at another to a post-office clerk wearing a brown beard that made him look like M. Robert Darzac, whom he wished to ruin.

Yes, the right end of my reason brought together those two people, or, rather, *the two halves* of that one person which I had never seen at the same time — Frédéric Larsan and the unknown man — and made of them the mysterious and formidable being whom I was pursuing — the attacker.

That revelation completely threw me. I tried to recover by concentrating on those external clues which had, up till then, led me astray, and which, naturally, I had to bring within the circle drawn by the right end of my reason.

What, in the first place, were the principal external signs which on that night had led me away from the idea of Larsan as the attacker?

(1) I had seen the unknown man in Mlle Stangerson's room, and, running to Frédéric Larsan's room, I had found him there, dull with sleep.

(2) The ladder.

(3) I had placed Frédéric Larsan at the end of the side gallery, and told him I was going to burst into Mlle Stangerson's room and try to capture the attacker. Then I returned to Mlle Stangerson's room, where I drew a blank!

I was not worried about the first external sign. It is likely that when I came down the ladder, after having seen the unknown man in Mlle Stangerson's room, he had already finished what he was doing there. Then, while I was going back into the chateau, he went back into Larsan's room, quickly changed his clothes and, when I knocked at his door, showed the face of Frédéric Larsan, as sleepy as could be.

The second sign — the ladder — did not worry me either. It was clear that if the attacker was Larsan, he did not need a ladder to enter the chateau, since his room was next to mine; but that ladder was there to make people believe that the attacker had come from outside – something vital to Larsan's plan, since, that night, M. Darzac was not at the chateau. Finally, that ladder was there in case of emergency, to facilitate Larsan's escape.

But the third sign altogether misled me. Having placed Larsan at the end of the side gallery, I could not see why he had taken advantage of the moment to return to Mlle Stangerson's room while I went to the left wing of the chateau to see M. Stangerson and Old Jacques. It was a most dangerous thing to do. He risked being caught and he knew it. And he very nearly was caught, not having time to return to his post, as he certainly had hoped to do. He must have had a very urgent reason for returning to Mlle Stangerson's room. As for myself, when I sent Old Jacques to the end of the straight gallery, I naturally thought that Larsan was still at his post at the far end of the gallery; and in going to his post, Old Jacques himself, to whom I had given no detailed explanation, did not look to see whether or not Larsan was at his post.

Old Jacques only thought of carrying out my instructions as quickly as possible. What, then, was the unforeseen reason that had induced Larsan to go to the room for the second time? What was it? I thought it must have been some obvious clue indicating that he had been there – a sign that would betray him. He had forgotten something of great importance while in that room. What? Did he find it? I remembered the candle on the parquet floor and the man stooping. I asked Mme Bernier, who used to clean the room, to search it thoroughly. Mme Bernier found a pince-nez in a crack in the parquet flooring – *this pince-nez*, Monsieur le Président!'

Rouletabille drew from his pocket the pince-nez with which we are already acquainted.

'When I saw this pince-nez,' he continued, 'I was dismayed. I had never seen Larsen wearing spectacles. If he did not wear them it was because he had no need of them. He had still less need of them at a moment when complete freedom of action was so precious to him. What did this pince-nez mean? It did not fit in my circle. Unless it belonged to a long-sighted person! This thought flashed across my mind. As a matter of fact, I had never seen Larsan reading. He might, then, be long-sighted.

They would certainly know at the Detective Department whether he was or not. They would, perhaps, know this pince-nez, the pince-nez of *long-sighted Larsan*, found in Mlle Stangerson's room after the incident in the gallery. That would indeed have been disastrous for Larsan! That explained Larsan's return to the room. And, in fact, Larsan-Ballmeyer is indeed long-sighted, and this pince-nez, which they will probably recognise at the Detective Department, is his property. You see now, Monsieur, what my system is,' Rouletabille continued. 'I do not call upon external clues to tell me the truth; I simply ask that they do not go against the truth which the right end of my reason has indicated to me.

To make quite sure of the truth in regard to Larsan, I made the mistake of wanting to see his face. I have been well and truly punished for it. I really think my reason avenged itself by punishing me for not having – since the incident in the gallery – leaned solely and confidently upon it. I ought indeed to have simply given up the search for proof of Larsan's guilt anywhere but in my reason. Then, Mlle Stangerson was attacked again.'

Rouletabille stopped, coughed. He was deeply moved.

'But what did Larsan intend to do in that room?' asked the judge. 'Why did he twice attempt to murder Mlle Stangerson?'

'Because he adored her, Monsieur le Président.'

'That is evidently a reason.'

'Yes, Monsieur, a most pressing reason. He was madly in love, and because of that and many other things, was capable of committing any crime.'

'Did Mlle Stangerson know this?'

'Yes, Monsieur, but, naturally, she was ignorant of the fact that the man pursuing her was Frédéric Larsan, otherwise he would not have been allowed to install himself at the chateau, and could not, on that night in the mysterious gallery have gone into Mlle Stangerson's room with us after the mysterious incident. I noticed, moreover, that he remained in the darkest corner of the room and kept his head lowered. He must have been searching for the lost pince-nez. Mlle Stangerson had been compelled to bear the attacks of Larsan under a name and disguise unknown to us, but which *she* may already have known.'

'And you, Monsieur Darzac,' asked the judge, 'you may perhaps have heard something on this point from Mlle Stangerson. How is it that she has never spoken about it to anyone? That might have put the police on the track of the attacker, and, assuming you are innocent, would have spared you the pain of being accused.'

'Mlle Stangerson has told me nothing,' replied M. Darzac.

'Does what this young man has said appear possible to you?' the judge asked.

M. Robert Darzac replied imperturbably:

'Mlle Stangerson has told me nothing.'

The judge turned again to Rouletabille:

'How do you explain that, on the night of the murder of the gamekeeper, the attacker brought back the papers stolen from M. Stangerson? How did the attacker gain entrance to Mlle Stangerson's locked room.'

'Oh, as to the last question, I think that is easily answered. A man like Larsan-Ballmeyer could have secured, or had made, the keys he required. As for the theft of the documents, I believe that Larsan had not at first thought of it. Keeping a close watch on Mlle Stangerson, and having made up his mind to prevent her marriage to M. Robert Darzac, he followed her and M. Darzac into the Magasins du Louvre one day and got possession of the bag which had been stolen from her or which she had lost. In that bag there was a key with a brass head. He did not know the importance of it till it was revealed to him by the advertisements which appeared in the newspaper. He wrote to Mlle Stangerson, poste restante, as the advertisement requested. No doubt he asked for a rendezvous, informing her at the same time that he, who had the bag and the key, was the person who had for some time pursued her with his love. He received no answer. He went to post office

No. 40 and ascertained that his letter was no longer there. He had already adopted the manners and bearing of M. Darzac, and, as far as possible, had dressed like him, for, having decided to win Mlle Stangerson at any cost, he had prepared everything, so that, whatever happened, M. Darzac, Mlle Stangerson's beloved, M. Darzac whom he detested and whom he was resolved to ruin, would be deemed the guilty party.

I say "whatever happened" but I believe that Larsan had not yet thought that he would go as far as murder. In any case, he took care to compromise Mlle Stangerson disguised as M. Darzac. He was very nearly the same build as M. Darzac, and had almost the same size feet. It was not difficult for him, after having taken an impression of M. Darzac's footprints, to have similar boots made for himself. Such tricks were mere child's play for Larsan-Ballmeyer.

Well, he received no answer to his letter; no appointment was fixed, and he still had the precious key in his pocket. Since Mlle Stangerson would not come to him, he would go to her. His plan had long been formed. He had gathered all the necessary information about the chateau and the pavilion. One afternoon, while M. and Mlle Stangerson were out for a walk, and while Old Jacques was away too, he climbed in through the hall window. He was alone for a moment and was in no hurry. He examined the furniture and noticed a small, rather curious cabinet, resembling a safe, and with a small keyhole. Ah, that was interesting! As he had with him the little brass key, he naturally connected the two things.

He tried the key in the lock, the door opened. The cabinet was full of papers and documents. They must be very precious to have been put away in so peculiar a cabinet, the key to which was clearly of such importance. That might prove useful – a little blackmailing – it might assist him in his amorous designs. Quickly he made a parcel of the papers and took it to the washroom in the hall.

Between his visit to the pavilion and the night of the murder of the gamekeeper, Larsan had had time to see what those papers were. What was he to do with them? They were rather compromising. That night he took them back to the chateau. Perhaps he hoped that by returning those precious documents – which represented some twenty years' work – he might win some sort of gratitude from Mlle Stangerson. Anything is possible with a man like Larsan-Ballmeyer. In short, whatever his reasons, he took the papers back and was happy to be rid of them.'

Rouletabille coughed and I understood what his cough meant. It was clear that he felt constrained at this point in his explanation by his wish not to give away the true motive for Larsan's terrible feelings for Mlle Stangerson. His argument was too incomplete to satisfy everybody, and the judge would no doubt have made some remark about it, had my quick-witted friend not cried out suddenly:

'*Now we come to the explanation of the Yellow Room!*'

In the court, there was a general scraping of chairs, rustlings and energetic shushings. Curiosity had reached its highest pitch. The judge said:

'It seems to me, according to your hypothesis, Monsieur Rouletabille, that the mystery of the Yellow Room is wholly explained. It was Frédéric Larsan himself who explained it to us, merely deceiving us as to the identity of the attacker, by putting M. Robert Darzac in place of himself. It is obvious that the door of the Yellow Room was opened when M. Stangerson was alone and that he allowed the man, who was coming out of his daughter's room, to pass without stopping him – perhaps even on her own entreaties – to avoid all scandal!'

'No, Monsieur le Président,' protested the young man. 'You forget that Mlle Stangerson was stunned and consequently unable to make such an appeal; neither could she have locked and bolted herself in her room. You also forget that M. Stangerson has sworn that the door was not opened.'

'That, however, is the only possible explanation, Monsieur. The Yellow Room was as tightly locked as an iron safe. To use your own expression, it was impossible for the attacker to make his escape by ordinary, or even extraordinary, means. When the others entered the room, he was not there. Therefore, he must have escaped.'

'Not at all, Monsieur le Président.'

'What do you mean?'

'He did not need to escape, *because he was not there.*'

'Not there?'

'Obviously not! Since he *could not* be there, he *was not* there! One must always lean on the right end of one's reason, Monsieur le Président.'

'But what about all the marks he left behind,' the judge objected.

'That, Monsieur le Président, is the wrong end of your reason. The right end indicates this: From the time when Mlle Stangerson shut herself in her room to the moment when her door was broken down, it was impossible for the attacker to escape from that room; and since he was not found there, it was because, from the moment when the door was closed to the moment when it was forced open, the attacker was not in the room!'

'But the marks!'

'Ah, Monsieur le Président, once more, they are merely external, such as have led to so many miscarriages of justice, because they make you say what they want you to say. They must not, I repeat, be used to reason with. One must reason first, and afterwards find out whether the external clues fit the circle of one's argument. I have a very small circle composed of incontrovertible truth: the attacker was not in the Yellow Room. Why was it assumed that he was? Because of the marks he left behind him. But he may have been there before. Nay, reason tells me that he *must* have been there before. Let us examine these marks, and whatever else we know of the affair, and see whether these marks do not agree with the idea of his being there *before* Mlle Stangerson shut herself in her room, in the presence of her father and Old Jacques.

After the publication of the article in *Le Matin* and a conversation which I had with the judge during the journey from Paris to Epinay-sur-Orge, the proof appeared to me to be complete, that the Yellow Room was sealed off and that, consequently, the attacker had left it before Mlle Stangerson went into her room at midnight.

The external signs then appeared to contradict my reasoning. Mlle Stangerson had not been her own attacker, and those marks attested that it was not a case of attempted suicide. The attacker, then, had come *before*. But how was it that Mlle Stangerson had not been attacked until *afterwards*, or, rather, appeared not to have been attacked until afterwards? Naturally, I had to reconstruct the affair in two phases – two phases that occurred several hours apart. The first phase, during which an attempt really had been made to murder Mlle Stangerson, an attempt which she had kept secret; the second phase was the effect of a nightmare she had. Those who were in the laboratory believed she was being attacked!

At the time, I had not yet been in the Yellow Room. What were Mlle Stangerson's injuries? Marks of strangulation and a bad blow to the temple. The marks of strangulation did not trouble me much; they might have been made before and Mlle Stangerson had possibly hidden them beneath a collar, a scarf, anything. For, since I was obliged to divide the affair into two phases, I was compelled to think that Mlle Stangerson had concealed all the events of the first phase; she, no doubt, had her reasons for doing so, since she had said nothing to her father and was forced to tell the story of the attempt made on her life by the attacker – whose presence in her room she could not deny – to the judge, as if it had taken place in the night, during the second phase. She was compelled to say that, otherwise her father would have asked: "Why did you hide this from us? Why did you remain silent after such an attack?"

She had concealed the marks made by the man on her throat, but what about that blow to the temple? That I could not make out. The less so when I learned that the weapon, a cudgel made from a sheep's bone, had been found in her room. She could not hide the fact that she had been struck on the head, and yet that wound appeared to have been inflicted during the first phase, since it required the presence of the attacker. I imagined that this wound was much less severe than it was said to be – in this I was wrong – and I thought that Mlle Stangerson had concealed the wound by wearing her hair parted in the middle.

As to the mark on the wall, made by the hand of the attacker, wounded by Mlle Stangerson's revolver, it had evidently been made *before*, and the attacker had, necessarily, been wounded during the first phase, that is to say, when he was there. All traces of the attacker's presence in the room had naturally been left during the first phase – the cudgel, the footprints, the old beret, the handkerchief, the blood on the wall, on the door and on the floor. It is absolutely clear that if those traces were still all there, Mlle Stangerson – who wished to keep the whole matter secret – had not yet had time to remove them. This led me to suppose that the first phase of the affair had taken place not very long before the second.

If, after the first phase – that is to say, after the attacker's escape – after she herself had hastily returned to the laboratory where her father found her working, if she could have gone back into her room for just one minute, she would, at least, have hidden the cudgel, the beret and the handkerchief lying on the floor. But she did not do so, since her father did not leave her alone. After the first phase, then, she did not re-enter her room until midnight. Someone had entered it at ten o'clock: Old Jacques, who, as was his practice every night, closed the shutters and lit the nightlight. Owing to her disturbed state of mind – while at the desk in the laboratory, where she pretended to be at work – she had, doubtless, forgotten that Old Jacques would be going into her room! She was startled; she begged Old Jacques not to trouble himself, not to go in there. All this was mentioned in the article in *Le Matin*. Old Jacques went in anyway and noticed nothing, it being so dark in the Yellow Room.

Those must have been terrible moments for Mlle Stangerson! However, I imagine that she was unaware that the attacker had left so many traces behind in her room. She had probably – after the first phase – only just had time to conceal the marks of the man's fingers on her throat and to hurry from her room. Had she known that the cudgel, the beret and the handkerchief were on the floor, she would have gathered them up when she retired at midnight. She did not see them, however, as she undressed by the faint glimmer of the nightlight. She went to bed exhausted by so many emotions and by sheer terror — a terror that had made her retire as late as possible to her room.

I was thus forced to consider the second phase of the drama, in which it appeared that Mlle Stangerson was really alone in the room, since the attacker was not found there and I had, naturally, to make the external signs fit the circle of my reasoning, as I have explained.

But there were other external signs and they required explanation. Shots had been fired during the second phase. Cries of "Help! Murder!" had been raised. What conclusion could the right end of my reason draw from such circumstances? First, with regard to the cries, they must have been caused by a nightmare, since there was no attacker in the room!

There was a lot of noise. There seemed to have been a struggle, furniture had been overturned. On reflection, I was forced to this conclusion: Mlle Stangerson was sleeping, haunted still by the terrible events of that afternoon. She dreamed. Nightmares filled her fevered brain with images of crime, of murder. She again saw the attacker hurling himself upon her; she screamed "Help! Murder!" and wildly felt for the revolver she had placed within her reach on the table by her bedside. But her hand hit the table hard enough to overturn it. The revolver fell to the floor, and, in falling, went off, lodging a bullet in the ceiling. From the outset, this bullet in the ceiling appeared to me to have been the result of an accident. It revealed, at least, the possibility of an accident, and fitted so well with my theory of the nightmare that it was one of the reasons why I ceased to doubt that the crime had been committed much earlier and that Mlle Stangerson, being a most determined woman, had kept it secret.

Mlle Stangerson woke up in a terribly agitated state. She tried to get up, but fell to the floor exhausted, overturning some of the furniture and even crying out. She then fainted.

However, *two* shots were said to have been fired that night during the second phase. My theory demanded that two shots should have been fired, one in each of the two phases, and not two in the last phase – one *before*, to wound the attacker, and one *after*, at the time of the nightmare. Now, was it certain that, during the night, two shots had been fired? The shot was heard in the midst of the noise of falling furniture. When questioned by the judge, M. Stangerson spoke of a *dull* sound which he had heard first, followed by a *ringing* sound. What if the dull sound had been caused by the marble-topped table falling over? That explanation had to be the right one. I became certain that it was, when I learned that the caretakers, Bernier and his wife, although quite close to the pavilion, had heard only *one* shot. They had said so to the judge.

Thus, I had almost reconstructed the two phases of the drama, when, for the first time, I entered the Yellow Room. The seriousness of the wound on the victim's temple, however, did not fit the circle drawn by my reason. This wound, then, had not been made by the attacker with the cudgel during the first phase, for it was too serious a wound; Mlle Stangerson could not possibly have concealed it by arranging her hair so that it parted in the centre and concealed part of her forehead, as I had supposed. Had that wound, then, necessarily been made during the second phase, during the nightmare scene? I asked this of the Yellow Room and the Yellow Room answered me.'

Rouletabille drew from the same little package a piece of white paper, neatly folded in four, and took from it an invisible object, which he held between his thumb and forefinger, and carried to the judge.

'This, Monsieur le Président, is a hair, a blonde hair, from the head of Mlle Stangerson. I found it sticking to one of the corners of the overturned table, the marble top of which was also stained with blood, only a very tiny stain, but most important, for it told me that, on getting up bewildered from her bed, Mlle Stangerson had fallen heavily against the corner of the marble top, and had been wounded on the temple. The hair remained stuck to the marble.'

The crowd applauded again, but, as Rouletabille immediately continued his deposition, silence was instantly restored.

'Besides the name of the attacker, which I only discovered a few days later, I still had to find out when the first phase of the drama had taken place. The interrogation of Mlle Stangerson and that of M. Stangerson, though calculated to deceive the judge, revealed this to me. Mlle Stangerson described very exactly how she had filled her time that day. We had established the fact that the attacker had got into the pavilion between five and six o'clock; let us say, then, that it was a quarter past six when the professor and his daughter resumed their work. The drama could only have been enacted while the professor was away. What I had to do, then, was to find within that short space of time *the moment when the professor and his daughter were not together*. Well, as for that moment, I found it in the interrogation which took place in Mlle Stangerson's room, in the presence of M. Stangerson.

It was said that the professor and his daughter had returned to the laboratory at about six o'clock. M. Stangerson made the following statement: "At that moment, my gamekeeper came up to me and detained me for a while." The professor then had a conversation with the gamekeeper. The man spoke to him about thinning out the woods and about poachers. Mlle Stangerson was no longer there. She had already gone to the laboratory, since the professor said further: "I left the gamekeeper and rejoined my daughter, who was already at work."

The drama must needs have occurred during those few brief moments. I can clearly see Mlle Stangerson returning to the pavilion and going to her room to take off her hat, finding herself suddenly face to face with the scoundrel who was pursuing her. The man had been in the pavilion for some time. He had arranged it so that everything would take place at night. He had taken off Old Jacques' boots; he had removed the papers from the cabinet and, afterwards, had slipped under the bed. The time must have dragged for him. He had got up, gone back into the laboratory, then into the hall, looked out at the garden and seen, coming towards the pavilion, Mlle Stangerson – *alone*! He would never have dared to attack her at that time if he had not thought she was completely alone. For him to suppose she was quite alone, the conversation between M. Stangerson and the gamekeeper must have taken place at a bend in the path where there was a clump of trees which hid the two men from the attacker's sight. His plan was decided upon. He would be more at his ease then, alone with Mlle Stangerson in the pavilion, than he would in the middle of the night, with Old Jacques above him, sleeping in the attic. And so he shut the hall window, which explains why neither M. Stangerson nor the gamekeeper, who were at some distance from the pavilion, heard the shot.

The criminal went back to the Yellow Room. Mlle Stangerson probably cried out, or tried to. The man seized her by the throat. He was perhaps going to strangle her, but her hand had sought and grasped the revolver which she had kept in the drawer of her bedside table ever since she had begun to fear the man's threats. The attacker was already brandishing over her head that weapon which is so terrible in the hands of Larsan-Ballmeyer – that cudgel made from a sheep's bone. She fired. She wounded her attacker in the hand; the cudgel fell to the floor, covered with blood from the man's wound. He staggered, clutched at the wall for support, leaving his handprint on it, and, fearing another bullet, he fled.

She saw him go into the laboratory. She listened. What was he doing in the hall? He was at the window for a long time. At last he jumped out of it. She flew to the window and shut it. Had her father seen? Had he heard? Now that the danger was over, she thought only of her father. Gifted with superhuman energy, she would hide everything from him, if it were still not too late. And so, when M. Stangerson returned, he found the door of the Yellow Room closed and his daughter in the laboratory, bent over her desk, already at work!'

Rouletabille turned towards M. Darzac.

'You know the truth,' he cried 'tell us, then, if that is not the way things happened.'

'I know nothing about it,' replied M. Darzac.

Rouletabille folded his arms, and said:

'You are a hero, M. Darzac, but if Mlle Stangerson were in a state to know that you had been accused of her attempted murder, she would release you from your oath; she would beg you to tell everything that she confided to you, moreover, she would herself come here to defend you!'

The prisoner did not stir nor did he utter a word. He merely looked sadly at Rouletabille.

'Well, then,' said the young reporter, 'since Mlle Stangerson is not here, I must do it myself, but, believe me, M. Darzac, the best way – the only way – to save Mlle Stangerson and to restore her reason is for you to be acquitted.'

Thunderous applause greeted this last remark. The judge did not even attempt to quell the crowd's enthusiasm. Robert Darzac was saved. It only needed a glance at the jurors to be certain of it. Their faces bespoke their belief in his innocence.

The judge then said:

'But what is this mystery that makes Mlle Stangerson, whom somebody has twice tried to murder, conceal such a crime from her father?'

'That, Monsieur le Président, I do not know,' said Rouletabille. 'It is no business of mine.'

The judge once more endeavoured to force M. Darzac to speak.

'You still refuse, Monsieur, to tell us what you were doing while the attempts were being made on the life of Mlle Stangerson?'

'I cannot tell you anything, Monsieur.'

The judge appealed to Rouletabille.

'One may well suppose, Monsieur le Président, that M. Robert Darzac's absences were closely connected with Mlle Stangerson's secret. That is why M. Darzac feels bound to remain silent. Suppose that Larsan, who in his three attempts did everything possible to throw suspicion on M. Darzac, had arranged certain meetings with M. Darzac in compromising places, meetings where the mysterious affair was to be discussed, and these all corresponded exactly to those three occasions! M. Darzac would rather be condemned to death than explain anything connected in any way with Mlle Stangerson's secret. Larsan was clever enough to have planned even that!'

The judge, half-convinced but still curious, asked again:

'But what can that mystery be?'

'Ah, Monsieur, I cannot tell you!' said Rouletabille, bowing to the judge. 'Only I think you know enough now to acquit M. Robert Darzac – unless Larsan should return, which I very much doubt!' he added, with a happy, hearty laugh.

Everybody laughed with him.

'One more question, Monsieur,' said the judge. 'If we accept your theory, we know that Larsan wished to cast suspicion on M. Robert Darzac, but why cast suspicion on Old Jacques?'

'He wanted to show himself to be a marvellous unraveller of intricacies, by himself destroying the proofs he had created. That was very clever indeed. It is a trick that had often enabled him to divert suspicion from himself. He proved the innocence of one person then accused another. You must understand, Monsieur le Président, that such a plan as this must have been thought out and prepared a long time in advance by Larsan. I can assure you that he had seen to every detail, and knew all there was to know about the people and about Glandier. If you would like to know how Larsan became acquainted with the place, let me tell you that he had at one time made himself the official messenger between the Detective Department's laboratory and M. Stangerson, who had been asked to carry out certain experiments for it.

In that way he had been able to enter the pavilion twice before the crime was committed. He was disguised in such a way that Old Jacques did not recognise him afterwards, but he, Larsan, had taken advantage of his presence in the pavilion to steal a pair of Jacques' old boots and a beret, which the servant had tied up in a handkerchief, probably intending to take them to one of his friends, a charcoal burner on the road to Epinay. When the crime was discovered, Old Jacques, who naturally recognised those objects as belonging to him, pretended not to know them, at least, not immediately. They were too compromising, and that explains his confusion at the time when we spoke to him about them. All this is perfectly obvious. I drove Larsan into a corner and made him confess the whole thing. He did so, indeed, with pleasure. For although he is a villain – which, I hope, no one now doubts – he is also an artist! He has his own way of doing things. He acted in a similar manner in the case of the Banque de Crédit Universelle, and in the case of the gold ingots. Those cases will have to be reviewed, Monsieur le Président, for a good many innocent persons have been sent to prison since Larsan-Ballmeyer has been employed in the Detective Department!'

CHAPTER XXVIII

In which it is shown that one cannot always think of everything

Excitement, murmurings, applause! Maître Henri Robert asked for an adjournment of the trial to another session, to allow for further investigations. The judge agreed. The affair was postponed. M. Robert Darzac was provisionally freed and Mathieu was unconditionally released, his innocence having been established. Larsan was sought in vain. M. Darzac at last escaped the frightful calamity which had for a while threatened him and, having called on Mlle Stangerson, was able to hope that, with constant and devoted care, she would one day recover her reason.

As for Rouletabille, he was, naturally, the hero of the hour! Newspapers all over the world published accounts of his great achievements and reproduced his photograph; and he, who had interviewed so many famous people, became famous himself, and was in turn interviewed. I must say that it did not seem to go to the modest young man's head.

We returned from Versailles together, after having dined at the Dog and Pipe. In the train, I asked Rouletabille all sorts of questions which, during our meal, I had refrained from putting, knowing he did not like to mix work and pleasure.

'My friend,' I said, 'this Larsan affair is quite sublime, and worthy of your heroic brain!'

He stopped me and begged me to talk more simply, saying he would be inconsolable if so fine an intellect as mine should fall into the hideous abyss of imbecility by my admiration of him.

'I will come to the point, then,' I said, a little nettled. 'None of what I have said explains to me why you went to America! If I understood aright, when you last left Glandier you already knew all about Frédéric Larsan. You knew that he was the attacker, and you had nothing more to learn as to how he had carried out the attacks.'

'Exactly! And you,' he said, trying to change the subject, 'you suspected nothing?'

'Nothing!'

'Amazing!'

'But, my dear friend, you took great pains to hide your thoughts from me, and I really don't see how I could have guessed what they were! When I arrived at Glandier with the revolvers, did you already suspect Larsan?'

'I did. I had just been reasoning out the "mysterious gallery" affair, in the way I explained to the judges this afternoon, but the reason for Larsan's return to Mlle Stangerson's room had not yet been made clear to me by the discovery of the pince-nez. Moreover, my deduction was only theoretical, and the idea of Larsan being the attacker appeared to me so extraordinary that I had resolved to wait for some further external signs before venturing to take it any further. Nevertheless, the idea worried me and I sometimes spoke to you of the detective in a manner that ought to have roused your suspicions with regard to him. I no longer mentioned his good faith, as I had before; I no longer said to you that he was mistaken; I spoke of his system as a miserable one and my contempt – which you thought was intended for the detective – was really, in my mind, aimed less at the detective than at the *criminal* I already suspected him to be! Remember in what tone I once asked you: "Now is Larsan really misled by this idea? That is the question, that is the question, that is the question!" Those words, repeated three times, ought to have given you some inkling of my suspicions. But I watched you; you did not seem to guess my secret meaning, and I was pleased, for I was not absolutely certain of Larsan's guilt until the discovery of the pince-nez. After that discovery – which explained Larsan's return to Mlle Stangerson's room – I was really happy, ecstatically happy! Oh, I remember it all! I rushed into your room like a madman and cried: "I'll beat Larsan, I'll beat the great Frédéric!"'

Those words referred to the criminal, not the detective. And that same evening, when M. Darzac asked me to keep watch over Mlle Stangerson, I did nothing until ten o'clock, dining with Larsan, taking no special precautions whatever. I kept quiet and did nothing, because he was there opposite me! At that moment, again, you might have suspected that it was that man alone I feared. And, again, when I said to you, in reference to the imminent arrival of the attacker, I said: 'I am quite sure that Frédéric Larsan will be here tonight.'

But there was one important object which ought at once to have told us the identity of the criminal, a thing which denounced Frédéric Larsan, and which we both missed, you and I. Have you forgotten the story of the walking stick? Yes, apart from the reasoning which, to any logical mind, denounced Larsan, there was the story of the walking stick, which alone should have denounced him to all observant minds.

I was amazed to note that, during the trial, Larsan made no use of the walking stick to incriminate M. Darzac. Had not that cane been purchased by a man whose description fitted M. Darzac? Well, a little while ago, before he stepped onto the train that took him away, I asked Larsan why he had not made any use of that stick. He replied that he had never had any intention of using it in the way I was suggesting, that he had never imagined using it against M. Darzac, and that we had much embarrassed him that evening at the inn near the station at Epinay, by proving that he was lying to us!

You remember that he told me that he had obtained that stick in London, whilst the mark on it showed that it had come from Paris. Why, at that moment, instead of thinking, "Frédéric is lying, he was in London; he could not have got this Paris cane in London!" Why did we not say, "Frédéric is lying! He was not in London, because he bought that stick in Paris!" Frédéric is a liar! Frédéric was in Paris at the time of the crime! That would be a starting-point for suspicion! And when, after your inquiry at Cassette's, you told me that the stick had been bought by a person dressed like M. Robert Darzac, when we were positive – having M. Darzac's word for it – that it was not he who had purchased the stick and, further, when we were sure – thanks to the post restante business – that there was a man in Paris pretending to be M. Darzac, and we wondered who this man could be, who, disguised as Darzac, went to Cassette's on the evening of the crime and bought a stick which we found in Larsan's hands, why, why, why did we not instantly think, "What if this unknown person, disguised as Darzac, who buys a walking stick which Larsan has in his hands, were Larsan himself?"

Of course, his position as a detective did not favour such a supposition, but when we saw the eagerness with which Larsan gathered evidence against Darzac – the zeal with which he pursued the unfortunate man – we might have been struck by Frédéric's great lie. Now, how was it that he never used the cane when near M. Darzac? It is very simple, so simple that we never thought of it!

Larsan bought it after having been slightly wounded in the hand by Mlle Stangerson's bullet, solely for the look of the thing – to keep his hand continually closed – not to be tempted to open it and thus let the wound be seen. Do you understand now? Larsan told me all this himself, and I remember having often remarked to you how strange it was that Larsan never let go of that cane! At table, when I dined with him, he would only let go of his cane to take up a knife with his right hand, which he then never put down throughout dinner!

I remembered all these details when I finally fixed on Larsan – that is to say, too late for me to use them. For instance, on the evening when Larsan pretended to be asleep, I bent over him and surreptitiously looked at his hand. There was only a small piece of plaster hiding what remained of a very slight wound – so slight, indeed, that Larsan might have said it had been made by anything but the bullet of a revolver. Nevertheless, so far as I was concerned, that new external sign fitted perfectly in the circle drawn by my reason. The bullet, as Larsan told me this afternoon before disappearing, only grazed the palm of his hand, but caused an abundant flow of blood.

If we had been more perspicacious at the moment when

Larsan lied, he would doubtless have used the very story we had imagined – the story of the discovery of Darzac's stick – in order to ward off suspicion. But events happened so quickly that we forgot all about the cane. All the same, we considerably worried Larsan-Ballmeyer, without suspecting we were doing so!'

'But, my friend,' I said, 'if Larsan had no intention of using the cane against Darzac when he bought it, why did he disguise himself to look like him when he went to buy it?'

'Because he had only just reached Paris, after having committed the crime at Glandier, and had, immediately afterwards, disguised himself as Darzac – a disguise which he has repeatedly used in his criminal activities, with what intention you already know. But already his wounded hand was worrying him, and, as he was passing the Avenue de l'Opéra, he thou he would buy a stick, and he did so at once. It was eight o'clock. Think of it! A man, looking like Darzac, had bought a cane which I had found in the hand of Larsan, and I, who had guessed that the drama had already taken place, that it had, in fact, taken place at about that time, I, who was almost persuaded of Darzac's innocence never suspected Larsan! Really, there are moments when . . .'

'There are moments,' I said, 'when the greatest intelligence . . .'

Rouletabille stopped me there, and, although I kept asking him questions, I found that he was no longer listening to me; he was sound asleep and I had the Devil's own job to wake him when we reached Paris!

CHAPTER XXIX

The mystery of Mlle Stangerson

During the following days, I continued to ask Rouletabille why he had gone to America. He did not give me any more precise answer than he had in the train from Versailles, and he always turned the conversation to other points of the affair.

At last, one day, he told me:

'I needed to find out the truth about Larsan.'

'No doubt,' I replied, 'but why go to America to find it?'

He puffed on his pipe and turned his back on me. Evidently I was encroaching upon the mystery of Mlle Stangerson. Rouletabille had thought that this mystery, which bound her and Larsan together in such a terrible manner – a mystery of which he, Rouletabille, could find no explanation in her life in France – must have its origin in her life in America. And so he had crossed the Atlantic in search of a solution. There, he would discover who this Larsan really was and would acquire the necessary information by which he could compel him to remain silent.

Rouletabille went to Philadelphia.

And now, what was this mystery which had ensured the silence of both Mlle Stangerson and M. Robert Darzac? After so many years, after all the stories invented by scandal-mongering newspapers, now that M. Stangerson knows and has forgiven everything, the full story may be told.

There is but little to say, but it will serve to put the record straight, for there have been people who have dared to speak ill of Mlle Stangerson!

From the very beginning of this sad affair, Mlle Stangerson has always been the victim.

That beginning goes back a long way, to when, as a young girl, she lived with her father in Philadelphia. There at a party, at the house of one of her father's friends, she met a compatriot, a Frenchman who succeeded in fascinating her with his attractive manners, his wit and his love. He was said to be rich. He asked the famous professor for his daughter's hand in marriage. M. Stangerson made inquiries about this M. Jean Roussel and very soon realised that he was dealing with a swindler. 'M. Jean Roussel' was only one of the many aliases used by the celebrated Ballmeyer, who, being wanted by the police in France, had fled to America!

M. Stangerson did not know this, nor did his daughter. She only found things out for herself in the following way. Not only did M. Stangerson refuse M. Jean Roussel his daughter's hand, he banned him from his house. Mathilde, whose heart had opened to love, and who saw nothing in the whole world more beautiful and better than her Jean, was outraged. She did not conceal her discontent from her father, who, to keep her quiet, sent her to the banks of the Ohio, to the house of an old aunt in Cincinnati. Jean joined the young girl there and she, in spite of her great respect for her father, resolved to elude her watchful aunt and run away with Jean, taking advantage of the facilities afforded by American laws to get married at once.

They did so, but they got no further than Louisville. There one morning, someone knocked at the door of the newly wedded couple. It was the police come to arrest M. Jean Roussel, which they did, despite the tears and protestations of Professor Stangerson's daughter. At the same time, they informed Mathilde that her husband was none other than the notorious Ballmeyer!

Desperate, and after a failed attempt at suicide, Mathilde rejoined her aunt in Cincinnati. The old lady nearly died of joy to see her again. She had been looking for her niece for a whole week, and had not dared to tell M. Stangerson. Mathilde made her promise to tell her father nothing. This suited the old lady, for she felt somewhat responsible for what had occurred. A month later, Mlle Stangerson returned to her father, repentant, and with a heart dead to love. She only asked one thing: never again to see her husband, the terrible Ballmeyer – whose death was reported a few weeks later – but to be able to forgive herself for her mistake and to restore her self-respect through a life devoted to study and boundless devotion to her father.

She kept her word.

At the very moment, however – having confessed everything to Robert Darzac, believing Ballmeyer to be dead, having so completely paid for her sins – when she had promised herself the supreme joy of marriage to a true friend, destiny had revived Jean Roussel, the Ballmeyer of her youth! The man informed her that he would never allow her to marry M. Robert Darzac, that he still loved her, which, alas, was true!

Mlle Stangerson did not hesitate to confide in M. Darzac. she showed him the letter in which Jean Roussel-Larsan-Ballmeyer recalled the first hours of their union in the charming little vicarage which they had rented in Louisville. 'The vicarage has lost none of its charm nor the garden its brightness.' The wretch said he was rich and claimed the right to take her back there! She had declared to M. Darzac that if such a dishonour came to the knowledge of her father, she would kill herself. M. Darzac had sworn that he would silence Roussel, by threat or force, even if he had to commit a crime to do this. But M. Darzac was no match for a man like Larsan-Ballmeyer and would have been defeated but for the daring youngster, Rouletabille!

As for Mlle Stangerson, what could she do in the presence of such a monster? The first time when, after threats which had put her on her guard, he suddenly stood before her in the Yellow Room, she tried to kill him. Unfortunately, she did not succeed. From that time on she was the marked victim of this invisible being, who could blackmail her to the end of her days, who lived by her side without her knowing it, who demanded meetings in the name of their mutual love! On the first occasion, she had refused the meeting demanded in the letter addressed to her at post office no. 40 and the result was the tragedy of the Yellow Room. The second time, warned by another letter from him which reached her by post – and which found her in her sickbed – she had avoided meeting him by taking refuge in her boudoir with her maids. In that letter the wretch had informed her that, since, owing to her condition, she could not come to him, he would go to her, and would be in her room on such a night at such a time. Knowing that she had everything to dread from Ballmeyer's audacity, she had left her room empty. That was the mysterious episode in the gallery.

On the third occasion, she had arranged a meeting. That was because her persecutor, before leaving her empty room on the night of the mysterious gallery, had written her an ultimatum, which he had left on her desk. In that missive he insisted on a proper meeting for which he fixed the date and hour, promising to return her father's papers, but threatening to burn them if she continued to avoid him. She did not doubt that the man had those precious documents in his possession; she had, in fact, for years suspected him of being the thief who had stolen her father's papers in Philadelphia and she knew him well enough to understand that if she did not obey, the results of all that work, all those experiments and scientific theories would soon be reduced to ashes!

She decided to meet the man who had been her husband face to face, and to try to reason with him since she could not avoid him! She, therefore, arranged the meeting. What happened between them may be imagined. Mathilde's pleas, Larsan-Ballmeyer's brutality. He insisted that she must give up Darzac. She proclaimed her love for him. He struck her down, with the thought of sending the other man to the scaffold! For he was clever and the Larsan-mask which he would assume as soon as he left her, would, he thought, save him, whilst the other man would again be unable to account for his movements. In this respect, Ballmeyer's plot was well thought out, and the idea was very simple, as young Rouletabille had guessed.

Larsan blackmailed Darzac, as he blackmailed Mathilde; using the same weapons and the same secrets. He declared himself ready to do a deal, to deliver up all her old love letters, and above all, to disappear – if they would pay him his price! Darzac had to go to the meeting-place which Ballmeyer had appointed, under the threat of disclosure the very next day, just as Mathilde had been compelled to consent to the rendezvous which the man had forced upon her. M. Robert Darzac went to Epinay, where an accomplice of Larsan – a fantastic being whom we will meet again some day – held him by force and wasted his time. That same 'coincidence' which Darzac, when charged with the crime, refused to explain, could well have led him to the scaffold!

Ballmeyer, however, had reckoned without Joseph Rouletabille!

Now that the mystery of the Yellow Room has been explained, we do not intend to follow Rouletabille, step by step, on his journey to America. We know the young reporter, we know him capable of tracing the whole of the past lives of Mlle Stangerson and Jean Roussel. In Philadelphia he learned everything concerning Arthur William Rance; he learned of his act of devotion and of the rewards he thought himself entitled to claim for it! The rumour of his marriage to Mlle Stangerson had first found its way to the drawing rooms of Philadelphia. The young scholar's indiscretion, his tireless pursuit of Mlle Stangerson, even in Europe, the disorderly life he led on the pretence of drowning his sorrows, none of these things commended him greatly to Rouletabille, but they serve to explain the coldness with which the young man had greeted him in the witnesses' room. Moreover, Rouletabille soon saw that the Rance affair had nothing whatever to do with the Larsan-Stangerson affair.

He had discovered the extraordinary Roussel-Stangerson adventure. Who was this Jean Roussel? Rouletabille went from Philadelphia to Cincinnati. There he found the old aunt and made her talk. The story of Ballmeyer's arrest threw new light on everything. He went to see the vicarage, a pretty little dwelling in colonial style, which had, indeed, 'lost none of its charm'. Then, abandoning the trail of Mlle Stangerson, he followed that of Ballmeyer, from prison to prison, from crime to crime. Finally, on the New York docks, when he was returning to Europe, he learned that Ballmeyer had set sail from there five years previously with, in his pocket, the papers of a certain honourable French merchant from New Orleans, called Larsan, whom he had murdered.

Does the reader now know everything about the mystery of Mlle Stangerson? Not yet. Mathilde Stangerson had borne her husband, Jean Roussel, a child – a son. That child was born in the house of the old aunt, who had arranged things so well that no one in America ever knew anything about it.

What became of that son? That is another story, which I do not as yet have the right to recount.

About two months after these events, I met Rouletabille, sitting on a bench in the law courts, looking very melancholy.

'Well,' I said, 'what are you thinking about, my dear friend. You are looking rather sad. How are your friends getting on?'

'Do I have any real friends, besides yourself?'

'I hope that M. Darzac . . .'

'Of course . . .'

'And Mlle Stangerson – how is she, by the way?'

'Better – much better.'

'You have no reason then to be sad.'

'I am sad,' he said, 'because I can't forget the perfume of the lady in black.'

'The perfume of the lady in black! You keep coming back to that. Won't you tell me at last why the thought of it haunts you so?'

'Perhaps . . . one day, one day,' said Rouletabille.

And he gave a heavy sigh.

Afterword

When *The Mystery of the Yellow Room* was published in New York by Bretano as 'the book of the month' (August, 1908), it was hailed by one critic as 'the most extraordinary detective story of recent years.'

Nearly ninety years later, such an assessment seems entirely justified. Like *The Phantom of the Opera* (1910), the other work with which Gaston Leroux is nowadays most closely associated, *The Mystery of the Yellow Room* has established itself as a classic of the genre. 'It remains,' wrote Howard Haycraft in his pioneering history of detective fiction, *Murder for Pleasure* (1941), 'after a generation of imitation, the most brilliant of all "locked room" novels.' As recently as 1982 it was voted by a distinguished panel of writers and critics of detective fiction among the top three locked room and impossible crime stories of all time.

Although the concept of the story of a seemingly impossible crime committed in a room so secured that neither entry nor exit is possible had first been utilised by Edgar Allan Poe in *The Murders in the Rue Morgue* (1841), the form was largely ignored by later writers until Israel Zangwill rediscovered it in *The Big Bow Mystery* (1891). More recently still, Edgar Wallace, who like Leroux was a journalist, had employed it in his first crime story, *The Four Just Men* (1905), which he had published at his own expense. As a publicity stunt, Wallace, had omitted the solution as to how the Just Men had killed the Foreign Secretary in favour of a reward of £500 for each correct solution sent in. Unfortunately, so many readers exercised their ingenuity to good effect that Wallace lost money on the venture.

Most commentators dwell on the formal complexity of the

puzzle which is at the heart of *The Mystery of the Yellow Room*. Howard Haycraft, for example, is particularly laudatory: 'For sheer plot manipulation and ratiocination – no simpler word will describe the quality of its Gallic logic – it has seldom been surpassed.' Although this is certainly the case, it is also to underestimate the extent of Leroux's achievement. After all, a plot, however ingenious, can be employed but once. *The Mystery of the Yellow Room*, on the other hand, played a seminal role in the development of detective fiction as a genre. The true measure of Leroux's success was that he managed to combine the weird, creepy atmosphere of the nineteenth-century thriller with the meticulous logic of the Sherlock Holmes story while also exploiting many of the techniques of early twentieth century sensationalist journalism. In so doing, he continually challenged the reader to find a rational solution to the mystery – a clear anticipation of the direction which detective fiction would take in the hands of authors such as Agatha Christie, Dorothy Sayers and S. S. Van Dine in Britain and America in the 1920s and 30s.

Gaston Leroux was born in 1868 and spent his childhood and adolescence in Normandy before gaining a law degree in Paris in 1889. Until 1893, he practised at the Paris bar, turning to journalism only in his mid-twenties when he was asked by an evening paper to cover the trial of an anarchist by the name of Auguste Vaillant who had thrown a bomb in the Chamber of Deputies (Vaillant was executed in 1894). Almost immediately, Leroux was poached by a more ambitious daily paper, *Le Matin*, which had only been founded ten years earlier. This was the ideal moment to move into journalism as a career as the details of a succession of crimes, corruption charges, and other newsworthy events (especially car and railway accidents) was devoured by a readership avid for news: the trial and execution in 1892 of Ravachol, whose death inaugurated a two-year anarchist reign of terror culminating in the assassination of President Carnot in Lyons in 1894; the Panama scandal, said to have touched more than a hundred deputies (1892–93); the Dreyfus affair (1894–1906); Jack the Ripper on one side of the Channel (1888) and his French equivalent,

Vacher l'Eventreur, on the other (1895–97). Nonetheless, when Leroux joined *Le Matin* in 1894, the circulation had stagnated at less than 30,000 copies. Ten years later, the circulation had risen to more than 300,000; by the outbreak of the First World War it had reached a million. As *Le Matin* expanded Leroux was offered more exciting assignments abroad: Madeira in 1904 (to cover the return of an expedition to the South Pole); Russia in 1905 (reporting on the 1905 Revolution); Morocco in 1907.

Both *The Mystery of the Yellow Room* and *The Phantom of the Opera* owe much to Leroux's journalistic background. As a writer, Leroux is not only terse but also highly inventive. Thus, the narrative is continually interrupted by fresh developments, just as a story is when it breaks over a period of days or weeks in the popular press – and when, for structural reasons, this is not possible, the author has recourse to other devices, such as the use of crime reports and hurriedly scribbled notes, to provide pace and stylistic variety. In the hands of Gaston Leroux, the detective novel becomes the fictional equivalent of investigative journalism.

Given that such practices inform *The Mystery of the Yellow Room*, it is perhaps only to be expected that Gaston Leroux would provide us with a detective who earns a living as a newspaper reporter: Joseph Rouletabille. Rouletabille was once described as remarkable for his ordinariness, as if Leroux was consciously rebelling against the eccentricities of Poe's Chevalier Dupin and Conan Doyle's Sherlock Holmes. And as Dupin and Holmes have their faithful scribes, Rouletabille has his admiring friend, Sainclair. But even if Rouletabille is the very opposite of the bookish detective, though this is perhaps just an effect of his extreme youthfulness, his pronouncements often resemble those of his famous predecessors: 'The evidence supplied by the senses only is no proof at all,' he remarks in Ch. XVIII of *The Mystery of the Yellow Room*. 'I too am bent over superficial clues, but only to demand that they come within the circle drawn by my reason.' Like Holmes, Rouletabille can be the very incarnation of intellectual arrogance.

Though a classic detective story, *The Mystery of the Yellow Room* is also more than a detective story. So strange and inexplicable is the murderous attack on Professor Stangerson's daughter which is investigated by Rouletabille that the novel hints on more than one occasion that an adequate explanation might not be found in the rational world – indeed, there is mention of some fearsome local creature called the Good Lord's Beast (surely a *clin d'oeil* at the hound of the Baskervilles), talk of hypnotism and magic, and the ever-present question as to the nature of Professor Stangerson's research into the 'dissociation of matter'. Not only this, but Leroux sets the novel in an isolated château in the middle of the Forest of Montlhéry of sinister renown (French readers at the beginning of the century would have been more familiar than we are today with the myths and legends emanating from the reign of Philippe le Bel). Finally, Leroux's masterstroke was to clearly signpost with the title that the crime under investigation is situated in the 'yellow' 1890s. Even before the trial of Oscar Wilde, this was a colour which had become associated in the mind of the general public – in France, Britain and America – with all that was unhealthy, corrupt, exotic and strange. Thus, the reader of *The Mystery of the Yellow Room* is continually forced to navigate between the rational procedures of a contemporary criminal investigation and a world teetering on the verge of science fiction, feudal superstition and the bizarrerie of the *fin-de-siècle*.

In a talk given in Nice, where he died in 1927, Gaston Leroux provides us with a privileged insight as to how he achieved such a tremendous synthesis of influences, ideas and styles. 'However fantastical my imagination, it has always been anchored in something real,' he claimed. 'Perhaps that is why so much indulgence has been shown to my work, a work which has no pretences except to distract the reader without overstepping the boundaries of propriety. How many times I have been asked how I came up with such strange combinations! Well, I shall tell you how I did it – and it has nothing to do with rising with the larks. It was by sleeping! Yes, sleep! I would go to sleep with some half-formed idea in my head and

the next thing – tap, tap – something would wake me up . . .
I've no idea who or what it was . . . But there was the answer,
the solution to the problem, I had found the mystery . . . All
that was left for me to do was write it.'

How easy Leroux makes it sound! Yet some French writers
and critics have begun to see his work – particularly his sense
of the fantastic – as anticipating the Surrealist revolution of the
1920s. Whatever the truth of this, *The Mystery of the Yellow
Room* also remains – as it was described at the time – 'a classic
tour de force on the "least-likely-person" theme.'

– Terry Hale